Under cover of a t... **tried to put more d... noted her resistance and ... little lower, coaxing her into a twirl.**

He returned her deftly to their original position, but now they were even closer than before. Worse, his hand kept shifting slightly against the small of her back in a way that was probably not apparent to observers but would have merited a sharp rebuke from any respectable partner.

"I *am* appreciating your tactics, my lord. They are most...persuasive. Though at the moment they are sitting rather a shade too low on my back. I think if you shift your hand a tad higher, you could achieve the same effect without risking gossip."

"Like this?"

His words were as smooth as his hand as it eased the silk of her gown against her back, his fingers finding and tracing her spine until they reached the stiff barrier of her stays. His finger teased that line and the tingling continued its path unimpeded, wrapping around her ribs, over her shoulders, creeping up her cheeks.

It was all done as he turned her from the very edge of the dance floor, and by the time they were back in the fray of the other dancers, his hand was decorously settled precisely where the strictest of dancing masters would approve.

LARA TEMPLE

—

A Match for the Rebellious Earl

HARLEQUIN
HISTORICAL

HARLEQUIN®
HISTORICAL™

**Recycling programs
for this product may
not exist in your area.**

ISBN-13: 978-1-335-50602-3

A Match for the Rebellious Earl

Copyright © 2021 by Ilana Treston

This edition published by arrangement with Harlequin Books S.A.

For questions and comments about the quality of this book,
please contact us at CustomerService@Harlequin.com.

Harlequin Enterprises ULC
22 Adelaide St. West, 40th Floor
Toronto, Ontario M5H 4E3, Canada
www.Harlequin.com

Printed in U.S.A.

Lara Temple was three years old when she begged her mother to take dictation of her first adventure story. Since then she has led a double life: by day an investment and high-tech professional who has lived and worked on three continents, but when darkness falls, she loses herself in history and romance—at least on the page. Luckily her husband and two beautiful and very energetic children help weave it all together.

Books by Lara Temple

Harlequin Historical

Lord Crayle's Secret World
The Reluctant Viscount
The Duke's Unexpected Bride

The Return of the Rogues

The Return of the Disappearing Duke
A Match for the Rebellious Earl

The Sinful Sinclairs

The Earl's Irresistible Challenge
The Rake's Enticing Proposal
The Lord's Inconvenient Vow

The Lochmore Legacy

Unlaced by the Highland Duke

Wild Lords and Innocent Ladies

Lord Hunter's Cinderella Heiress
Lord Ravenscar's Inconvenient Betrothal
Lord Stanton's Last Mistress

Visit the Author Profile page
at Harlequin.com for more titles.

Chapter One

'Useless fops…' *thump* '…the lot of them!' *thump* 'What is the point…' *thump* '…of having a stable of stallions…' *thump* '…if not one of them has sired an heir?'

Thump, thump, whack!

Genny straightened the small table that had fallen victim to Lady Westford's enthusiastic cane-wielding. Her tantrums were always accompanied by a militant tattoo, but today she seemed intent on wearing a hole in the carpet. It didn't help that Carmine, Her Ladyship's off-key canary, accompanied the thumping with contrapuntal warbling and frenetic leaps about his large gilded cage.

Mary and Serena sat stiffly in their chairs, dark and light heads bowed, hands folded in their laps. With their lovely profiles aligned they looked like women posing for a tableau of penance.

Genny plucked a stalk of hay from her skirt and began stripping it into slivers, imagining it was Lady Westford's cane she was shredding.

Or, better yet, Lady Westford.

'And now the family is headed by a wastrel and a rogue who did not even see fit to attend his grandfather's funeral, and never cared one snap of his fingers for the Carringtons.'

'To be fair, Lady Westford, other than Emily and Mary, I haven't seen that the Carringtons have ever cared one snap of the fingers for him either. Quite the opposite, in fact,' Genny intervened—and immediately regretted her impulsive comment. Her object was to soothe the dragon, not throw oil on its fiery breath.

Lady Westford's cane slashed the air towards her. 'We gave that doxy's boy everything and he repaid us by shaming us even further! This is what we are brought to... Oh, go away, all of you!' she exploded, her voice cracking. 'You are no use to me. You've had your chance and failed. You two...' her cane slashed the air again, now towards Mary and Serena '...you were gifted the finest of the Carrington men and you brought them both to nothing. Now all you do is feed off the Carrington teat like the empty vessels you are. Soon I shall follow Alfred to the grave and leave the Carrington tree bare of fruit. I'm surrounded by nothing but fops and rogues and barren women and hangers-on and... Oh, go away!'

They did as they were told and Genny sighed as she closed the door behind her.

'Well, that will teach me that silence is golden,' she said far more lightly than she felt as she surveyed her sister.

Serena Carrington was ashen, her hand pressed tellingly to her abdomen, as if the pain of her third stillbirth was as sharp inside her as it had been two years ago.

'Come out to the garden, Serena,' Genny suggested, but her sister gave her a slight smile and shook her head.

'I think I shall rest a little, Genny.'

Mary and Genny stood in silence until the door to her room closed.

'Well, this cannot continue,' Genny said, taking Mary by the arm and guiding her downstairs to the library. 'Serena will never recover from losing Charlie and her babes if that harridan keeps flaying her every single day.'

'Lady Westford is suffering too, you know, Genny,' Mary reproached gently. 'Losing three sons, her favourite grandson and a husband is enough to turn anyone sour.'

'I know she is suffering, Mary, but that is no excuse to torment Serena. I know Lady Westford never thought my sister good enough for the heir to the title, but she has the biggest and truest heart in the world. When Grandfather died she fought for me to come live with her, despite their objections. I cannot stand by and watch her ground to dust by that Medusa. I *will* not. She deserves better.'

'Of course she does.' Mary clasped Genny's hand between hers and their comforting warmth sparked a long-gone memory of her mother, holding her hand as they walked down to the village.

'I'm tired, Mary.' The words burst out of her before she could stop them. 'I'm tired of watching the person I care for most in the world suffer. I'm tired of living on the fringes of Lady Westford's charity. Soon there will be nothing left of Serena and nothing left of me, and I want... I need to *breathe*...'

She choked the words to a stop. The urge to lean against the older woman and cry was so strong Genny pulled her hands away and went to look at the rainbow of spring colours out in the garden.

'I know we must do something—but what?' Mary asked. 'We cannot change Lady Westford.'

'I don't intend to change her. My grandfather always said that if you cannot choose your enemy, try and choose your battlefield. Lady Westford is most bearable when surrounded by her cronies and whist partners in London. We could convince her to hold a...a ball for Emily in Town, perhaps to celebrate her upcoming marriage.'

Genny watched the idea take root in Mary's mind, her handsome face softening. Envy flicked at Genny's heart— partly for herself, but mostly on Serena's behalf. She'd seen how her sister watched the bond of love between Mary and her daughter when she thought no one was looking.

Finally, Mary smiled. 'You're tired, I'm frightened, and Serena is…lost. What a trio we are, Genny. You are quite right: it is high time we return to the living. But how shall we convince Lady Westford? She might consider it a betrayal of Alfred's memory.'

'The way to convince Lady Westford is to offer her something she wants. Leave that to me.'

'The only thing she seems to want is for her grandsons to produce an heir. And that, unfortunately, is highly unlikely. They are all well past thirty, and none of them has shown the slightest inclination towards matrimony.'

'Yet,' said Genny, and headed towards the door.

'Where are you going?' Mary asked behind her.

'To make a deal with the she-devil. And then I shall have a word with one of her useless fops.'

'Useless, perhaps, but I take offence at being called a fop,' Julian said as he shifted some papers off the sofa.

Genny raised her veil and sat down in the cleared space, glancing around the room. She'd never been to Julian's rooms on Half Moon Street. They were not quite what she'd expected. The place looked as if a whirlwind had just passed through and left it littered with papers, books and instruments.

'I suppose there is some method to this madness?' she asked and Julian leaned against the table, a rueful smile on his handsome face.

'There is always method to my madness, Genny. I hope there is some to yours? It would be much safer to stick to our arrangement and summon me to Dorset.'

'Desperate times call for desperate measures.'

'I'm not going to like this, am I?'

'Probably not. I told your grandmother I might accept your proposal after all.'

Julian's abrupt movement almost knocked over a precariously placed miniature orrery. The planets set to dancing giddily and he steadied it, glaring at her.

'That was three years ago! And, as you may recall, you turned me down, Genny.'

'I never actually turned you down. I merely pointed out that marrying me to gain your aunt's legacy was a poor bargain for both of us. And since it turned out she meant to leave it to Marcus all along, it is lucky we didn't wed.'

'Well, you cannot just resurrect a proposal when it's convenient. Why don't you stop beating about the bush and tell me what it is you really want, Genny mine?'

She smiled. 'I need your help to appease your grandmother.'

'How?' he asked, still suspicious.

'She is lonely and bored and hasn't had a decent game of whist in months...'

'I am *not* playing whist with my grandmother, Genevieve Maitland. I would rather walk naked down Piccadilly.'

She wrinkled her nose. 'That's not a pleasing image, Julian.'

'I protest. Some would call it a very pleasing image indeed.'

'I'm sure they would,' she said placatingly. 'In any case, I don't expect you to play whist—you are a terrible player. What I mean is that I plan to bring her to London, where she can meet all her old cronies.'

'That sounds sensible. Where is the catch?'

'There is no catch.'

'Of course there is. There's always a catch with you, Genny.'

'Well, it is not precisely a catch... The Carrington

women have been in mourning and away from London and society for two years. They will need a supporting arm to ease them back into society. If you could convince Marcus to come to London for a show of familial solidarity...'

Julian grinned. 'And there it is. So this whole proposal nonsense was merely to make the alternative seem more palatable.'

'Julian Carrington, how ungallant of you!'

'Genevieve Maitland, how devious of you!' he replied, in a falsetto that had little in common with her husky voice.

She laughed. 'Well, will you help? You might even find someone new to finance your projects.'

'I doubt it, but I promise to attend a couple of entertainments of your choice.'

'Not a couple. Nine.'

'No, you madwoman. I said a couple.'

'A couple is hardly anything at all. Eight, however, is a nice round number.'

'Eight isn't round.'

'It is—it goes round and round like a snake.'

She traced a slow figure eight on the table, leaning forward to provide a nice display of her low bodice. Julian had always told her she'd been blessed with one of the loveliest bosoms of his acquaintance, and at the moment she was not above using any weapons at her disposal.

Predictably his gaze flickered between her suggestively sweeping finger and her bodice. 'For heaven's sake, Genny, you are shameless. Three, and not one more.'

'Seven.'

'Four.'

'Six.'

'Five.'

'Seven.'

'Six... Damnation. That's not fair—you reversed direction.'

'Oh, very well, only six,' she said demurely.

He planted his hands on the table. 'You are lucky I am fond of you, you cunning pixie.'

'I am not only lucky, but grateful. Will you try and convince Marcus to come as well?'

'I'll try. Why not command me to go down to the docks, prostrate myself before our new Lord and Master and beg him to attend as well, while you're at it?'

'Lord Westford is in London?' she asked in surprise. Mary had told her he planned to attend Emily's wedding in Hampshire, but she'd said nothing about him arriving in London.

'Docked only yesterday.'

'Oh, no—that isn't good.'

Julian's brows rose. 'I agree, but I didn't think you shared my distaste for my very inconvenient cousin and the new head of the misbegotten Carringtons. You and Charlie used to leap to his defence every time any of us dared speak ill of your precious Captain Christopher Carrington.'

She raised her chin, a little embarrassed. She had been very careful to patrol her true thoughts on the Carrington clan when she'd gone to live with Serena and Charlie, well aware of the tenuous nature of her position. But she'd been so shocked by the way they'd vilified Captain Carrington that she'd been goaded more than once into defending the man her grandfather had considered his most trusted officer during the year he'd served with him.

'I defended him because I thought it terribly unfair and disrespectful the way you and Marcus and your grandparents spoke of him, when in truth it appears you hardly knew him, since he'd spent so little time at the Hall.' She saw Julian gather himself to argue old grievances and hurried on. 'But, in the interests of fairness, I admit his behaviour since he sold his commission has hardly been exemplary—and as Lord Westford he is abysmal. Do you know that neither the lawyers nor the steward have heard from him since your grandfather died, apart from a perfunctory letter from some solicitor in London to direct all correspondence to him?'

'Ah. So you have discovered your idol has feet of clay?'

'I have never idolised anyone in my life—not even my grandfather, and I respected him more than anyone I know. I admit I did expect a modicum of accountability from Captain Carr—from Lord Westford, but since he seems to have shed his scruples along with his uniform, I must find other means to pursue my ends.'

'Meaning me?'

'Precisely. So concentrate your efforts on bringing Marcus. If you find it rough going I shall have a word with him.'

'The threat of that alone should be enough to convince him to come, darling.'

'Thank you, Julian.'

'Huh. Now, you'd better be off before I'm tempted to demand recompense for being so useful.'

She smiled and lowered her veil once more. 'Now, now, Julian. Think of how much worse it might be.'

'It might?'

'Yes, I might have agreed to marry you three years ago, and you would have been saddled with my devious ways for good.'

Chapter Two

'A month ago I was swimming stark naked in the Bay of Alexandria,' Kit said as he leaned against the bulwarks of the *Hesperus* and surveyed the fog. He could see no more than a few yards into the noxious soup, but occasionally the outline of the warehouses formed, like a hulking beast pacing the docks, waiting for the unwary to step ashore.

It might be April in the rest of the world, but it was darkest, dankest December in the London docks. Beneath him Kit could feel the sluggish pull of the Thames towards the sea. The temptation to weigh anchor and slide just as sluggishly out of the grip of his home town was powerful.

'This fog—it is a bad omen, *Capità*,' Benja said, and spat into the sluggish water of the Thames below.

'Why is it you always turn superstitious when we come to England, Benja?'

'Because it was on a day like this that your father brought his ship to England for the last time.'

Kit grinned. 'No, it wasn't. I may have been only eleven, but I remember well we docked in Portsmouth in full sunshine.'

'I remember fog. There is always fog in England…' Benja stopped as a voice called up from the dockside.

'You there, is this the *Hesperus*?'

An equally muffled voice answered from the deck. 'And what will you be wanting with the *Hesperus*, my fine cock?'

Kit smiled at the surly Kentish tones of his bosun, Brimble. He suspected people rarely, if ever, addressed Julian Carrington with that degree of disdain.

He nudged Benja. 'Do me a favour and fetch that fine cock and bring him to my quarters, Benja.'

Benja leaned over the bulwarks to get a better look and clucked his tongue. 'I don't like it. He looks like a Borgia. You know him?'

'I do. That, *amic*, is one of the two men at the top of the very long list of those who would like to see me feeding the fish at the bottom of the ocean.'

'You wish to invite your enemy on board the *Hesperus*?'

'He's worse than my enemy, Benja. He's my cousin.'

'Huh. Looks expensive. Are those rubies real?'

Kit watched as Julian held the filigreed music box to the lamp, turning it under the light. His cousin might be something of a wastrel, but he clearly had a good eye for value. Kit wondered if he'd have to do an inventory once his cousin left the ship.

'Of course they are real. I keep all my forgeries in the false hold, in case any excise officers decide to come calling.'

Julian replaced the box with the same swift, charming smile Kit remembered from his childhood. And had mistrusted just as long.

'Yes, I've heard you've turned respectable of late, Cuz.'

Kit sat down by the wide wooden table, fingering the edge of the map of the Mediterranean spread out on it.

'And I've heard the opposite of you, Julian. We neither of us should believe everything we hear.'

'Or read, apparently.'

Julian sat on the other side of the table and pulled out a folded sheet of a newspaper from his pocket and tossed it across the table.

There was nothing particularly informative written on it—merely broad hints that the new Lord Westford had not even been invited to his own half-sister's ball, so as to spare the family's blushes.

Kit didn't know whether to be annoyed or amused. There was something juvenile about the whole archly told tale—like children whispering behind a hedge.

'I knew you were a favoured target of the gossip columns, Julian, but I didn't know you read them.'

'I don't. This was brought to my attention by Marcus. He is part owner of the *Gazette* and he plans to have a sharp word with the author of this piffle. But that is hardly the point. The point is that they have a point.'

'Of course they do. I'm an uncouth, low-born pirate and our grandmother would as soon spit at me as be in the same room with the black sheep of the family. That is hardly a newsworthy revelation and I don't see why it should bother you. In fact, I would think you would be delighted to see me reviled. You've done it often enough yourself.'

'In private. However, family gossip is bad for business.'

'What business?'

'Our business,' Julian said flatly.

Kit went to fetch a bottle of wine, pouring out two glasses.

Julian sniffed at his, his dark brows rising. He drank and gave a surprisingly happy sigh. 'The rumours are not completely wrong, then. Your taste in wine is impeccable. Where is this from?'

'A day's ride from Rome.'

'What a happy life you lead, Lord Westford.' Julian's voice was light, but as acid as a third-rate vintage.

'Why have you come tonight, Julian? The last time we

saw each other you called me everything short of Beelzebub himself. Now you're here, on enemy territory, complimenting my wine and showing a completely disingenuous concern for my reputation. What is it you want? Money?'

Julian's hand tightened on the glass, his handsome mouth twisting. Strange, thought Kit, that his cousin looked far more like Kit's father than he himself did. If he hadn't had the Carrington eyes, Kit had little doubt his cousins would have thrown the slur of bastardy at him, as well as low birth.

'I'm no happier coming here than you are to see me, believe me,' Julian said at last. 'I admit our last encounter was unfortunate. It was very bad taste to air old grievances when your father had just been buried.'

'I appreciate the near apology. But, since I am certain you still haven't told me the reason for your presence here, I'll reserve judgement.'

'You always were a suspicious bastard, Kit.'

'And you always were a devious one, Julian.'

'You should be grateful I'm employing those skills in your favour at the moment.'

'Are you?'

'Yes. You asked why I'm here… I'm here to determine if you're presentable.'

'If I'm…what?'

'Presentable. To polite society. Our last encounter was inconclusive. None of us was at our best. Except poor Charlie—but then he was always the only ray of light among the heathens, as Grandmama would have said.'

'I wouldn't insult heathens by comparing them with the cursed Carringtons. And as for presentability—I don't see why it matters. The only society I plan to encounter is the family of Emily's betrothed in Hampshire, and they, unlike London society, apparently do deserve the epithet *polite*.'

'Damn, I'd forgotten you talk like a book when you're

angry. Just like your father. My point is that it won't do. You can't hide here in the fog while everyone knows you're in Town and practically on their doorstep. If you're so concerned for Emily and Mary, it would have been far better for them if you'd docked somewhere else entirely and sneaked up to the wedding and away again without anyone being the wiser. By the time the ball comes round they'll have you painted as a misshapen ogre holding pagan rites at the rise of the new moon—if you could ever see any moon through the sludge they call air down here.'

'Aunt Mary never said anything about gossip when I met her only yesterday.'

'That's because she's Mary. She's been putting a smile on things ever since her family sold her to our grandparents to take your father's mind off your mother's death. She wouldn't risk scaring you off, in any case, would she? You can always sail away, but she has to live with the old bat. Oh, and I doubt she appreciates you still calling her *Aunt Mary* as you did as a boy. It might have been a fine compromise when you refused to call her *Mama* back then, but she's only a few years older than you, and it's a tad aging to have your grown stepson calling you Auntie.'

Kit felt a sharp twinge in his jaw and realised he was grinding his teeth. Damn, he hated his cousins.

Julian's mouth quirked into a smile. 'I daresay your sweet stepmother didn't even meet you at Carrington House, did she?'

'That was at my suggestion,' Kit said, aware that he was sounding defensive. 'I don't wish to see my grandmother any more than she wishes to see me.'

'Well, once the festivities begin, either leave Town until she returns to Dorset, or do your bit for the family.'

Kit smiled, slowly. 'Are you ordering me to leave London?'

'That was my intention when I came aboard, but I've changed my mind. I think you should come to the ball.'

'Is this some new attempt to make my life hell?'

'At least in this instance, making you miserable isn't my primary objective. I've been asking around, and it seems you haven't been trading in contraband recently. Is that because you aren't, or because you've bribed the excise officers?'

'If you're asking whether my trade is above board, it is. Whatever sins I've committed, I've kept them far from England. In any case, I've become tediously respectable in the last few years.'

'Good—it would put a damper on the festivities if you were hauled out in the middle of the ball for smuggling, or worse.'

'I'm not coming to the damned ball. Putting me in the same room with Lady Westford is a recipe for disaster. Doing it in front of the whole of the London Ton, which is only waiting for the stain of my birth to out, is a recipe for the apocalypse. I don't want Emily's wedding tainted by scandal.'

'Well, it's a little late for that. As you can see, now the inhabitants of our little social swamp know you're in Town their cauldrons are bubbling with cackling conjecture. And a ball is the perfect place for the two of you to face each other across the green, since that's the one occasion she'll not risk showing her true face. You want the rare experience of Grandmama holding her tongue? That's practically the only time you'll find it, *Pretty Kitty.*'

Kit tightened his hand on his glass, breathing carefully.

'Oh, I forgot you didn't like your pet name,' Julian said with his most disingenuous smile. 'Marcus and I never meant for it to reach your school. Bad luck that. If you hadn't been such a pretty little thing it likely wouldn't have stuck. Still, I think it was rather extreme of you to force everyone to stop calling you Kit and call you Christopher instead.'

Kit was very tempted to show Julian precisely how he'd forced everyone to stop echoing his cousins' epithet. The only benefit of their mischief was that he'd learned to defend himself at a very young age, but for years he'd allowed no one to call him Kit other than Mary and Emily.

To everyone else he'd become Christopher Carrington.

And now, unfortunately, Lord Westford.

He sighed impatiently.

'If you're done drinking my wine and trying to goad me into losing my temper, Julian, you can take yourself off.'

Julian laughed. 'Foiled. You used to be so much more susceptible once. But don't let your dislike of me dissuade you from coming to the ball. I'm curious to see how you and Marcus rub along. At least I think Marcus will be there. He also has no intention of attending, but no doubt Genny will find a way of twisting his arm.'

'Genny?'

Julian stood and gave Kit a quizzical smile. 'Serena's sister—Genevieve Maitland. You've been away a while, but don't tell me you've forgotten Charlie's widow and her sister? The granddaughters of your old commanding officer General Maitland?'

'No, but what have they to do with any of this?'

'Since they live with Lady Westford, they will obviously be at the ball.'

'I didn't know they were living with our grandmother.'

'Where else would they be? Since Grandfather swore after the umpteenth time Charlie invested in some ill-fated agricultural venture that he'd not give him another chipped farthing, Serena has been left with all his debts, poor woman. And of course Genny wouldn't leave her to face Grandmother's bludgeoning alone.' He drained his wine and went to the door. 'Don't forget you promised me a case of that wine.'

Kit didn't bother to point out that he'd promised no such thing. Still, a case of wine was cheap compared to the funds Julian had received from the Carrington coffers over the years.

He was standing as the door closed and was still staring at it when Benja entered.

'Well, *Capità?*'

'Not well at all, Benja. In fact, I'm afraid I shall have to visit a tailor. My wardrobe does not stretch to acceptable evening wear.'

Benja clucked his tongue morosely.

'I knew it. The Borgia—they always bring bad news.'

Chapter Three

So far, so good.

Genny stood by the musicians' dais at the end of Carrington House's crowded ballroom and surveyed the product of her plotting. She didn't know what was more impressive: the fact that Emily's ball looked set to be one of the Season's successes, or that Lady Westford was actually smiling.

She was most pleased to see that Mary and Serena were occasionally leaving the matrons' corner to dance, and that even Marcus and Julian were behaving. Thus far. Well, Marcus was his usual reticent self, but Julian's easy charm was fast convincing many ambitious matrons that perhaps his lack of funds might be overlooked after all.

There was only one fly in the ointment, and she very much hoped it didn't transform itself into a whole hornets' nest.

One of the chief reasons the Ton had thronged to Carrington House tonight was not because of the Carringtons who were present, but because of the one who was absent.

For the past few weeks the gossip columns had continued to jab their poison pens into the enigmatic figure of Lord Westford as he'd lurked in the London docks. Genny had been particularly impressed with one of the engravings, depicting a cloaked and masked hunchback skulking along a darkened dock as brawny sailors scattered in fear before him. The text was hardly any better. An improbably salacious tale of his misdemeanours interlaced with what the Ton would probably consider even more scandalous facts about his origins and occupation.

They might smile at Lady Westford, but behind their fans they clucked their tongues because the once respectable Carrington name was now in the hands of a man whose maternal grandfather might well have been a bastard, whose mother had been not only a shopkeeper's daughter but an actress, and whose only protection from gaol and transportation might be the title he had never been meant to inherit in the first place.

It was all simply *too* delicious.

And Genny might curl her lip at the Ton's avid prurience, but she had to appreciate its effect—the ballroom was full to bursting. So long as the cause of that gossip kept himself to himself, Genny was content.

Still, she kept a close watch on the circling of the vultures, and was just beginning to relax her vigilance when the buzzing began—like a swarm of wasps shifting direction across the dance floor.

She knew that sound—it was the sound of gossip rippling across the fetid pond of London society, and it usually boded ill for someone. She had little doubt that this time it boded ill for the Carringtons.

It was at times like this that she wished she were taller.

She pasted a cool smile on her lips and worked her way towards the centre of this rising swarm. It was a bevy of eligible young women, many of whom were on her list of possible brides for Julian and Marcus. If either of them was fomenting trouble, this would be a good place to hear of it.

The girls had gathered in one of the alcoves that lined the ballroom wall, where weary dancers could rest between sets. Each alcove was flanked by tall Doric pillars which provided ample cover for Genny's eavesdropping.

'I'm telling you, Papa recognised him,' said Lady Sarah Ponsonby. 'Just as we stepped out of the carriage, we saw him walking up the street.'

'Is he truly a hunchback?' This excited whisper sounded like Lady Calista, the Duke of Burford's youngest granddaughter.

'Heavens, no. He looks nothing like the illustrations in the newspaper. In fact, he is by far the handsomest man I have ever seen. *Far* handsomer than Lord Byron.'

'No!'

'He is also far more scandalous…' whispered another voice.

'They say he's a *pirate*!' Lady Calista contributed again.

'Not a pirate—a privateer,' clarified Calista's sister Lady Sophronia, with a careful little cough. 'Though there are tales that he has engaged in…smuggling.'

'Well, I heard the men on his boat are escaped prisoners, even *murderers*.'

A hiss of satisfied gasps rippled through the small group.

'And *I* heard he has a harem on board.'

'What is a harem?' asked a timid voice. 'Is it some kind of animal?'

'Animals. Plural,' answered Lady Sophronia. 'It means women, Miss Caversham. *Not* respectable women.'

'He sounds dreadfully exciting. It is such a pity Grandpapa wouldn't approve of him,' said Lady Calista, and sighed.

'Why not?' Lady Sarah demanded, a trifle defiantly. 'He might be all those things, but now he holds the title and the estate he is bound to put all that behind him and settle down.'

'There is, however, the issue of his…birth.' Lady Sophronia lowered her voice and there was a swishing of skirts as the group huddled closer. 'His maternal grandfather was not only a foundling and a shopkeeper, but he trod the boards. There is some talk his mother did the same.'

'She trod on what?' asked the timid Miss Caversham as the others gave a gratifying gasp.

'She was on the stage,' Lady Sarah Ponsonby said impatiently. 'An *actress*.'

'*And* she was five years older than his father. They say she bewitched him. Truly! They eloped and set out to sea, and the present Lord Westford was born on a *ship*. That is how he became a pirate—just like Captain Drake.'

'Ooh! How thrilling!'

'Thrilling' wasn't the word Genny would employ.

She left the safety of her pillar and headed towards the entrance to the ballroom. Halfway there she was intercepted by the head footman, Henry, his face carefully devoid of expression.

'Mr Howich wonders if you could be spared for a moment, Miss Maitland.'

Genny followed him into the hall and Henry closed the door behind them, muffling the rumbling rush of human noise.

'What is it, Henry?'

'His Lordship, Miss Maitland. He is *here*.'

This was said with such a portentous tone Genny couldn't help smiling. Henry would have made a fine chorus for a Greek tragedy.

'Here...where?'

'In the library, miss. He asked for Mrs Carrington, miss, but she's in the lady's retiring room with Miss Emily, who's gone and torn her flounce, so Mr Howich sent me to fetch you, miss.'

'Very good, Henry. You needn't wait.'

Henry nodded and hurried off, rather in the manner of

someone being released from a cage shared with a prowling lion.

Genny entered the library, thinking fast. She had not gone to all this trouble to bring Serena back into the land of the living only for Lord Westford to waltz in and scupper all her efforts. There was too much at stake.

She stopped just inside the door, her thoughts stuttering to a halt. The man by the library window had turned at her entrance, candlelight shifting over his face and distorting its sharp lines. For a moment she was certain that Howich had made a mistake and admitted the wrong man. Eight years had passed since she'd last seen Captain Carrington, but she must have been a child indeed to have forgotten how handsome he was.

Strange.

And—even more strange—she felt a stab of inexplicable disappointment.

She pushed it aside and focused on the man who held her sister's fate in his hands. And therefore hers as well.

Lady Sarah was right—even in the gloom there was no denying that he was an exquisite specimen of manhood. Julian and Marcus were unfairly attractive men, but Lord Westford was close to being an ideal of thoroughly male beauty.

Scandalous or not, Genny sincerely doubted the new Lord Westford was about to receive the cold shoulder—at least not from the female half of the Ton. And perhaps not from a good portion of the male half as well.

His dark brown hair caught the candlelight, shining with the faintest hint of auburn, and his sun-darkened skin made the famous Carrington blue eyes gleam like shadowed sapphires. He was dressed in the height of fashion, but without a glint of colour to break the chiaroscuro landscape. Even the pin in his cravat was made of something dark, obsidian, perhaps.

If those young ladies were expecting a pirate, they might be surprised by the reality of Lord Westford, but Genny doubted they would be disappointed.

He moved away from the window and his eyes narrowed as they inspected her, a little puzzled. He probably was having difficulty placing her—which didn't offend her in the least. She would rather not be instantly memorable as the scrawny, taciturn seventeen-year-old he'd known while serving under her grandfather in Spain.

Then a faint smile that would most certainly please the likes of Lady Sarah curved his mouth.

'Well, well… Genevieve Maitland.'

Ah. She remembered his voice. Her grandfather had always said he had a natural voice for command.

'Lord Westford,' she replied, moving into the room. 'You choose your moments.'

His mouth quirked and those dark blue Carrington eyes narrowed, flashing with either annoyance or humour. 'Shall I leave?'

'That might be a good idea…'

His eyes widened, surprise wiping away the smile, and Genny continued.

'However, I think it is a little late for that. You were seen entering the house and the ballroom is already buzzing in anticipation. It would only make matters worse.'

'Worse for whom? And worse than what?' His smile was back as he approached the table, where she saw Howich had cleverly set out a decanter of wine. 'Would you care for some wine? I have a feeling I shall be needing it.'

'Probably.'

'That bad?'

'That depends.'

'On what?'

'On you, Lord Westford. We did not know you were planning to attend.'

He poured her a glass and approached her. His smile was still there, but it had changed into something of a warning, and in a way she was grateful for that. He was an intelligent man—there was little point in playing games. There was also very little time to beat around the bush.

'This is my house, Miss Maitland,' he said with quiet emphasis as she took the glass from his long fingers. 'I am not required to announce my comings and goings.'

She smiled at the rebuke. Her memories were returning with each word he spoke. 'Certainly not, my lord. But unless it is your express purpose to put Lady Westford… and thus your family…at a disadvantage, I think it is best that we ease her into the knowledge of your arrival at her first big social appearance since coming out of mourning. Which, unless I am mistaken, is why you sent for Mary rather than going directly to the ballroom.'

He leaned back against the table, gently swirling the wine in his glass as he listened to her. 'I can almost hear your grandfather when you speak, Miss Maitland. Where *is* Mary, by the way?'

'I believe she is helping Emily with a torn flounce. Howich will fetch her the moment she is available. I think it best that she and Emily accompany you into the ballroom, and after I have a word with your grandmother I shall ensure Marcus and Julian are on hand for a show of family solidarity. This is best done during the pause in the dancing and before everyone goes in for supper. When the dancing recommences after supper you should dance with several of the young women, starting with the Duke of Burford's granddaughters as the Duke is a particular friend of your grandmother. Mary will make the introductions. Marcus and Julian have already done so, and it will be expected. Oh, and you should take Her Grace the Duchess of Firth in to supper. She has precedence.'

His brows rose and rose as she spoke. 'Anything else, Miss Maitland?'

'No. My grandfather always said that of all his officers you were the one with the greatest degree of common sense and self-discipline, and I trust his judgement implicitly. I also infer from what Mary has told me over the years that you care deeply for her and Emily and would do nothing to jeopardise their happiness.'

'Good God, you do nothing by half-measures, do you?'

'There isn't time. By now everyone in the ballroom will be waiting for your grand entrance. Some are expecting a hunchback. Others are hoping you have brought a few members of your harem with you.'

'Hell and damnation.'

'Yes. Now I must go and prepare your grandmother and your cousins…' She paused as the door opened and Mary hurried in, a smile lighting her face.

'Kit! I didn't think you would come!'

Lord Westford straightened away from the table, his smile changing again, softening.

'I wasn't going to—but then guilt overcame good sense. I should have warned you.'

'Nonsense! I'm delighted you decided to come after all, and Emily will be *aux anges*. Come…'

She took his arm. But Lord Westford merely threw Genny a slightly cynical look. 'In a moment. Miss Maitland has to smooth my path first, apparently.'

Mary, utterly guileless, smiled. 'Oh, that is probably best. When should we follow, Genny?'

'Ten minutes—no more.'

'Such faith in oneself is admirable,' he murmured. 'Go to it, Miss Maitland.'

Genny ignored the undercurrents in his voice. She didn't need Lord Westford to like her. He was intelligent enough to do what was right without being coaxed. Still, his tone pinched at her as she left the room, as if her laces had been tugged by an inexperienced maid.

She found Julian and sent him to prepare Marcus, then went in search of Lady Westford. That lady was still holding court in the dowagers' corner, a densely packed jungle of jewelled and feathered turbans, shawls and politics. Two patronesses of Almack's, one duchess, and three countesses flanked Lady Westford, and it was evident from their watchful smiles as Genny approached that they had heard the gossip. Genny, who had hoped to speak with Lady Westford in private, realised that would be a mistake.

She widened her smile. 'Wonderful news, Lady Westford, Kit has arrived!'

Her tone sounded a little over-bright to her own ears, and for a moment she wondered if Lady Westford would spoil her hand. Then the heavy lids lowered, and when they rose Genny knew that Lady Westford's self-interest had won over her antipathy.

For the moment.

'How marvellous, my dear Genevieve. I don't believe you have yet met my grandson, Lord Westford, have you, ladies? He has been much away these years.'

Genny happily fell into the background as the seasoned dames of society made polite enquiries while they awaited the grand moment. Again she tensed at the sound of society ruffling its feathers as Lord Westford finally entered, but to her relief he exhibited none of the antagonism she'd felt roll off him in the library. He looked completely at his ease, with Emily on his arm and Mary by his side.

Julian, bless him, approached them, and the two men spoke with every external sign of amiability. Marcus didn't follow suit, but came to stand beside Lady Westford as the cavalcade proceeded, a faint smile playing at his mouth as he watched. Genny was tempted to poke him in the back with her fan, but remained where she was. There was always a point at which any additional act was likely to do more ill than good.

Talk rose and fell like gusts of wind about the room, and the musicians, as instructed, played a subdued but cheerful tune in the background. Lord Westford finally reached Lady Westford and stopped, his gaze holding his grandmother's.

'Good evening, Grandmama. You must tell me your secret. You haven't changed at all since last we met.'

There was the faintest grunt of amusement from Marcus, and Genny waited in mute agony for Lady Westford's reaction. Finally, her gloved hand was extended, quivering a little before Lord Westford took it and bowed over it. The silence felt a trifle too long, but then it was over, and Lady Westford was introducing him to the ladies seated beside her.

Howich, with impeccable timing, opened the doors to the supper room and Lady Westford rose. The Duke of Burford's corset creaked as he hurried towards her, while Lord Westford extended his arm to the Duchess of Firth and all the rest fell into their designated pairings with the ease of long practice.

Genny watched the procession, her shoulders lowering as it advanced. She realised she had a death grip on her fan, and eased her hands before the poor thing cracked under the pressure.

Chapter Four

Genny had always agreed with Wellington's words after Waterloo: *'Next to a battle lost, the greatest danger is a battle gained.'*

It was precisely what kept her from declaring the battle gained, despite supper passing without incident and nothing horrid happening as the new Lord Westford led damsel after damsel on to the dance floor for the next hour.

If he noticed her watching him like a hawk, he gave absolutely no sign. Like Julian, he possessed the skill of seeming to bestow his total attention upon his partners, and as she'd predicted, the Ton was at least temporarily bowled over by his external attributes, more than willing to be indulgent of this new and exotic toy dropped into its pen.

Finally, exhausted from her vigil, Genny relaxed enough to leave the ballroom in search of Howich. Barring any disaster yet to occur, the final verdict on the success of the Carringtons' return to society would not only be measured in the family's behaviour, but in the quality of the supper, the musicians, and the uninterrupted flow of spirits. There was no more she could do in the ballroom, but at least she could ensure the flow of wine to the card rooms.

She had just reached the hall leading to the servants' entrance behind the main staircase when a voice hailed her.

'A moment, please, Miss Maitland.'

Oh, dear, what now?

Genny didn't speak the words aloud as she turned to face Lord Westford, but her face must have expressed her thoughts quite faithfully.

His smile was mocking as he surveyed her, and there was no sign of the charm he'd recruited in the supper room and on the dance floor. The shadow cast by the rise of the stairs softened the hard-cut lines of his face. It should have dimmed the impact of his unfairly handsome visage and imposing size, but it merely added a predatory threat.

But if he meant to intimidate her by looming over her like that, he would be sorely disappointed. She'd never responded well to intimidation.

'Well, Miss Maitland?' he asked as she remained silent.

'*Well*, Lord Westford?' she echoed.

'*"Well"* as in did I pass muster?'

'Surely you don't need a subaltern's opinion on that, Captain Carrington?'

'Hardly a subaltern. Come.'

'Where?'

'Time to face the music, Genevieve Maitland.'

'What does that mean?' She frowned, her nerves tingling.

'It is a phrase I learned from an American friend after the wars. It means answering the call of the bugles into battle.'

'Oh, no, what has happened now?' She was too weary to keep the exasperation from her voice, and a strange look, almost of satisfaction, crossed his face.

'You shall see.'

She squared her shoulders and allowed him to lead her back into the ballroom. She scanned the landscape, but nothing horrible was apparent. There were fewer people than before supper, but that was to be expected as some of the older guests had left after supper, or gone to sit down and ease the effects of overeating in one of the dimly lit drawing rooms set up for that purpose.

She noted with resignation that Marcus was nowhere to be seen, but she wasn't overly surprised. At least Julian was still there. He was dancing with a rather dashing countess whose husband was always the first to populate the card tables. He caught her glance and his cheek twitched in something approaching a wink.

She sighed and frowned up at Lord Westford. 'I don't see anything…untoward. What is it?'

'Your penance. Come.'

He took her arm, directing her towards the dance floor and instinctively she resisted.

'No.'

His hold tightened. 'That frightening Mrs Drummond-Burrell is watching us. You wouldn't wish to blight Emily's chance of entering the hallowed halls of Almack's by leaving me standing on the dance floor, would you?'

Genny snapped her mouth shut and they moved forward again. To her further dismay, the musicians, who had finished a sedate country dance, were beginning the first strains of a waltz. Unlike the waltzes before supper, this was not at *trois temps* but at *deux*, its slower tempo more suited to the now pastry-and-champagne-heavy guests. Now she wished she'd not requested this modification from the musicians—the faster waltzes made talking rather difficult, and she was not feeling amiable enough to smile and converse with Lord Westford.

'It cannot be helped now, but in future you should ask a lady before presuming she wishes to dance,' she said under her breath.

'Just as you asked each and every one of us if we wished to be dandled from your puppet strings this evening?'

'I see. So this is by way of revenge?'

'For making Emily's first ball a success? I am not so petty. Besides, I don't think any of my partners these past couple of hours considered their dances with me punitive.'

'I am certain you can be charming when you wish, Lord Westford. But, although I am also certain you did not notice, I have chosen not to dance tonight. Dancing with you now, and in particular a waltz, will occasion precisely the kind of comment I was hoping to avoid during this already challenging evening.'

'You are wrong.'

'You may be an expert in many fields, Lord Westford, but this is not one of them.'

'I wasn't referring to my social skills, or lack thereof. Merely that I did notice you were not dancing. Mary has told me you prefer to focus your energies on ensuring that the grand return of the Carringtons to the bosom of the Ton goes smoothly.'

'Then why insist on dancing with me?'

'Because I wished to?'

She didn't reply to this blatant provocation, and fixed her gaze on the dark grey fabric of his waistcoat.

It was hard to remain aloof when one's hand was resting on one's partner's shoulder, and their differing heights were forcing one to lean one's forearm against the soft fabric of his sleeve.

He and his cousins were all tall men, and she'd danced with Julian often enough in the past, but the simmering tension and anger Lord Westford masked so well was beginning to slip its leash, and it intensified the impression that he was looming over her.

'Why *did* you come tonight?' she asked at last. 'It would have been far more sensible to conduct your first meeting with Lady Westford in private.'

'I don't wish to see her in private. I came for Emily and

Mary. My memory of my grandmother led me to believe she would not risk showing her distaste for me in public.'

'I see. So appearing in the middle of her ball was by way of forcing her civility?'

For the first time that evening he gave her a wholly genuine smile. The deep blue eyes caught glints of gold from the chandeliers, and the thin lines fanning out beside them added a human frailty to what in repose was a far too statuelike face. She'd watched him use this weapon to excellent effect that evening, in order to push back at society's deep suspicion of chimeric half-breeds like him.

She resisted the urge to smile back, though it was hard. When he finally spoke she realised that the smile might be genuine, but so was his dislike of her.

'You should appreciate my tactics, Generalissima, not condemn them,' he murmured, using the nickname that had sometimes been tossed at her in Spain by her grandfather's soldiers. 'In fact, I have been waiting all evening for some sign that you approve of my performance. If there is one thing I learned from your grandfather, it is that one should always show one's subordinates appreciation where it is due. Especially if you wish to encourage your men to fulfil your every need in future...'

His voice kept going lower, trickling like warm honey down her back. Her shoulders rose, as if to shake it off, and under cover of a turn in the dance she tried to put more distance between them.

He clearly noted her resistance, and his hand slipped a little lower, coaxing her into a twirl. She had no choice but to follow his lead or end up colliding with him. He returned her deftly to their original position, but now they were even closer than before. Worse, his hand kept shifting slightly against the small of her back, mirroring the rhythm of the music in a way that was probably not apparent to observers, but would have merited a sharp rebuke from any respectable partner.

She knew he was waiting for her to comment, which was precisely why she didn't. She also knew that there was nothing more to this mild seduction than a typical male show of power, like a peacock flashing its tail. She'd been through this with the other Carrington men at one point or another. It seemed second nature for them to make use of their considerable physical charms to get their way. To their credit, neither Julian nor Marcus had held a grudge when rebuffed.

She shouldn't be offended Lord Westford was like his cousins, but strangely she was. She had told Julian she had let go of her high opinion of Captain Carrington years ago, but it seemed some of her grandfather's high expectations lingered.

Not that she was surprised he was as smooth as his cousins at this game. Someone with his looks, innate charm, and intelligence was likely to have played it often enough. She just didn't like it that he was playing it with her. Still less did she like the fact that her body disagreed with her. In fact, it was now humming happily at the friction, and trying to make her breathe in the warm scent of sandalwood and musk that emanated from him.

Just a couple more minutes, she told herself, and then this little reminder of who was in control would be over. If she was wise, she would allow him this victory after an evening that must have been rubbing him the wrong way in a hundred different directions. Then he would be so much easier to manage.

So said her mind. Her tongue, however, had other ideas.

'I *am* appreciating your tactics, my lord. They are most…persuasive. Though at the moment they are sitting rather a shade too low on my back. I think if you shift your hand a tad higher, you will achieve the same effect without risking gossip.'

His smile turned inwards again, assessing. 'Like this?'

His words were as smooth as his hand as it eased the silk of her gown against her back, his fingers finding and tracing her spine until they reached the stiff barrier of her stays. His finger teased that line and the tingling continued, its path unimpeded, wrapping around her ribs, over her shoulders, creeping up her cheeks.

It was all done as he turned her from the very edge of the dance floor, and by the time they were back in the fray of the other dancers his hand was decorously settled precisely where the strictest of dancing masters would approve.

Genny's colouring did not lend itself to blushing, but she could feel an uncomfortable pinching sensation cresting her cheekbones. She refused to drop her gaze, locking it with the angry challenge in his dark blue Carrington eyes. She knew full well this was no attempt at seduction. He was paying her back.

Against all the advice she would have given herself, had she been in a more amiable frame of mind, she went to cut him off at the knees. 'I hope… I very much hope, Lord Westford…that you haven't been practising that particular sleight of hand with your other dance partners. It is shockingly bad Ton.'

His hand flinched against her back, dragging her momentarily too close and almost making them stumble. Then it relaxed again, and although there was a slight darkening of the tanned skin of his sharp-cut cheekbones, there was no other sign of discomfiture or anger when he spoke.

'I know it's been dogs' years since we met in Spain, but unless you have changed drastically it's not like you to antagonise people unnecessarily. Certainly not people who have a hold over you.'

She was about to deny that he had a hold over her, but since she lived in what was actually his home, and was currently wearing clothes that had been indirectly paid for by him, she kept her mouth shut. In fact, she was beginning to wonder why she was finding it so hard to play her own game with him.

No, she knew why. Julian had been right about her. She was angry with Captain Carrington. More than angry—she was *furious* with him.

She could not get over her almost childish expectations of the Captain Carrington her grandfather had so admired. When the old Lord Westford had died, so soon after Charlie, Genny had been convinced it was merely a matter of time before the new Earl arrived to untangle the mess left after his grandfather's death.

But, although she knew he had learned of it, arrive he hadn't. Instead, Mary and Emily continued to receive letters with tales of Askalon and Stamboul and Alexandria and Nafplio, and Genny had wondered at what point Mary and Emily might begin to doubt, as she did, his priorities.

But as months had passed and their little cage had shrunk, 'Darling Kit' had remained Darling Kit, unblemished by expectation and disappointment. Genny wouldn't have been surprised if his half-sister and stepmother had thought of some excuse for him, had he decided he was too busy to come to Emily's wedding.

She took a deep breath and forced a smile. 'You are quite right, Lord Westford. I apologise. It has been a long day. Thank you for the dance.'

His smile held, but now it was purely surface—under it she felt something flicker…perhaps an echo of the anger she hadn't even realised was boiling so hotly inside her.

'You're welcome, Miss Maitland. And thank *you*. This was by far the most…enlightening dance I have had this evening.'

The music slowed and faded. He still held her hand, and now tucked it over his arm as if to lead her back to Lady Westford, but for a moment they stood unmoving at the edge of the dance floor, like two wary dogs.

She meant to move away, back into the orderly motion of the evening, but for a moment she could not remember what it was she was supposed to do next. It was as if she had walked into a room and now stood there, wondering what on earth she had come for.

She knew hesitation was to society what a rustling in the bushes was for a hunting dog. Every alarm bell in her head was pealing, but she couldn't think of the right course of action.

Without turning her head, she could see Lady Sophronia and Lady Sarah Ponsonby watching her and Lord Westford with unmasked curiosity. Then she saw Julian approach and gave an audible sigh of relief. Lord Westford watched him as well, with that same half-smile on his face—not unpleasant, but certainly not pleasant.

He nodded to Julian, and Julian returned the nod but addressed Genny. 'My turn, Genny?' he asked, holding out his arm.

She placed her hand on it with relief, and was surprised to see Marcus back in the ballroom as well, watching them without a flicker of expression on his face. Clearly Julian had been orchestrating some action of his own since he'd seen Kit lead her onto the dance floor. No doubt he'd lined Marcus up to dance with her next, and perhaps some other cronies of his.

She felt like a fox that had tumbled into a wolves' den. Her newly discovered dislike of Lord Westford rose a notch.

'Thank you, Julian,' she said softly as they went down the dance.

'No need. I thought it would be best to spread us Carringtons about a little. I thought you weren't planning on dancing tonight, though?'

'I wasn't. He forced my hand.'

Julian glanced over his shoulder. 'Strange. Perhaps he doesn't enjoy being ordered about by you as much as I do. Never mind—he'll get used to it if he hangs about long enough.'

That stung as well, but she tried to smile. 'I was doing it for you lot, you ungrateful wretch.'

'Sheath your claws, love. I *am* grateful. Resistant, but grateful. Difficult combination to carry off well. Marcus is doing rather poorly with it, and I think my unwelcome cousin is at the end of his rope as well—which is understandable, given this evening's baptism of fire. You'd think people would refrain from gossiping about a man in his own home, but this vicious flock of carrion crows can't seem to help themselves, and I've no doubt he was meant to overhear quite a bit of it. It's like bear baiting for the Ton—prod the beast and see what he does. All told, I am impressed with his performance, since as far as I can tell he hasn't bitten off anyone's head…yet. But if you'd like me to thrash him for you I'll be happy to oblige,' he said hopefully.

Genny smiled at his light-hearted nonsense. She felt better already, and was wondering why on earth she'd allowed herself to become so unsettled.

It was merely the natural outcome of her concerns for Serena.

Nothing more.

Chapter Five

Kit resisted the urge to snatch his grandmother's cane and toss it out of the window. The constant tapping was almost as aggravating as her words.

'I would have preferred...' *thump* '...you give warning...' *thump* '...of your arrival...' *thump* '...last night...' *thump* '... Christopher.'

Thump, thump, thump.

She looked like a wizened dancing master, marking out the rhythm for a group of disappointing pupils. Or perhaps the steward at a medieval court. Kit did rather feel like an errant courtier, summoned to an audience before an aging queen. Instead of a court jester she had Carmine the canary cackling in a cage by her armchair. And on the other side she had her three ladies-in-waiting, seated in a neat row, watching him being dressed down.

Three heads—corn-yellow, honey-brown, and dark wood—were bent over three embroidery frames. Two of the ladies were even embroidering.

Serena's design was an abundance of flowers in sedate lavenders and blues. Mary was completing a shepherdess, surrounded by a rather overweight flock. Both were rich in detail, and would no doubt bloom into fine cushions or screens one day.

Genevieve Maitland, on the other hand…

Kit wasn't in the least surprised to see that she wasn't doing much more than prodding her stretch of fabric with her needle. The result was either a surly cat or a shifty-looking toad.

He turned away from the monstrosity and sighed. He'd been annoyed to find that his grandmother had assembled an audience for their first *tête-à-tête* in almost ten years. He didn't mind Mary's presence—she'd always been a calming influence on the stormy Carrington sea—but he wished the Maitland girls weren't there.

Thump, thump, thump.

'Having stayed away this long, Kit,' his grandmother continued after she had recalled his attention, 'it is rather unfortunate you could not have postponed your return until closer to Emily's nuptials. Still, now you are returned it is highly improper that you remain living in the docks like a common sailor. There is nothing for it but that you shall have to come and stay here with the family.'

He squeezed his hands more tightly behind his back. He'd been in plenty of skirmishes with hostile navies, and even more hostile pirates, but his preferred tactic had always been to elude, not engage. He resorted to brute force only when necessary, no matter how satisfying it could be. One always paid a price for violence.

He reminded himself of how well this had worked for him over the years even as he dreamed of turning a good three hundred guns on his grandmother. He couldn't resist a shot across her bows, though. Just a warning…

'Thank you for the invitation to stay in my own home, Grandmother.'

'Do not be flippant, Kit. It was always understood that I shall have use of the Carrington House for my lifetime.'

'It being *understood* is not a contract.' He knew before the words were out that they were a mistake.

She gave a slight superior smile. 'Not in *trade*, perhaps. But a gentleman's bond is above such vulgar considerations.'

Damn. Brute force was looking as seductive as Aphrodite rising from the waves right now.

He gave a slight bow. 'Thank you for the clarification, Grandmother. I shall consider your invitation.'

'I don't see that there is anything to consider, Kit. Surely we both want what is best for Emily? You are not *au courant* with society's ways, but I assure you that now you have stepped into its world, were you to immediately retreat to your…*boat*…and attend no more events, the brunt of society's thrust would be felt by your half-sister.'

He didn't answer. He couldn't think of anything he wanted to say that he wouldn't later regret.

'I am certain Emily would be delighted if you joined us here before she departs with Peter for his grandparents' house in Hampshire, Kit,' Mary said, searching in her sewing bag and extracting a pair of silver scissors. 'And she does worry that you must be dreadfully uncomfortable, sleeping in a ship's cabin.'

'My cabin is very comfortable, Mary, and the docks are not very far away. Carrington House is actually quite conveniently situated, so far east of the fashionable centre of town.'

'Berkeley Square is eminently fashionable,' Lady Westford protested, rising to the bait like the most succulent trout.

A slight dimple formed in Miss Maitland's cheek, but she kept her head bent over in her pretence of embroidering. He had no doubt the last thing she wanted was anyone interfering with her sway over this all-female household.

'I will consider your invitation, Grandmother,' he repeated, wandering over and picking up a Sevres figurine of a shepherdess with a sheepdog half hidden by her broad skirts. It was one he'd bought for Emily for a long-ago birthday. He turned to Mary. 'Where is Emily, by the way?'

'She has gone with Peter's mama and his younger sisters to visit the Menagerie,' Mary replied. 'The younger girls have never been to London, and are trying to see as much of Town before they depart. Tomorrow we are attending a lecture on Roman treasures at the museum. Do say you will come.'

He smiled at her enthusiasm, weighing the blushing shepherdess in his hand. 'Tomorrow, I am afraid I cannot, but I shall try to come here in the evening if you aren't engaged elsewhere.'

Mary hesitated, and Miss Maitland's head dipped a little further. This time it was Serena who spoke, her pale blue eyes lighting with sudden and surprising pleasure, like a child waking and remembering it was her birthday.

'Oh, but we are going to see Kean play Sir Giles Overreach at Drury Lane tomorrow. We have not been to a play in…in years, and only last night Miss Dalrymple was telling us how marvellous it is now they have rebuilt the theatre after the fire. She said it is as pretty as a music box—all white and gold, with tableaux from Shakespeare and the most opulent boxes. Oh, you *must* come…'

'I do not think Kit would care to attend a theatrical entertainment,' Lady Westford said with finality, her cane hitting the floor with a sharp snap.

It knocked Serena out of her reverie and sent a flush up her pale cheeks. It was such a sharp transformation that Kit stepped into another pit he would have never thought he would enter in a hundred years.

'On the contrary, Grandmother. I am curious to see how Drury Lane has changed since I was last there… How long ago was it? Twenty years? You might better remember. We were there together, weren't we?'

He saw the memory rise along with a faint flush on her papery cheeks.

'I do not recall.'

'Don't you? Perhaps once we are all there tomorrow evening it will spark your memory.'

He turned away from the flash of anger in his grandmother's eyes and caught sight of Serena's face. Her pale blue eyes were wide and a little red, as if she was about to cry. He noted too that Miss Genevieve Maitland's hands were tight on her tambour frame, her gaze on her sister's profile.

He pulled tight on his temper and smiled at Serena Carrington. 'Thank you for the suggestion, Mrs Carrington. It is not a play I am familiar with, but I am certain that anything with Mr Kean is well worth watching. I shall depend upon you to tell me what the play is about.'

The three women in a row smiled in unison. Serena with relief, Mary with pleasure…but most surprising of all was Miss Genevieve Maitland. Her smile was utterly different from any he had seen her wear the previous night. Gratitude lit her face, softening her carefully held mouth and bringing two dimples to full life in a way her society smiles hadn't.

So he had inadvertently discovered how to tame the little general—defend her pack.

But Lady Westford was not done with him yet. Having been foiled, she abandoned subtlety. 'Do you think that wise, boy? People are bound to comment on your choosing to appear at the theatre of all places. I think it best to confine your appearances to less contentious settings.'

There were limits.

He turned back to his grandmother, but Miss Maitland spoke first.

'Perhaps you are right and that is best, Lady Westford.

We shall already be quite crushed in the box, as Julian will be joining us, as well as Lord Ponsonby and Lady Sarah.'

'That is hardly reason for Kit not to be present in his own box, Genny,' Mary reproved a little sharply.

Lady Westford looked between the two of them with a rather malevolent smile that made Kit's jaw clench even harder.

Before he could comment, Genny Maitland rose, her eyes downcast as she folded her embroidery and laid it in the basket. 'I didn't mean... Of course you're quite right, Mary... Pray, excuse me. I must go. I must see Mrs Pritchard about the menus...'

When the door had closed behind her, Lady Westford turned to Mary. 'Well done, Mary Carrington. Do her good to have her wings clipped. Too used to having her own way by half.' Several decisive thumps of her cane sent Carmine trilling in a rare show of harmony.

'I didn't mean...' Mary looked contritely at the door.

'But Genny *agreed* with you, Lady Westford.' Serena said hesitantly, a thread of hurt in her voice.

'I don't need people agreeing with me, girl. If there's one thing I can't abide, it's toadies!'

Carmine broke into syncopated chatter and Lady Westford rapped his cage with the knob of her cane, silencing him.

'Help me upstairs, Serena. I am tired. And, Mary, you ring for Mathers and tell her to come up to me.'

The two women sprang into action with an alacrity that Kit would have commended in any of his men, but now made him wish more than ever that he could toss both his grandmother and her cane out of the window.

He waited for the door to close behind her before turning to Mary. 'How the devil can you stand it?'

Mary shushed him with her hands, her worried gaze on the door. 'Hush, she is not that bad. Losing your grandfather has been dreadfully hard on her. It is a good thing Genny convinced her somehow to end her mourning and come to London, for she looked likely to stay there sunk in a brown study indefinitely. She has not yet recovered her spirits.'

'She seems plenty recovered to me. I had forgotten what a poisonous snake she is. You *cannot* stay with her, Mary.'

'I cannot leave her. Where would I go? I do not wish to become a burden to Emily when she is about to begin her married life, and I cannot imagine setting up house alone. And, more to the point, I cannot leave poor Serena all alone with her. That would be quite unfair.'

There was a finality in her voice that checked Kit. His stepmother's soft-spoken kindness was often mistaken for weakness, but he knew better. When something mattered to her, she could be as stubborn as his grandmother. It was a pity she'd chosen this hill on which to make her stand.

Still, he made another attempt to dislodge her from it.

'She wouldn't be alone. Having seen Genevieve Maitland's *modus operandi* last night, and today, I would say she provides ample protection for her sister. I'd back her against the old crone any day.'

'Pray do not make fun of Genny.'

'I'd as soon make fun of Napoleon. But that is beside the point—which is that guilt is a poor reason to remain in purgatory.'

'It's not guilt, Kit. It is duty.'

His skin must have thinned considerably since his return to London, because her comment pierced it and prodded his temper back into life. 'Ah, here comes the reprimand.'

She flushed. 'I did not intend it as a reprimand. It is a fact. The one balm of my existence during these years, other than Emily, has been my friendship with Serena and

Genevieve. I will not leave them here at your grandmother's mercy.' She hesitated. 'Or her at Genny's.'

'Are those two constantly at war?'

'Oh, no. Nothing so obvious. Genny is…' She frowned, her eyes on the row of figurines, and pointed to the one he'd set down. 'She's like that sheepdog. She herds. And when there's a fox prowling she can…well, she can be protective in her own way.'

'So you and Serena are the sheep?'

'You are being harsh again. Oh, I do wish I had not chastised her as I did. You do not know how much she has done for us since she came to live with Serena. She is the only one who could manage your grandfather and grandmother.'

'All the more reason to leave her to it.'

'But that is wrong—can you not see? She isn't even a Carrington. Perhaps if she had married Julian when he offered…'

'*Julian* offered for her?'

'Oh, several years back. But it came to nothing and they remain good friends. My point is that, unlike Serena and myself, she has no duty to your grandmother.'

'Nor do you. That old bat treats you worse than she does her cacophonous canary.'

'That is only because she is unsettled. I think she feels guilty that she is enjoying coming out of mourning and seeing her old friends after so long. We must be patient.'

Kit realised that at least was true. As had been Mary's comment about her lack of choice. She had been living for other people since her marriage to his father, when she was seventeen, and the birth of her daughter the following year. He could see that, for her, the thought of setting up her own household must be almost unbearably daunting.

If he wished to remove Mary from his grandmother's influence he would have to provide a suitable alternative.

The only problem was that he had no idea what that alternative might be. The best thing for her would be to marry again, but playing matchmaker was well beyond the scope of his skills.

'Very well,' he conceded, rolling back his guns. 'I won't press.'

'Thank you, Kit. And you will come with us to the theatre?'

He looked down at her pretty, hopeful countenance and felt a wave of gratitude roll over him. She'd been younger even than Emily when she'd found herself in a marriage of convenience, and yet she'd tried so hard to be a good wife to a grief-stricken man and a caring stepmother to his equally grief-stricken son.

She was still trying. He ought to do the same.

'Of course I will come, Mary.'

Chapter Six

'He's drinking, Miss Genny,' said Mrs Pritchard as she gazed down at the basket resting on a bale of hay in the stables. 'And he had a little sliver of mutton just now.'

Genny smiled at the housekeeper and crouched down to inspect the tiny cat. The basket was a trifle large, for it had recently been populated by three ginger kittens a stable hand had found abandoned in the alley between Carrington House and the mews stables.

Likely their arrival at the house had scared the mother away, and only one of the litter had survived the week. Genny had learned not to name them until they could feed on their own. Even now she hesitated, waiting for some sign that it wouldn't suddenly weaken and fade as the other two had.

'Well, I'd best be about my duties, miss. I'll keep an eye on him.'

'Thank you, Mrs Pritchard.'

When she had left, Genny sat on the bale of hay and plucked the tiny cat from the basket. It circled itself into a ball on her lap, the agate eyes slitting and razor teeth flashing as it yawned.

'Did you like your mutton, you stubborn little ball of fluff? You did, didn't you, sweetheart?'

She purred encouragingly as she ran her finger from its little bony head down the curve of its soft back. She could feel its vertebrae shift like a bead necklace as she traced it again and again, murmuring foolish words to this sole survivor.

The kitten stiffened suddenly and Genny stopped, realising someone was standing in the alley. She turned, expecting to see one of the servants.

'This is an unusual place to hide, Miss Maitland. I take it your need to see the housekeeper was an excuse for a strategic retreat?'

His voice was even deeper in the confines of the stables. Genny considered standing as he approached, but remained where she was. She was at distinct disadvantage, seated on her bale of hay, but standing in this confined space would be even worse. His tone clearly indicated that he was intent on attack, and if she must be loomed over she preferred to do it from her throne of hay with a kitten between them.

'If you wish to think so, my lord, then it was.'

'What I wish for and what I am likely to obtain around here are evidently two altogether different things.'

'Dear me—should I feel sorry for you? How quickly you have fallen from prodigal son to mere sacrificial lamb.'

He sank down on his haunches with a suddenness that made her lean back slightly.

'Don't mistake me for a lamb of any kind, Miss Maitland. I'm not a good subject for whatever herding games you like to play in this household.'

His eyes, more silver than blue in the gloom, were fixed on hers, a hint of a smile softening his sharp-cut mouth.

'I don't play games, Lord Westford. What I do, I do for a reason.'

'Which is?'

She wanted to look away, but strangely she couldn't.

She also felt the urge to swallow, but knew he wouldn't miss that tell-tale sign of unease.

'To get through the day,' she replied, keeping her voice light.

'Yes, I remember that,' he said slowly, his gaze moving over her, his cheekbones catching the faint light from the doorway. 'You were always on your guard. Your grandfather said you could have made your mark in the army, had you been a boy.'

A stab of pain pierced her between abdomen and chest. It was cruel of him to use her grandfather's words and unfulfilled wishes against her. She didn't want him talking about her grandfather as if he owned part of him.

'I'm well aware of my failings, Lord Westford.'

'He meant it as a compliment,' he said, and his voice softened, as if in regret. 'He also said he was likely to go off tilting at windmills like Don Quixote, if not for his Sancho Panza.'

'That is certainly not a compliment to either of us. I may be short, and secondary, but no one could say of my grandfather that he was a deluded romantic.'

'Don't twist what I said, Genny. Your grandfather was a brilliant and generous man, but like everyone he had his blind spots, and he trusted your judgement, despite your youth. It might have upset some of the men under his command to have you hovering in the wings, but anyone with an ounce of sense knew better than to underestimate your impact on him.'

'I think I prefer the comparison to Don Quixote and Sancho Panza. Now I sound like a scheming harridan and he a malleable fool.'

'Now you are merely twisting my words in the other direction. You understand me very well.'

'You certainly appear to think *you* understand *me* very well, Lord Westford.'

'Let us say I am beginning to remember quite a bit from those days.'

'Surely you have better things to occupy you than my relationship with my grandfather?'

'I do, but since you appear to be impacting upon most of those "better things", in a rather surprising manner, I find I am curious about my old commanding officer's *eminence grise.*'

'So now I am not only short, and scheming, but also grey? And there I was, believing Mary when she said your reputation for deadly charm was well deserved.'

He smiled—his first real smile for her.

'You must have some French fencing blood to go with that name, Genevieve. You parry beautifully—though a little forcefully. If I were a gentleman, I would have been grovelling a dozen times by now.'

'Well, I'm glad you're not. I hate grovelling. I'm too tempted to kick snakes when they're down.'

'Ouch. I've never been likened to a snake before.'

'It's better than a peacock.'

His smile widened, causing the same softening about the eyes that had had such an unsettling effect on her on the dance floor.

'Nothing pea-sized about me, sweetheart. Certainly not my—'

'I don't need you to flash your feathers for me, Lord Westford,' she interrupted hastily, grateful for the gloom of the stables. 'There are plenty of young women in Town all too willing to oblige if you need your vanity fluffed.'

'It's not my vanity that needs fluffing, Generalissima.'

'No, that needs a good flattening.'

'You're doing a damn good job of that,' he said musingly. 'You're still winning this parrying game.'

'It's not a game, Lord Westford, and I'm not your enemy.'

He didn't answer, his gaze holding hers as if he would force some revelation out of her that she herself wasn't aware of. She tried very hard not to waver, but her breath began to fall out of rhythm, as if she was forgetting the most basic of physical actions.

Finally, he moved—but only to sit on a bale of hay next to her.

She wished he would leave. *She* should leave, but somehow she didn't want to. It was damnably confusing, and she didn't like feeling so stretched and pulled in opposite directions.

She especially didn't like feeling suddenly so young. As if somehow his vision of her as a taciturn, cautious, almost-eighteen-year-old was forcing her back to that strange time where she'd been clinging to her world by untried claws like the little ginger cat.

She stroked the ball of fur and the kitten, which had been happily asleep, gave a mewl, its tiny claws pressing into her skin.

He glanced down at it. 'I remember that too. Genevieve…patron saint of strays.'

His voice was low and soft, and the undercurrent of hostility was gone. She felt a strange flush spread out from the knot between her abdomen and lungs.

He leaned closer, stroking the arching back of the ginger cat with one finger. The kitten's eyes narrowed to blissful slits as he ministered to it, making long, gentle strokes from the crown of its scruffy head to the brash burst of its tail, stopping just short of her fingers. She held herself against the need to tighten her hands about the kitten as its purring went from silken to rough velvet against her palms.

'Where did this fellow come from?' he asked.

'He was found with two other kittens in the alley by the stables. The mother never returned and now he's the only one left,' she murmured, keeping quite still as the kitten wallowed in shivering bliss. She felt Lord Westford's gaze shift to her, but his stroking didn't lose rhythm.

'He's a good size already. He'll make it.' He spoke in a voice almost with the timbre of that purr. 'I'm sorry about the others.'

'There's no point in being sorry. They rarely survive. This one shall have more mice to choose from in the stables. And too many cats upset the dogs.'

He looked around. 'There are dogs here as well?'

'Not here. At the Hall in Dorset. Milly and Barka. Barka is too old to chase anything, and spends most days dozing in the stables, but Milly has enough energy for both of them. Hopefully by the time we return there Leo will be large enough to stand his ground.'

He stopped stroking, resting his elbows on his knees as he remained leaning towards her. 'Leo? He doesn't look like much of a lion.'

'Leo is short for Leonidas.'

'Good God, poor fellow—' He broke off with a soft laugh. 'Are Milly and Barka also named for long-dead warriors?'

'I'm afraid they are. Militiades and Hannibal Barka. I had to name them something...'

'What is wrong with dog names like Bouncer, or Dancer, or Rover?'

'I've used them all through the years. Also Juno, Thunder, Lovely, Lady, Lovely Lady, Hector... That one gave me the idea of going to the Greeks, so then there was Mars, who was a brute, and Zeus who was spoilt and ill-tempered, and Athena, who was quite the least intelligent dog I ever had.'

His laugh was every bit as beautiful as he—a warm rumble that reverberated through her far more deeply than Leo's purring.

'I remember you gave some odd name to that great scruffy brute who adopted you in Talavera. What was it?'

'Oh, Archidamus! Archie was a dear, but already quite old by the time he found me.'

Kit smiled, leaning back to look up at the wooden beams of the stables as if they were opening up and beyond them was a view of some long-ago memory.

'That's true. Strays of all forms did seem to find you. Your grandfather used to grumble that whenever we barracked for longer than a few days the place soon began to resemble a menagerie.'

'That wasn't my fault. Soldiers always attract foraging animals during a war. I didn't feed them any more than the others did.'

'Yet they always seemed to follow you about. Like that Archie fellow. I never did understand why he left the village with us; he must have lived there all his life.'

'The mayor's wife told me his family had been killed. Maybe he wanted to start anew, go on an adventure before...' Her words ended on a strange intake of breath. She let it out slowly, stroked the ginger kitten once more, and replaced him in the basket, where the little ball of fur curled up into soft sleep.

'Before he died,' he completed.

The shaft went home, surprising her with its sharpness. And with a strange hurt that *he* had driven it home.

His hand touched hers briefly and drew away just as abruptly, leaving a trail of sensitised fire and her nerves twanging like an angrily plucked harp.

She shrugged. She had no clear idea how he had gone from an inquisition to this strangely intrusive sympathy. She didn't *want* his sympathy. The inquisition had been less unsettling.

'They all do. It was a long time ago.'

'Two trite rationalisations that have little to do with the pain of losing someone you care for,' he said.

She bent to pluck straw from her skirt, pressing back the completely unexpected threat of tears.

She'd never succeeded in putting Captain Carrington in a safe box, so she'd done her best to keep her distance from him during that year in Spain. Now she could see her instincts had been completely justified. He did not play by any rules that she could see. He seemed to adapt himself to whatever situation he found himself in and yet remain aggravatingly, impenetrably, the same.

She had no idea why he seemed to think she'd succeeded in parrying his thrusts. She felt like an emotional pincushion. Perhaps he'd learned that annoying skill as the Captain of a less than respectable ship—adjusting to capricious oceans and whatever political games were being played out on the grand chessboard of the world's powers.

Whatever the case, she knew he wasn't…*safe*.

'I'd best go inside.' She stood and then hesitated. '*Are* you coming to the play tomorrow evening? I didn't mean to dissuade you.'

'I'm aware of that. Now. That little manoeuvre was aimed at cornering me into agreeing to attend, wasn't it?'

'Not cornering. Prodding. Society will make a deal of it whether you join your grandmother at the theatre or stay away. Sometimes bold is best.'

He remained seated on the bale of hay, looking up at her, his eyes catching the faint light from the stable entrance. Like the sea under a heavy cover of cloud. She felt absurdly nervous suddenly.

'Sometimes it is…' he replied at last, with surprising hesitation. 'I admit I allowed you and my grandmother to goad me into saying I would come, but I don't wish to do Emily any harm.'

'If there is one thing I have learned since I came to live

with the Carringtons, it is that you should never give society the upper hand. That means never revealing a weakness. Individually, people can be kind, but as a group they are vicious and unforgiving.'

'All the more reason not to tempt them to lash out. I don't care what they say of me, but I don't wish my contribution to Emily's nuptials to be an even heavier cloud of scandal.'

'You should come.' The words were out before she could think them through, and she scrambled to explain them to herself as much as to him. 'Last night was a success because you appeared to take it for granted that they would accept you.'

He gave a short laugh. 'I take nothing for granted.'

'I know—which is excellent and precisely why it worked. It might just as easily have been a complete disaster, but you have several serious advantages, Lord Westford. Your title, your inheritance, and your good looks. Not to mention the dash of romance your piracy brings to the table.'

He shifted on the bale of hay, his gaze falling from hers, and she wondered if she'd embarrassed him.

'I was never a pirate. And, believe me, that is not something one should consider romantic.'

'I don't. But then much of society—including our esteemed and rotund King—consider war to be the height of romance.'

'True... Idiots. I'm glad Emily found herself a nice country husband and not one of those dandies.'

'Peter is a darling, isn't he? But the point is, I think it best not to allow the one weakness in your flank to become your Achilles heel. If you try to hide it, that will only make the enemy all the more determined to pitch their arrows at it.'

'So you suggest I flaunt it?'

'No. Merely treat it—or rather their opinion of it—as a matter of no great import. You wish to go to the theatre, so you will go to the theatre.'

'I *don't* wish to go, but you are right.'

'Why don't you wish to go? Do you dislike plays?'

He seemed a little surprised by her question, and for a moment she thought he wouldn't answer.

'Did Mary tell you I was raised on a ship?' he asked.

'Yes. Until your mother died—' She broke off, wondering at her insensitivity.

'Yes. Well, the *Hesperus*…the original one…was a rather unusual ship. My father loved the theatre—which was where he met my mother. My maternal grandfather was, amongst other things, an actor, and she often went to help at the theatre. She was several years older than my father, to add to all her other sins, and if my father was Captain of the *Hesperus*, she was definitely captain of everything else on board. She regularly held plays on deck, and made all the sailors take part.'

Genny felt her jaw slacken at the image of a theatrical pirate ship and she shut her mouth, trying not to smile. 'How marvellous! What roles did you play?'

'None. I didn't inherit a smidgen of her or my grandfather's talent. Our star was Benja, who is my first mate now. The best I could do was fetch and carry, and then I would climb the mizzen mast and play audience.'

'I see…'

His mouth quirked. 'What *do* you see, Genevieve Maitland?'

'Drury Lane. All that pomp and grandeur and scent and noise compared to a wind-blown seaborne stage with sailors playing Hamlet and Ophelia. It won't be the same.'

In the silence she could hear the huffing of the horse in the adjacent stable, and Leo's rumbling purr.

'No, it won't be. But you are right. It is probably best to grab this bull by the horns. I hope the play is worth it.'

'Kean's playing of it is likely to be well worth it. But I must go now. Do tell Emily if you are coming—she will be delighted.'

'Yes, miss. Anything else I must do?' he asked with utterly unconvincing meekness as he leaned back further on the bale of hay.

'No, that will do for now,' she replied, unable to resist adding, 'But you really must learn to play by the rules. Such as not remaining seated when a woman stands.'

He grinned up at her. 'But I was being chivalrous, Miss Maitland. You should commend me.'

'For what?'

'I have noticed you dislike being loomed over.'

He rose from the bale of hay and she had to admit he had a point. His superior height seemed to shrink the already confined space.

'Besides,' he murmured, 'I rather liked looking up at you. You look good from all angles, Genevieve Maitland.'

'You aren't required to flirt with me, you know,' she said, hating the uncertainty in her voice.

'You should be happy. I'm honing my social skills. Drilling makes the soldier.'

'"Drilling" doesn't involve shooting at the side of a barn at five paces.'

'I had no idea you were that susceptible, Genny,' he said, with utterly unconvincing surprise, before adding, 'And I would never be so ungentlemanly as to think of you in terms of a barn—though you *are* rather liberally covered in hay at the moment. You might want to do something about that before you go inside, or the servants will get the wrong idea.'

Genny searched for something suitably cutting, and

then decided that ignoring pests was sometimes the best
policy.

'Thank you for your concern, Lord Westford. Good
day.'

Kit watched her brush the hay from her skirts as she
left the stables. The material stretched against her hips
and legs, and for a moment, as she swung open the gated
door, sunlight permeated the summery fabric and outlined
a figure that made it clear she'd changed a great deal since
Spain...

The image was overlaid with another from years ago, of
a much younger version of Genevieve Maitland, brushing
dust from her skirts after helping clear one of the General's
billets in a small hill town by the Pyrenees. She'd been
only a girl then, but already seeming far older than most.

He couldn't remember Serena ever pitching in to help.
But then it probably hadn't been her fault. The General had
split his paternal and maternal instincts between his two
granddaughters, and to be fair both had appeared quite
content with the division, and had expected it to be repli-
cated within the cadre of officers.

Serena, with her pure English beauty, pale blue eyes and
corn-gold hair, had expected and received universal admiration. Genny had snapped impatiently at anyone who'd
tried to flirt with her, but immediately fallen in with anyone who came to her with a problem to solve.

People new to the General's command had often been
surprised to learn that Serena and Genevieve were sisters.
Genny must have inherited some of her grandmother's
Latin blood, and though her hair had been a broad palette
of browns, from chestnut to pale honey in the light, her
skin had used to take the sun like a Spaniard's, making her
deep grey eyes look even larger in an almost gaunt face.

Well, she was gaunt no longer. In fact, she'd filled out

very nicely indeed. Serena had remained fashionably reed-thin, but Genny was a pure pocket Venus—small, but perfectly proportioned, and with a bosom worthy of a portrait of its own.

And yet she still possessed that strange quality that managed to keep curious males at bay. He'd seen them watching her the night of the ball, their eyes flickering over her lush curves, but amazingly not one of them had dared breach the invisible but very palpable battlements she carried about her.

No, that wasn't true—she'd let Julian in with a smile, which wasn't perhaps surprising if they'd nearly been betrothed. Marcus as well, though not quite as happily—there had been more resigned acceptance than affection between them. Still, it showed she had the capacity to let men in if she chose.

Strange…

She was strange. He could not understand what she was still doing here. She was not a beauty, like her sister, but she was far more interesting—and leagues more intelligent. Strange that someone with her skills at manoeuvring people had not yet married.

She must be…what? Twenty-five or six? Given the less than impressive scions of some of the nobility, he didn't doubt she could have found herself a husband to mould to her needs. Still, it appeared that for the moment all her skills were being used in aid of his family, for which he should be grateful.

For which he *was* grateful, he told himself. Reluctant, and uncomfortable, but grateful.

War made strange bedfellows, and it appeared he had just slipped into bed with Genevieve Maitland.

He waited for the rush of warmth that swept through him at the unfortunate analogy to fade.

Not a good idea.

Not that there was much to be read into his physical reaction to the pleasure of a battle well played and a very luscious figure and stormy eyes. Little Genny Maitland had been transformed into a very attractive woman and, more significantly, a puzzling one.

He had a weakness for puzzles. Especially those scented like orange blossoms.

Still, she'd been right to call him to attention—just as she had been right last night, when he'd stepped over the line into a literally heavy-handed attempt to test her defences.

Well, he'd best step back behind it. Uncharted waters might be enticing, but they were far more likely to hide treacherous reefs than treasures.

Chapter Seven

'As pretty as a music box' was an appropriate description for Drury Lane Theatre. Everything was designed to impress and awe—the grandiose foyer with its Doric columns, the brightly lit rotunda, crowded with the cream of the Ton, the boxes lit with rows of gaslight chandeliers, and finally the forty-foot-high stage.

Kit, who had entered the theatre with all the wariness of a man entering a scorpion-infested cave, wasn't certain whether he was relieved or disappointed that it looked nothing like his vivid memory of the place. But if it was relief, the feeling was very mild compared with the other emotions seething inside him.

Only a fortnight ago, if anyone had asked what it would take for him to accompany his grandmother to a play at the Drury Lane Theatre, under the viciously watchful eye of the Ton, he'd have said it would take an act of God to do the trick. He wondered if acts of God came in the guise of his sister's happiness coupled with a little devious manipulation by a general *manqué*.

Still, the happiness on his sister's face now, as she settled into her seat in the box between him and Peter, was a balm to his rumbling temper. She was practically bouncing, her gaze moving with patent awe over the theatre and her hand holding Peter's tightly.

'It is simply enormous! There must be *hundreds* of people here!' she whispered.

'Don't gawp, girl!' Lady Westford admonished, and Emily sat back, abashed.

Peter, his pale cheeks turning rather red, placed his hand on Emily's and leaned forward, clearly preparing to take up arms in his beloved's defence. But Kit's wish to see Emily's serious-minded betrothed tackle Lady Westford was dashed as Genevieve, seated on Peter's other side, touched his arm, drawing his attention.

'Do you know, Peter, I think Drury Lane was the first theatre in London to introduce gas chandeliers? It is rather amazing to think they are all connected to a warren of gas pipes. It seems quite impossible—and rather frightening.'

Peter, his clever, practical mind latching on to this engineering challenge, rushed into a reassuring speech about temperatures and pipes and counterweights. And Kit was rather amused to see Emily regard this serious monologue with far warmer admiration than she'd shown for the *Who's Who* of London society filling the theatre.

He was even more impressed when she interrupted with an objection about Archimedean points of leverage. The happy couple then descended into a heated but amicable discussion of how best to prevent all this piping from causing another catastrophic fire, and the rest of the world—the theatre included—was clearly forgotten.

His gaze briefly met Genny Maitland's. Her mouth was primly holding back a smile. It was let loose for a moment as he looked at her, and her eyes lit with shared laughter, a momentary flash like faraway lightning.

Then Julian walked in, paused for a moment to listen to the heated discussion, and then bent to whisper something in Genny's ear. The look she cast him over her shoulder would have felled a tree, but he merely raised his hands with a grin and settled deeply into his chair.

Lady Westford threw him an exasperated look. 'Sit up, do, Julian. What is it with you young men these days? You dress like footmen, lounge like hackney drivers, and behave in all manners as if you were the hoi polloi.'

'Hoi polloi, Grandmama,' Julian said with suspicious meekness.

'That is what I said.'

'No, you said *the* hoi polloi. *Hoi* is the plural for *the* in Greek, and *polloi* is *many*. Saying *the* hoi polloi is unnecessarily repetitive.'

The cane hovered ominously above the floor, but then a party including the Duke of Burford entered the box opposite them and the cane was lowered. When Lady Westford spoke again it was with a wholly unconvincing smile.

'I don't know why you bother to come at all if you mean to be unpleasant, Julian.'

'I don't *mean* to be, Grandmama. It just happens.'

She snorted and turned her back to him. Julian caught Genny's frown, winked at her, and raised an imaginary quizzing glass to ogle her bosom. Her frown dissolved into a rueful smile and she shook her head and turned her back on him too. Julian, balked of his view, sighed and settled into his slouch.

At least in this respect Kit could empathise with his cousin. Genny Maitland might not be a beauty, like her sister, but she had been endowed with a body that could launch quite a few ships.

She'd worn a relatively modest evening gown during the ball, and although her present gown was also far from elaborate, its simple square-cut bodice and silky material the colour of ripening Turkish apricots moulded over her curves and displayed her exquisite bosom like the work of art it was, promising that what lay beneath was a hundred times more appetising than that sweet fruit.

Kit was not in the least surprised that a connoisseur of feminine charms like Julian would appreciate the view. What surprised Kit was the degree of ease between Genny and Julian. Perhaps even intimacy?

Not that there was anything wrong with that. Genevieve Maitland was of an age to do as she willed, and she had a degree of maturity to her that outstripped her widowed sister, and in a way even Mary. As far as he was concerned, so long as it did not adversely impact upon Emily and Mary, she could—and probably would—do as she wished.

Kit forced his attention to the stage as a buzz of cheering signalled Edmund Kean's entrance. He hoped the performance of the actors on stage would compensate for the performances off it.

To his surprise, it was excellent. As Sir Giles Overreach, Edmund Kean was ambition and rancour personified. He reminded Kit a little of Lady Westford. And the crowd, from the boxes to the pit, was enthralled with Sir Giles's vicious destructiveness towards everyone around him. He had no redeeming qualities but the sheer force of his will to win.

Kean's portrayal was so convincing Kit found himself completely in accord with the muffled cries of 'Shame!' and 'Poor show!' that punctuated his increasingly convoluted attempts to destroy and discredit everyone about him.

'Why, he is the most contemptible worm that ever was! If I were his daughter I would set the dogs to him!' hissed Emily, practically writhing in her seat. She looked ready to descend onto the stage, fill his pockets with chops, and drag him out to the dogs herself.

Kit smiled at his half-sister's uncharacteristic bloodthirstiness and let his gaze slip past her to Genny. She appeared as engrossed by the play as Emily, her whole body canted forward in a manner that might have drawn his grandmother's condemnation if she hadn't already slipped into a fitful doze.

Like this, Genny looked years younger—as if surrendering to the passion of the drama had peeled years off her. One fisted hand was clenched to her sternum, pressing her bosom into an even more impressive display of perfect curves as she leaned forward. Kit realised his own hand had fisted too, and he released it. But it fisted again, involuntarily, as she raised her hand to her mouth as if to stifle a gasp at Kean's latest masterpiece of evil.

He turned back to the stage himself, a little annoyed at his green response to her surprisingly girlish show of enjoyment, coupled with her wholly female show of curves.

She'd had those rare moments in Spain as well, when she'd been caught up in the heated discussions that had often brewed around her grandfather's dinner table in the barracks. Her careful mantle of control would slip, and her excitement and determination would be bared in service of whatever cause she'd felt worth defending. Then some comment would check her, and she'd withdraw like a fern, furling back as night fell, her gaze glacial, as if challenging anyone to remind her she'd been on fire only a moment before.

The contrast with the soft and frothy Serena had been even more obvious during those vivid eruptions and retreats. From his lofty age of twenty-five he'd thought it merely a sign of a girl hovering on the tricky bridge between youth and womanhood, and he'd felt both sorry for her and strangely proud, as if he was as invested in her awkward intelligence as her grandfather had been.

But she had not appreciated his stilted attempts to smooth those moments over and, looking back, he couldn't blame her. Charlie had done it much more successfully by poking fun at her at the same time as making his awe of her unburnished intelligence clear.

She'd certainly managed to leash that awkwardness over the years, but right now she looked precisely as she had in the heat of passionate argument. Her eyes glistened a strange vulpine silver, like snow deep in the shadows, and her generous mouth was parted and moving faintly, the sheen of the chandelier dancing on the soft curve of her lower lip. She seemed to be echoing the soliloquy below, and in a strange twist of acoustics he seemed to hear the words emanate from her—a tortured, hopeless call to arms against everything and everyone.

As if aware of being watched, she turned, her face alight with surprising excitement, her light grey eyes catching the gold flickers of the chandeliers like sun flicking off an ice-bound sea. She seemed hardly to see him, caught wholly in the deep human drama on the stage.

He turned away, rubbing his tingling fingers surreptitiously on his trousers, a little ashamed to have distracted her with his schoolboy gawking. He was here to watch the play and make Emily happy—not to ogle the woman who had become his unexpected nemesis.

He managed to insert himself back into the play, but was relieved when the crowd rumbled in a mix of protests and cheers that marked the departure of Sir Giles Overreach from the stage.

Genny Maitland sat back with a faint exhalation and in the same moment turned. Their eyes met once more. Her smile, already soft and faraway, deepened, encompassing him, inviting him to appreciate something extraordinary.

It caught at him. The immensity of the theatre, the strange abandonment that came from being told a bedtime story on a grand scale. He could feel the beating heart of the audience, the wonder, the passion, the escape…

That sensation was strange enough, but then her smile

made the theatre shrink and fall away, and he saw only a young woman freed for a moment from everything that held her down. It stripped him raw, and he had the unsettling conviction that she was looking right inside him to something he hadn't even realised was there.

It was merely a short, sharp moment. Then Julian rose, blocking his sight of her.

By the time he passed towards the door of the box she had turned back to the stage, her head tilted as Serena spoke to her. Though she was still smiling, the wonder was gone from her face, replaced by the slight crease between her brows that she'd worn for most of the ball.

The managing Miss Maitland was back.

'Is it true that pirates bury their treasure?'

This question, blurted out by the youngest of the Duke of Burford's granddaughters, caused a sudden break in the buzzing voices that surrounded them in the foyer of Drury Lane Theatre. Several pairs of eyes, from the brown of the two Burford girls to the blue of Lady Sarah Ponsonby and the pale green of a young woman whose name he could not recollect, were all fixed on him, awaiting his clarification on this crucial issue.

Kit, having twice already in the conversation disclaimed being a pirate, stifled a sigh. 'Burying is a rather risky way to treat your valuable belongings, Lady Calista. I don't know what pirates do, but I prefer to place mine safely in a bank.'

'Oh,' she said, clearly disappointed.

Her sister and the green-eyed girl appeared only slightly less disaffected with this prosaic approach, but Lady Sarah Ponsonby smiled a trifle condescendingly.

'I told you burying treasures made no sense, Cally. It is shockingly risky. Anyone could be watching and might make off with it the moment you sail away.'

'But you don't *have* banks at sea, do you?' Lady Sophronia pointed out, hurrying to her sister's defence.

Lady Calista perked up. 'That is quite true, Ronny! Perhaps you could place a curse on your treasure to stop other pirates from making away with it?'

'My mother taught me that it is impolite to curse,' Kit replied, once again debating and abandoning the idea of arguing with the 'other pirates' categorisation. Denial only appeared to fuel conviction.

He cast his gaze over the perfectly coiffed heads surrounding him and searching the crowd in hope of salvation.

His grandmother, who'd positioned him in this crowd of debutantes and then wandered off with the Duke of Burford, would be no salvation, and despite his height he could not see the other members of their party.

'Was your mother a pirate as well?' asked Lady Calista, and was met with a hiss of warning from the other young women. The youngest Burford flushed and added hurriedly, 'Oh, I forgot…she was an actress.'

Dead silence.

Now all the young women were all red as lobsters—even Lady Sarah Ponsonby, usually as cool and biting as ice. He took pity on them even as he cursed Genny Maitland for manoeuvring him into coming tonight.

'No, my grandfather was the actor, as well as being a bookbinder. Though my mother did enjoy the theatre very much. I learned my appreciation of Shakespeare from her—as well as my manners,' he added a little pointedly. 'Now, if you will excuse me? It has been delightful conversing with you, but I must find my sister.'

He ran Mary to ground behind one of the Doric columns, watching over Emily and Peter who stood in a small group of younger people.

She smiled at his approach. 'I cannot believe this is Emily's first time in a proper theatre! I have been very remiss.'

'From what I know of Emily, she is more likely to enjoy a visit to a foundry than a theatre. Still, I am glad she is enjoying herself.'

'Oh, dear. I take it you aren't?'

'I am surviving. Though if one more doe-eyed young woman asks me about pirates and treasure I might do something drastic and tell them I keep mine under my bed, along with the skulls of my enemies.'

'Kit! Pray be patient. They mean well, you know.'

He turned away before he told her what he thought of her naiveté. He spotted Serena Carrington, in conversation with two women by the stairs leading up to the boxes, but there was no sight of Genny.

'Where is Miss Maitland? I haven't seen her in the foyer.'

Mary glanced around her.

'Oh. I daresay she has remained in the box with Grandmama.'

'No, Grandmother is over there, with His Aging Grace. It was she who threw me to the sharks among the debutantes. Genny wasn't with her.'

Mary frowned as she scanned the crowded rotunda 'Perhaps she prefers to remain in the box on her own. She is like that sometimes.'

Kit felt a twinge of offence on Genny's behalf at Mary's casual unconcern for her whereabouts. Then he remembered Genny sitting in the stable at the house, conferring with the kitten, and how lost in rapture she'd been during the play. Now he thought of it, she had played the social game with consummate skill at the ball, but at no time had she looked to be enjoying herself. Perhaps she truly did prefer her own company. He of all people should be able to respect that.

'Or perhaps she is with Julian,' Mary continued, with

the same blithe unconcern, even as she turned away to greet two women approaching her.

Kit left her before he was roped into more piratical queries. They still had the second performance to sit through and he was already itching to leave.

He moved towards the stairs, wondering where Julian had gone. The Green Room, where actors entertained guests, was unlikely to be open for the usual influx of admirers until after the second play or musical piece, but no doubt Julian would find a way to wheedle himself into whatever room her liked.

Or perhaps he was, as Mary had said, with Genevieve Maitland.

He noted that Lord Ponsonby and his daughter were now standing with Serena by the stairs. Passing by them without stopping would be clearly rude, so instead he slipped into one of the side corridors and took a set of stairs leading upwards, hoping they would eventually lead to the boxes.

There were few lights here, and the narrow corridors were hushed. He smiled as he climbed the narrow stairs. It was fitting that he had turned into what was probably the servants' passage, or perhaps one of the passages where actors like his grandfather had once navigated the warren-like structure.

He'd barely heaved a sigh of relief at the quiet when he stopped. Two shadowy figures stood at the end of the darkened corridor, outlined by the hazy light coming through a window darkened with grime. They were standing quite close, their voices hushed, and they had not yet seen him.

Kit knew it was poor form to eavesdrop, but he stood silently, watching the dark-on-dark outline of Genevieve Maitland's profile. His cousin Julian was lounging against the wall, his hands shoved deep in his coat pockets, his chin tucked into the folds of his cravat.

'You promised me, Julian! I won't allow you to back out now.'

'I'm not backing out, love. Merely renegotiating. I gave in far too easily.'

'There is nothing to renegotiate.'

'There is *always* something to renegotiate.'

The same ease of long familiarity that he'd seen at the ball was even more evident here. Genevieve Maitland might be radiating annoyance, her arms folded like a disapproving headmistress and plumping up her bosom, to Julian's evident appreciation, but her voice was more resigned than angry, and the affection beneath it was as clear as her enjoyment of the play.

'I think you are being difficult for difficulty's sake, Julian.'

'All I am saying is that I think I deserve some incentive for being so…biddable.'

'Really, Julian. You do choose your moments.' She sighed with resignation, but there was a peculiar relief in her voice, as if she'd been expecting something worse.

'Do you know how much I adore being scolded by you, Gen…?' Julian's voice dropped as he moved even closer.

Kit moved into the corridor.

Genny turned and Julian stepped back. For a moment no one spoke.

Then Julian gave a rueful laugh. 'Your timing leaves a lot to be desired, cousin.'

'I could say the same of you, Julian. Wouldn't it be wiser, or at least safer, to conduct your flirtation at Carrington House?'

'Wiser, perhaps. Not quite as enjoyable. Knowing Grandmama is in the house is bound to put a dampener on one's enthusiasm.' He turned to Genny. 'Though we could continue our discussion at my rooms? I'll even clear the sofa for you this time.'

'Julian!'

Genny's voice snapped down on his name but he merely laughed and sauntered off around the corner.

For a building humming with hundreds of people, this corridor was as quiet as the hold of a ship. The murmur of the crowd from somewhere inside was like the soothing sound of water against the hull.

The comparison did nothing to ease the strange burning of anger inside him. He knew full well he was being irrational, and that if anyone was accountable for the charade he'd been forced to play out in the foyer it was his grandmother, not Genevieve Maitland. But all his frustration, exasperation, impatience, and discomfort homed in on her like light through a piece of glass. Its concentrated heat was searing a hole in him as surely as it would burn through wood.

He struggled for composure, but the words came out anyway. 'Are you in the habit of meeting Julian in darkened corridors in very public locations?'

'That is none of your concern, Lord Westford.'

'No? Since you are living in my house, I rather think it is.'

His eyes were now accustomed to the gloom, and he watched colour rush up her cheeks. But her tone remained as calm as before.

'Julian was trying to get a rise out of you. Apparently he has succeeded.'

'I will take that as a yes. Does Mary know?'

'Does Mary know what?'

'That the two of you are having an affair.'

Her indrawn breath was long, and gave him another display of her bosom that would likely have delighted Julian.

'It is amazing to me that men rule the world and yet they can never seem to think past their libidos. Or perhaps that is *why* they rule the world. Life is so much simpler when you are stupid.'

He ignored this clear attempt to divert his fire. 'You do realise that if it had been anyone else who had come up those stairs you and Julian would be in the centre of a very unpleasant little scandal?'

'Then we are lucky it was you, aren't we?' Her words were light but her eyes were still watchful.

'I would rather not depend upon luck protecting my family's reputation.'

'Interesting… I was rather of the opinion that was precisely what you have been doing ever since you sold your commission and adopted your…itinerant lifestyle.'

Damnation. The brutality of that thrust was only matched by the fact that she was absolutely right.

Still, what surprised him was the realisation, as sharp as a knife piercing flesh, that she was furious. With him. And she had been from the moment she'd walked into the drawing room the night of the ball. No, before he'd even returned to London.

Just as he made that discovery, he realised why.

'You think I'm irresponsible.'

She had turned away, as if to follow Julian's exit, but now she gave a strange little huff and turned back to face him. 'Yes.'

'I daresay you think Julian the soul of accountability?'

She shrugged, and turned again in the direction Julian had disappeared in, but he strode after her, capturing her arm and stopping her on the bottom step of another staircase leading upwards.

'Damnation, you don't get to throw around accusations—'

'I didn't accuse you,' she interrupted. 'I answered your question. Then *you* replied with a completely irrelevant statement. Now it is time to return to the box. The sheep are returning to their pens, and in this particular case I'm not a shepherd but a nice fluffy little sheep—and so are you. If you wish to meet me at dawn with pistols or cutlasses, Captain Carrington, I will be only too happy to oblige, but not now.'

He was so damn tempted to use every inch of his superior height and strength, but that in itself shocked him. He couldn't remember ever being tempted to use his physical superiority against anyone other than his cousins since his schooldays—let alone a woman. Genny Maitland was bringing out the worst in him.

He moved away but didn't quite let go of her arm. 'Damnation—how do you win each and every round?'

'I've won nothing.'

Her voice wobbled and his temper fell right off its high horse.

His hand slipped down to capture hers. It was cold. He was keeping her in a draughty corridor in a dress that probably weighed less than his waistcoat, doing his damnedest to force something out of her he didn't even understand.

An admission that he wasn't as black as she thought him?

He didn't need absolution from her, but he was still here, holding her hand, while she wished him in Hades and while the rest of the world was probably taking their places in the boxes.

With that realisation came a sly, unsettling thought… What would happen if they walked in together after the second play had begun? All that eager buzzing that surrounded him like wasps around a jam tart would turn deafening. And vicious.

He stepped aside. 'You'd best return to the others.'

She glanced down at the hand he still held. It didn't feel cold now. He let it slip against his as he withdrew, sensation shooting up his arm. She curled it into a fist and for one long moment he tensed as if for a blow, his whole body thudding with anticipation.

Then she slipped into the darkness.

Chapter Eight

'I'm so glad you decided to attend the theatre last night, Kit. Though I must say the second piece was not at all of the same quality as Kean's performance. But Emily found it engaging—especially the spectacle with the waterfall and the dog jumping out of the water. I still cannot understand how they did that, even after Peter's explanation…'

Mary's gentle flow of words accompanied Kit as he prowled the morning room. He'd arrived early, knowing his grandmother rarely descended from her rooms before the afternoon, but now he felt somewhat disappointed. At the very least he'd hoped that Emily would be there. She never failed to lighten his mood. But Mary had come down alone.

'Where is Emily? Is she worn out after her late night or off with Peter's family, exploring London again?'

'Neither. She and Genny have gone to Hatchards. Emily has discovered that Peter's library is composed primarily of scientific tomes, and though she shares his interests, she loves novels as well, and so has set about rectifying that fault before the wedding. You both inherited your father's love of literature, though Emily hasn't inherited his interest in history.'

As always when she mentioned his father, there was an

edge of sadness to her voice. Kit took a sharp turn towards the window. Sometimes her tendency to melancholy aggravated him. Today, it grated against his nerves. He wasn't in a mood to soothe her.

'She will be married in under a month. I think it is time we discussed your plans, Mary.'

'We have discussed this already, Kit,' she reproved. 'I shall remain with your grandmama. I know you are concerned, but I must say she is much improved this past week. Perhaps now she has had a chance to accept your grandfather's death she is coming to appreciate our presence—'

'Ballocks,' he interrupted indelicately. 'Don't fool yourself. She doesn't respect sweetness, Mary; she respects strength. If you'd once told her to shut the hell up, you'd have a better chance to stop her constant needling.'

Mary's pale cheeks flushed with mortification. He felt a complete bastard, but he couldn't seem to stem this newfound anger at his stepmother. Her sweetness might bring her much in life, but rarely what she most needed. He'd watched her allow her needs to fall to the very bottom of the Carrington pile time and time again, and he couldn't seem to convince her that she had the power to alter that order.

'I appreciate your concern, Kit, no matter how you express it… But I assure you she is not always as free with her criticism as you have seen her be these past days. In fact, her mood was much improved yesterday. She hardly made any cutting remarks at all.'

'Because we all obeyed her edicts and behaved ourselves on the social stage. And because—' He stopped, warned by the clicking of the cane on the marble of the hall. 'Ah, hell…'

Mary sighed and folded her hands.

Howich opened the door and Lady Westford entered, surveying the room.

'Where is Genevieve?' she demanded of Mary, not even bothering to acknowledge Kit's presence.

'Gone with Emily to Hatchards, Mama.'

'Huh…' Her gaze weighed Mary like a wolf eyeing a doe. 'Wasting my money again, eh?'

'Mine, Grandmother,' Kit corrected, drawing her fire, but she merely shrugged.

'Should have gone yourself, Mary. I need a word with Genevieve.'

'Perhaps I could help?' Mary asked.

Lady Westford gave a snort. 'Not likely. None of you have an ounce of her sense. Charlie should have married her instead of that golden sheep with no hips, then everything would have been a sight better all around. It's not looks we need; it's brains.'

They both watched as she limped out, and then Kit went to close the door behind her, resisting the urge to slam it.

'It's amazing none of you has shoved her down the stairs yet. She's the three witches all rolled into one and dipped in vinegar. And don't offer more excuses for her, Mary, or I might lose my temper.'

Mary kept her eyes on her embroidery, but her fingers shook. He took a deep breath and went to sit beside her.

'I'm sorry, Mary… I don't know why I'm being such an ass. Coming back here always brings out the worst in me. It's like being shoved back into the skin of a twelve-year-old. But that's no reason to make you miserable.'

'You aren't,' she said, not very convincingly. 'And I do understand it is hard for you. They truly were always horribly beastly to you. But I wish you could make your peace with her…with us. Keeping away is no solution. You need to come home—now more than ever.'

'It isn't my home, Mary.'

'It *could* be if you wished it.'

'Therein lies your answer. I wonder what the devil she's up to.'

'Who? Your grandmama?'

'She and the little field marshal.'

'Field mar…? Oh, you mean Genny? She probably wants her for something to do with the housekeeping. She's very hard on housekeepers, and both she and Mrs Pritchard find it easier to use Genny as intermediary. Mr Fletcher, the steward at the Hall, does so as well. It is easier that way.'

'I have no doubt. Clever how Miss Maitland has made herself indispensable…' His temper was beginning to climb, so he changed tack. 'Why hasn't Serena married again? She is still a handsome woman; she must have ad-mirers.'

Mary's mouth twisted a little. 'You forget—we had not yet come out of mourning for Charlie when Lord Westford died. Besides, admirers aren't suitors. A widow burdened with debt, who has shown she cannot carry a child to term, is not in high demand, no matter how pretty.'

Nor was a woman of thirty-seven who had had but one daughter in a dozen years of marriage.

Those words remained unsaid, but they sounded loud and clear.

'Well, it doesn't help that you have both been immured at the Hall for the past year and a half. Now you are in London for the next few weeks it might be different. Men are not all cut from the same cloth.'

Mary frowned. 'That was what Genny was hoping.'

'She was hoping to find a husband?'

'Not for her. For Serena. And for me. She doesn't wish for either of us to remain with your grandmother alone.'

'Why not for herself? Because of Julian?'

'Julian?'

'Is she holding a candle for him? There is definitely something between them.'

'It is true they have been good friends from the start, but I do not think it is any more than that. I certainly don't think Julian wishes to wed her—or anyone, for that matter. He only offered for her because he hoped his maternal aunt would grant him a legacy if he were betrothed, but in the end Marcus inherited it all. Poor Julian was quite put out. Your grandfather always said he was shockingly expensive, and I happen to know he has borrowed funds from Marcus. If he did marry it would most likely be for a dowry, but Genny hasn't a penny, you see…'

No, he didn't see. Since the moment he'd become entangled in the workings of this strange female-driven household he'd felt as if he was sailing through a fog and far too close to the reefs.

He hated that feeling.

Mary turned her head, listening, and he heard the murmur of voices in the hall.

'Speak of the devil…' he muttered.

Mary cast him an imploring look. 'Please don't cross swords with her again in front of Emily.'

'Again?'

'The two of you were so viciously polite to each other at the theatre after the intermission it was evident to all that you had had words. Emily spoke of it when she prepared for bed last night. She was very upset that two people she loves were at loggerheads.'

'We merely disagreed about the merits of the play.'

'Huh.' Mary gave an uncharacteristically indelicate snort.

He stood, moving restlessly towards the fireplace. 'You may enjoy being herded. I don't.'

'She isn't trying to herd *you*, Kit.'

'Well, I don't like her herding *you*, either.'

'I see. Only you are permitted to do that, then?'

'I don't… That is different,' he bit out, annoyed at the truth behind her words.

Before he could continue, the door opened and Emily hurried in, followed by Genny.

'Kit! We've had the most marvellous morning. I think we have cleared all the shelves at Hatchards and I have bought you the loveliest illustrated edition of Swift's *Travels*. Would you believe the clerk tried to dissuade me? He said it was not at all the thing for a young woman to read, but Genny soon routed him—didn't you, Genny? And in the sweetest possible way, so that the poor fellow was quite smitten and spent the next half-hour carrying around our purchases like a little lamb.'

Kit raised an eyebrow, throwing Mary a wry look over Emily's head. At least she had the grace to blush a little.

Unfortunately, Genny herself looked up from drawing off her gloves and intercepted their exchange.

He was damned if he would ascribe the same omniscience to her that Mary and Julian seemed to, but when those chasm-deep grey eyes were fixed on one, it was damned easy to believe in it oneself.

He took the book from Emily and opened it to the illustration of Gulliver tied down by the Lilliputians. Right now he felt a double dose of sympathy for the helpless fellow.

'It's beautiful, Emmy. Thank you.'

She touched the dark brown spine of the book. 'Some of my very first memories are of you reading to me whenever you came down from school. I would keep myself awake, watching for the light of your candle under the door as you came with one of your books. Mama would read to me too, but she couldn't do the voices like you.' She smiled at Mary. 'Sorry, Mama.'

Mary smiled back. 'Don't apologise, love. It is quite

true. I admit I would listen at the door when you read, Kit. George said you had Kathleen's gift.'

Had his father said that? It wasn't true, of course, but it felt like a rare gift. His memories of his father before and after his mother's death were of two different men: one strong and often laughing; the other silent and bowed.

Mary had received an ill bargain with only Emily as compensation. It was time to repay her. And that meant removing her from under his grandmother's dark cloud.

He looked past Emily and Mary to where Genny was sorting through a stack of correspondence by the desk. The sun filtered through her hair, creating a gold and amber halo. She seemed utterly absorbed in her task, and yet he could feel her awareness of everything that was happening in the room.

Now she gathered the correspondence and excused herself. Emily and Mary barely noticed—Emily was chatting to Mary about her new books, while Mary watched her daughter with a combination of love and wistfulness.

Kit excused himself as well, and went in pursuit of the Generalissima.

Chapter Nine

'Miss Maitland.'

'Yes, Lord Westford?'

Damn, he hated that tone. If there was anything less deferential than Genny in this mood, he had yet to encounter it.

He went to lean against the writing desk which dominated the study, watching as she sorted and stacked letters.

'How long have you been my grandmother's secretary?'

'I help when I can, Lord Westford. Serena and I are living on her charity, after all. Or rather, on yours. It soothes my conscience to make myself useful.'

'More straight dealing?'

'It is merely the truth.'

She laid out the correspondence in neat piles. Most, as far as he could see, was addressed to his grandmother. There were a couple of letters for Mary, and one Genny had placed face down. He reached for it but she placed her hand on it.

'That is mine.'

Her voice was without inflection, but a slight burn of colour feathered across her cheekbones. The temptation to slip it out from under her hand was sharp, but instead he focused on the others.

'I didn't know my grandmother was such an avid correspondent.'

'These are mostly invitations.'

'And these?' He tapped another stack.

'Responses from tradesmen regarding enquiries I have made about a Venetian breakfast.'

'Venetians don't eat breakfast. I've yet to meet a Venetian who wakes before noon.'

Her mouth quirked and a near-dimple hovered into being. 'A Venetian breakfast takes place in the afternoon and has nothing at all to do with Venice, unfortunately.'

'Have you been there?' he asked

She shook her head and the same wistful light sparked for a moment and was extinguished.

He picked up a bill, raising a brow. 'Three dozen lanterns?'

'Lady Westford wants to hold it in the garden. There are few houses in London with grounds like Carrington House.'

'But why lanterns? I thought you said it is held in the afternoon.'

'It might last well into the evening. One must be prepared.'

'You plan to entertain guests for a whole day in the garden? In April? In England? What if it rains? Or have you put in an order for sunshine as well?'

'It shan't rain.'

Her response was so bland he felt a momentary loss of balance. Not even a dimple quivered in her cheek now, but he knew, absolutely, that she was laughing at him. His resentment against her, which had been riding so high the past few days and had peaked sharply last night, faded like a fog lifting.

As if she sensed his lowering of some internal barrier she finally smiled. Not the vivid, almost blissful smile of last night, but a mix of relief and laughter still carefully held in.

'I would hate to play cards against you, Genevieve Maitland,' he admitted.

'I thought that was precisely what we were doing, Lord Westford. You did not follow me here to discuss your grandmother's social plans. You want something from me, correct?'

You want something from me.

It was the truth, but an unfortunate choice of words.

At the moment, with that playful challenging smile tilting up her eyes and softening her mouth so that is showed its full, lush promise, he could think of one thing in particular he wanted from her.

It was as disconcerting as hell that she could spark in him this mixture of confusion and attraction. In Spain he had thought of her only as his commanding officer's granddaughter. Yet his memory of her was quite a bit sharper than he would have thought reasonable. She'd had freckles then, coaxed to the surface by the Spanish sun that had lightened her wavy hair. She'd looked like a waif but acted like one of the Prussian mercenaries who served under Wellington—cool, focused, and as prickly as a hedgehog.

Except when she'd been with animals. With them she'd always been as soft and cooing as she'd been with the little kitten in the stables.

He had no idea which of those warring personas was at her core and he doubted she'd allow him to find out.

Not that it mattered.

She hadn't moved during his silence, but the light of laughter faded from her eyes and left them guarded. He had the strangest sensation of looking through the deep grey to something else entirely. But whatever it was, it was as elusive as ever.

On impulse, he touched her chin lightly. She didn't pull away but stood there, impassive and waiting.

'You used to have more freckles,' he said, simply for something to say.

His fingers were barely touching her skin but he felt it humming. Her throat worked, as if she was trying not to swallow, a sign of nervousness that gave him far too much satisfaction—he didn't want to be the only one unsettled.

He moved away to the other side of the desk. 'You are right, Miss Maitland. I followed you here for a purpose. First, I wish to apologise for my behaviour last night. I realise you think me the lowest of slackers...'

Her eyes widened and her hands flew up, stopping him. 'No, that is not... I had no right to say that.'

'As I recall, you didn't actually *say* anything aloud.'

'I made my sentiments clear, which is even worse than saying them aloud.'

'That is debatable,' he replied, a little mollified. 'But it brings me to the second reason I wish to speak with you. The truth is, I need your help.'

Once again the shield fell away. Her lips parted and he had the pleasure of watching Miss Genevieve Maitland surprised. Unsettled, even. Her eyes darkened as her pupils dilated, crowding the grey into a dusky violet at the rim. It reminded him of the deep waters of the ocean in the slow hours before dawn—when sailors felt most at the mercy of the endless emptiness.

'I don't understand.' She lowered her chin, her long lashes curling upwards in a wary question.

He glanced at the door. The last thing he wanted was either Mary or Emily bursting in on this conversation. After a quick glance into the empty corridor he locked the door. Her eyes had widened further during this manoeuvre and the faint flush that had warmed her skin had darkened.

Unsettling her hadn't been part of his agenda, but seeing her less than cool and collected was a pleasant change.

'I want Mary out of this house.'

Surprise was transformed into outrage. 'Kit Carrington! That is…beastly!'

'Hush! Damn—I keep forgetting this is my house. I mean I want her out of my grandmother's clutches. I want to find her a husband.'

Genny's flush turned livid and she pressed her hands to her cheeks. 'Oh, dear. I'm so sorry. I thought…'

'Yes, that I am a beast and an ogre and I toss widows out on the street in the cold dark hours of the night.'

She dropped her hands, her dimples flashing. 'No, that is not what I thought, but…'

She hesitated and he forged forward. 'I know you will say I am interfering, but she is still young, and now Emily is leaving she will be lonely. I don't want to return in five years and find her still crushed under my grandmother's thumb. She deserves better.'

'True, but…'

'And I know you wish to find someone for Serena as well.'

'How do you know that?'

'I saw you herding her towards Lord Ponsonby and Gresham—apparently two eligible widowers with independent means and a measure of charm. But though your methods are impressive, your information is flawed. Gresham is deeply in debt. I wouldn't encourage that connection.'

'I have heard no such talk.'

'Because you move in polite circles and Gresham is clever enough to secure his loans from sources that are anything but polite. It won't last, though. I would give him perhaps three months before he is forced to rusticate.'

'A pity. He is very knowledgeable about rhododendrons.'

'A man can like rhododendrons and yet be a villain,' Kit misquoted, and won a quick smile.

'So, Lord Westford, what do you want in exchange for saving my sister from an impecunious rhododendron-lover?'

'I told you—your assistance in finding Mary a husband. I am no hand at matchmaking. What do you say?'

'I don't know...' she replied a little helplessly.

'Don't know if you want the trade or don't know if you can use your considerable skills to find a match for Mary?'

He was beginning to enjoy the peculiar revelation of Genevieve Maitland utterly unmoored. Her colour was coming and going like a drunken sailor in a storm.

'That is not the point, Lord Westford.'

'Then what is? Is she beyond all hope? Too hideous? Old cattish?'

Her eyes flashed with silvered laughter. 'You know full well she is lovely and any sensible man should be delighted with someone like Mary. But men aren't sensible. They are too often either practical or romantic. Neither works in Mary's or Serena's favour. All men see when they look at them are two portionless widows of mature years. However...'

Her eyes turned murky and faraway again. Strange that he'd thought her cool and controlled—one had only to watch her eyes to see a whole panoply of tales being played out.

He watched her toil along some inward path for a while. Finally, she gave a sigh, not of despair but of resolution, and he allowed himself to prompt her. 'However...?'

Her gaze focused once more—determined, decided, and direct. His nerves, already clanging like fog bells, snapped to attention.

'I will do it.'

For a moment he felt a wave of relief, which was quickly followed by annoyance at himself. It was a bad sign if he was beginning to regard this pint-sized woman with the same blind faith as Mary did.

'What, precisely, will you do?'

She leaned against the desk and crossed her arms. 'I have some ideas, Lord Westford. But you may not care for them.'

'If it makes Mary happy, I'll bear the cost.'

'It wouldn't merely be monetary. You would have to do your part. And I cannot have you arguing with everything I do.'

What was he letting himself in for?

'Why don't you share your ideas and then I'll decide whether I want to come on board?'

'Very well. I am afraid the kind of entertainments I have been organising aren't enough for our purposes. You saw what happened at the ball, and again yesterday at the theatre. Mary lavishes most of her attention on Emily, and even when she doesn't she mostly relegates herself to the company of matrons and elderly men. She will never meet anyone eligible in that manner, let alone engage their interest.'

'So what do you suggest?'

'I suggest we concentrate on entertainments that attract the right kind of men and conduct them in settings where Mary and Serena have no choice but to interact with them.'

He almost felt sorry for these faceless fellows. 'I presume you have already have a list of likely candidates waiting to be summoned to their marital doom?'

'Of course—in the drawer right between my list of men guaranteed to bore you with their hunting exploits and my list of men who can dance a quadrille without breaking your toes.'

He crossed his arms, mirroring her stance, and smiled. 'Sarcasm is not an attractive quality, Genevieve Maitland.'

'You started it.'

'You sank to my level without a peep.'

'I thought it would be easier for you to converse down there. Being polite is evidently a strain on your faculties.'

'I will have you know that I have always been noted for my good manners.'

'Pointing out your own good manners is the very definition of ill manners. It implies I am either too vulgar to recognise civility or the cause of you losing yours.'

Her teasing cut uncomfortably close to the bone, but he couldn't help laughing. 'Then I shall try to recover my reputation by accepting full responsibility for any unpleasantness between us.'

'Excellent. Now you have put me in the wrong while redeeming yourself. A masterly move, Captain Carrington. Oh, dear, I apologise… I keep forgetting… I mean, Lord Westford.'

'I keep forgetting myself. I wish I could do so categorically.'

'Most men would give their eye teeth for a title and a fortune.'

'I'd take that trade if I could. It never should have been mine. If I'd known Charlie was in such straits…'

'I don't see what you could have done. If your grandfather had no luck dissuading him from investing in those ventures and travelling to Argentina, how could you?'

He was about to comment that he was surprised *she* had not managed to curb his worst tendencies, but thought better of it.

'In any case, we are straying from our task,' he said. 'Which is finding a husband for Mary. I'm afraid I don't know her taste in men, though.'

Her smile turned a little sad. 'Men like your father.'

He moved away from the desk and wandered over to the shelves. 'He was a fool.'

'I never met him, so I cannot attest to that, but from what I have heard he was hardly that. Just…lost. Perhaps he should have stayed at sea after your mother died. Giving up too much of the familiar when you are in pain can be hard to bear.'

He shrugged. He had opened the door to confidences. He could hardly object now to her delving into his father's psyche.

'In any case, I hope we can find someone more suitable for Mary. She hardly shared his naval interests. I remember she never even wished to come down to the bay.'

'No, but she certainly shared his interest in antiquities. I know you aren't acquainted with people in society, but surely your…dealings…have brought you in touch with men who share your interest in art and antiquities.'

'How do you know I share those interests?'

'Aside from the tales you told in the letters you sent Emily and Mary, there is the damning evidence at the Hall. One cannot enter a room without encountering one of your baubles.'

'Baubles?'

'Since Lord Westford passed, Emily has been placing the gifts you've sent her over the years throughout the Hall and it now resembles a museum…in the best possible way. I cannot believe anyone who trades in such artefacts doesn't know of men who share similar interests.'

The image of all those *baubles*, some of which were near priceless, being spread indiscriminately around Carrington Hall was a little unsettling. And before he could consider the wisdom of asking, the words were out of him.

'Did she place any of these "baubles" in your room at the Hall?'

She hesitated, lowering her eyes as she did when she

was uncomfortable. 'She let me choose. There are two jade dragons on my writing desk.'

'I remember those. I bought them in Macau. Qin Dynasty. They are almost two thousand years old, by all accounts.'

Her eyes widened. 'I should put them somewhere safe, then.'

'No, keep them there. They are meant to be appreciated, not tucked away.'

'I admit it seems sad to put them in a box. They glow so beautifully in the sun, and the way they are shaped, so that their bodies interlace…' She stopped, a wholly uncharacteristic flush rushing up her cheeks. 'In any case, once we produce a creditable list of eligible men we can arrange for them to attend our entertainments.'

'How precisely will we arrange that? You can hardly command their presence.'

'I never command. In this case I need not even manoeuvre. Not when I have the perfect bait for our trap.'

He smiled at the rather bloodthirsty relish in her voice. 'And what is that?'

Her gaze focused on him and she smiled. He added another facet to Genevieve Maitland—she could look as smug as a cat with a year's supply of mice.

'Why, you, of course, Lord Westford.'

Genny paused in the corridor outside Lady Westford's rooms. She needed a moment to gather her thoughts, which were still tumbling over themselves as she tried to make sense of her new pact with Captain Carr—with Lord Westford.

She'd made one clear discovery—he was just as unnerving when he was being playful and kind as when he was intent on attack.

She rubbed her hands against her skirts and breathed

in and out several times to push back at the tingling unease that had been chasing her since he'd appeared at Carrington House.

She was not at all certain she could trust him to see the campaign through. He might be charming and insightful, but he was also a drifter, and might at any moment change course and leave her stranded.

Which meant she must also pursue her own plans.

Now she only had to ensure Lady Westford was compliant.

She tapped on the door and entered. Carmine immediately set up a bouncing warble.

'Don't hover in the doorway, girl. Come in,' Lady Westford commanded from her bed, putting down the quizzing glass with which she had been perusing the newspaper.

Genny slipped a few seeds into Carmine's cage, buying a few moments of peace, and placed a chair by the bed. 'Is your hip paining you, Lady Westford?'

'Don't use that sweet tone on me, Genevieve Maitland. I'm not happy with you. I'll concede you made my grandsons show themselves, which is more than I expected. But a ball and a jaunt to the theatre isn't enough for those hungry young misses to tie them down. Those boys are too canny for that—blast them. Marcus has already hared off back to whatever he is concocting up north, Kit refuses to leave the docks, and Julian... I'm not blind, girl. He may flirt with you, but if he hasn't popped the question yet he ain't likely to do so now. The moment Emily weds they'll scatter, and it will all amount to naught.'

'I agree—which is why we must adjust our approach.'

Lady Westford's hand groped for her cane, but it was leaning by the bed, so she gave the covers a thump instead. 'Out with it.'

Carmine chimed in with a warning warble, poking his

beak through the bars. Genny scattered a few more seeds at his feet.

'I have convinced Lord Westford that it will be in Emily's and Mary's interests if we hold a series of select entertainments here at Carrington House, but that for them to succeed he must be in attendance. And in residence.'

'What do you mean, you have "convinced" him? How?'

'It hardly matters. The point is that both he and Julian have agreed to attend.'

'Marcus won't.'

'Probably not. But two out of three is fair odds.'

Lady Westford's pouchy eyes narrowed to slits. 'We shall invite the Burfords. Good blood, large dowries.'

'Yes. And I think Lady Sarah Ponsonby and Miss Caversham as well. Although we'll need some men to balance out the list. We cannot be *too* obvious.'

'Quite. But no dashing young bloods that might appeal to the Burford girls.'

Genny thought it would be hard to find *any* young men who could compete with the Carringtons, but since Lady Westford's concern paved the way for her plan, she nodded.

'Of course not. I think older men…solid but unexciting. The contrast, you see…'

'Yes, yes. But…' Lady Westford tapped her newspaper. Cleared her throat. 'Are you certain Kit is in agreement? He might pull a runner. He was a devil of a boy—always disappearing. George ran him down in Southampton once. He'd gone to look for that ship.'

Over the years Genny had occasionally come face to face with something elusive behind Lady Westford's crusted exterior. She had never been quite able to tell if it was love or pain or merely discomfort.

Genny's attempts to approach were usually firmly rejected, but she stepped tentatively onto the plank. 'How old was he?'

'How should I know? It was years ago. Eleven? Been at the Hall less than a year.'

'Before Mr Carrington married Mary?'

'Yes. One reason George remarried. Thought the boy needed a mother. Told us to choose someone nice. Well, Alfred found someone "nice" for him, didn't he? Pity she couldn't produce more than the one girl. But at least she was good to the boy.'

Poor Mary.

Poor George.

Poor Kit.

'Was it better for Kit after they wed?'

'I don't know. He was away at school, mostly.'

Genny steeled herself to ask the question she'd always wondered. 'Why did he not attend the same school as Charlie and Marcus and Julian?'

The pale blue eyes flashed to hers and away. 'Alfred thought it best. Didn't want the boys dealing with gossip.'

'I see.'

Lady Westford must have heard enough in Genny's tone to pull back behind her ramparts. 'Nothing wrong with Westminster. His best friend was a duke's heir.'

'But Kit must have known why you separated him from the others. He is no fool.'

'What else were we to do? If it wasn't bad enough for that dreadful grandfather of his to be a shopkeeper *and* an actor, he was also a foundling. For all we know he was born on the wrong side of the blanket—could be a Hottentot for all we know. When George eloped with that woman all of London was laughing behind their hands at us. At *us*! I'm the granddaughter of the Duke of Malby and the Carringtons can be traced back to the crusades! Now the Seventh Earl might well be of base blood, not to mention that he carries on like a veritable scoundrel.'

Genny rolled her shoulders, trying to remind herself

why she was here. Letting loose the fury pressing against her control would not further anyone's cause. Still, she could not resist a thrust.

'From what I have seen of the world, birth has very little to do with worth, Lady Westford. A man should be judged by his actions, not by his ancestors, and in that respect the Carringtons have every reason to be proud of Lord Westford. He was by far one of the best officers who served under my grandfather during the war, and that is saying quite a bit. My grandfather was an excellent judge of men.'

'You weren't born into this world, Genevieve Maitland, and you and I have different notions of pride. Why do you think my Alfred fell ill when poor Charles died? He knew what was likely to happen. That when his moment came the future of his family name would be in the hands of that…that vulgar hussy's son. You didn't know her. She hadn't an ounce of proper respect. Looked us straight in the eye and said she and George didn't need us and would make their own path in the world. Snapped her fingers at us as if she was a queen, no less. At *us*!'

Good for her, thought Genny, keeping her jaw tightly locked.

Lady Westford subsided with something between a sigh and moan. 'It killed my Alfred. Killed him!'

There was such confused pain in those words that, despite her antipathy and disgust, Genny almost reached out to touch her gnarled fists. Instead she sat in silence and waited.

Finally, Lady Westford unknotted her hands. 'Do what you need to do, girl. But I think you're wasting your time on Kit.'

'What?' Genny asked, startled.

'Trying to find a match for him. I'd like to see one of the Burford girls take my place as Lady Westford, but likely Kit won't be interested in either of them. I daresay if he ever marries he'll bring back someone wholly unsuitable, like a Saracen or one of those harem girls of his. If he lives that long. Still, you'd best invite Lord Ponsonby's daughter. Handsome thing—and clever. She might wheedle her way past his defences. But make your big push with Julian. He's a rake, but he needs funds for his hobbies so he's most likely to fall into the trap. The Ponsonby heiress might do even better for him. She's no one's fool and she'll keep his head above water. *And* she might not take offence at his flirting with anything in a skirt.'

'He is a touch more discriminating than that, Lady Westford.' She didn't mention that Lady Sarah, definitely no one's fool, had shown at the ball and at the theatre that her sights were set firmly on Kit.

'Hmm… Now, go away. I'm tired. And I don't appreciate you giving Carmine treats. He's getting fat.'

Genny left the room, accompanied by Carmine's shrill objections.

When the door had closed behind her she allowed herself a smile. There was nothing quite like recruiting one's enemies to fight one's battles.

Chapter Ten

Hell on earth.

Kit had been to many places that might have deserved that epithet. The top of his list was still the hold of a Barbary Coast pirate ship, where he'd spent three hellish weeks. But dinners at Carrington House were climbing to the top of that list faster than a monkey up a coconut tree.

And the night was still young.

The worst of it was that he had walked into this particular hell with his eyes, and his bank coffers, open. He had no one to blame but himself…

Actually, there was someone else with whom he could at least share the blame. He cast a reflexive glance halfway down the ludicrously long dinner table to where Genevieve Maitland was seated, between two of his grandmother's portly whist partners.

Since their discussion in the library, the pocket-sized Generalissima had taken the helm at Carrington House with a determination that had left the other members of the household, even his grandmother, breathless in her wake.

In the past week the threatened Venetian breakfast had not only taken place—in full sunshine—but had lasted well into the night as the famous songbird Madame Vestris had given a brilliant recital of Italian arias by the light of several dozen lanterns floating up into the evening breeze. Not a single cloud had dared make an appearance.

The following day Genevieve had transformed the ballroom into a lecture room, and half the directors of the British Museum had joined prominent members of the Antiquarian Society for a lecture on the latest developments in the deciphering of Egyptian hieroglyphs.

He'd actually enjoyed that—and not merely because Mary had been in seventh heaven. And, to be fair, not all the entertainments had been horrible.

It was mostly the dinners. They seemed to involve interminable hours spent discussing tedious topics and parrying even more tiresome questions.

Still, there were elements of interest even in the dullest of evenings. One was watching the inexorable tightening of Genny Maitland's net about a supremely unaware group of eligible men. The list of guests was being constantly modified as she reviewed, discarded and revised her objectives.

He didn't bother trying to keep track of the list—merely watched the dance with appreciation, trying to follow her moves as she slowly amassed an impressive group of eligible, intelligent and mature men. She was strict with her pawns too. When the hands of a brilliant and wealthy antiquarian had happened to rove casually to Serena's derriere, he had been promptly struck from the list.

There were other selections she had made that were more obscure to Kit. For example, he understood the imperative of inviting the Duke of Burford and his granddaughters, as the Duke was a close friend of his grandmother. But Kit could not see her reason to invite someone like Lord Ponsonby. He was relatively eligible, but he'd already gone through two wives and many more mistresses.

Not someone Kit would care to see choose Mary as his third wife.

There were also a few others who were regular invitees—possibly for reasons of familial connection that eluded him. Unfortunately, they too were possessed of an annoying number of daughters.

He would not have minded if only he did not have to sit next to them. But when he'd made that point to Genny after the first few days she'd brushed his objection away without a smidgen of sympathy.

'You are head of the family, so you don't have the luxury of choosing your dinner companions. And do remember you promised you wouldn't make a fuss.'

She'd wandered off with Mrs Pritchard before he'd been able to object, and so tonight once again he was flanked by Lady Sarah and Lady Sophronia. He had nothing against pretty girls—quite the opposite—and he appreciated beauty. But he was not in the mood for flirtation and that was pretty much all they wanted from him. That and tales of grand adventure he had no wish to indulge them with.

At least Julian was similarly besieged. The bubbly Burford chit—Lady Calista, or Calamata, or something—was doing her best to monopolise his cousin's interest, while on his other side was a pretty brunette someone had mentioned stood to inherit ten thousand pounds, who was casting him occasional birdlike glances of mixed interest and fear.

Kit watched in appreciation for a moment as Julian skilfully navigated both those very different flirtations. But then, in the moment of shifting his attention between the two women, he saw Julian fix his gaze upon Genny, who was seated opposite him.

It was the matter of a second—like a bird tipping its wing mid-flight before correcting course. Julian's smile changed from charming and attentive to rueful and real, and then went right back to one of flirtatious enjoyment as he engaged Lady Calista once more.

Kit's gaze went to Genny. She was entertaining the

elderly whist lovers while she kept an eye on the rest of the players at the table and remained in constant silent communication with the servants in the background. But, like Julian, for that moment she'd let her guard slip and smiled a real smile—also rueful, and a little weary. And in another moment, as Julian's attention was engaged elsewhere, her gaze fell to the table, her smile faded, and she looked…lost.

The clinking and buzzing and rumbling and chattering seemed muted, as if they'd all sunk below the water. Even the colours, bright and brassy in the light of dozens of candles, became hazy.

She didn't look like Genevieve Maitland at that moment, but the Genny she had been in Spain—slight, watchful, quiet, and much more that he hadn't seen then but realised now. She was full of fierce determination and carefully sheathed pain.

The officers had laughingly tolerated her hold over her grandfather, but Kit realised now that General Maitland had seen everything that his granddaughter was and everything life would never allow her to become and tried his best to give her…*something.*

It was not enough. All that force, and passion, and *need*—wasted on organising dinner parties, curbing his grandmother's temper, and now finding husbands for the Carrington women.

Then she straightened her shoulders, raised her chin, and turned and met his gaze. It felt like a slap. His whole body took the brunt of the blow, short and sharp and followed by a surge of molten heat, and he pressed back against his chair.

She held his gaze, held *him*, her cool grey eyes carefully blank. But her shields weren't doing their job. If she'd stood and upended the table—china, silver, crystal and all—it would have felt more natural than her sitting there in her pretty pale blue gown, with her rebellious hair tamed into Grecian braids.

He let the image come—her standing like Dido among the ruins of Carthage, her honey-and-fire hair set loose to brush over her skin, her cool eyes in full storm. She would come towards him and—

'Don't you agree, Lord Westford?'

Lady Sarah's question dragged Kit's attention back to reality as abruptly as the erotic image had dragged him out of it, and far less pleasantly. In the haze of confusion, he considered agreeing blindly to whatever politeness she'd offered, but something in her eyes stopped him.

He managed a smile. 'I apologise, Lady Sarah. What must I agree to?'

'I asked whether you preferred flower arrangements or epergnes as a centrepiece,' she replied with mock de-mureness.

He glanced down the dinner table to where a lovely ar-rangement of peonies did nothing to impede his vision of his grandmother. Thankfully his view of Genny was now blocked by one of the rotund whist partners. He turned to the fine view of his grandmother down the miles of linen. She glared at him.

'Whichever is taller,' he said, in reply to Lady Sarah's enquiry.

She cast a quick glance down the table and hid a giggle in her napkin. 'I quite see your point. I had never thought of an epergne as an aid to digestion, but one learns some-thing new every day.'

'That is a positive outlook on life. What else have you learned today, Lady Sarah?'

'The same thing I learned yesterday, unfortunately. That my host would far rather be elsewhere.'

He raised a brow in surprise. This was a very direct approach.

He decided to meet candour with candour. 'I'm sadly deficient in that role, aren't I?'

'Not at all. You are usually engaged in discussions of greater interest than epergnes, or the weather, or the latest *on dits*. It is merely unfortunate that so many men with similar interests are assembled here. It makes it hard for those of us not up to snuff in matters of antiquity to compete for attention. I must endeavour to improve myself.'

He could almost hear his mother, chiding him for his ill manners. 'You do not need improving, Lady Sarah. You might equally claim that us old bores must improve *ourselves*, by broadening our horizons to matters other than musty antiquities.'

'But they aren't in the least musty. You have such beautiful treasures here.'

He smiled, waiting with resignation for some mention of pirates, but she surprised him again.

'For example,' she continued, 'that wonderful little vase in the drawing room that looks as if it has caught the sunlight, so you can see the little drawing as if the people are dancing.'

He frowned, trying to place it. 'Ah, yes. The alabaster vase. It is Egyptian, and probably some two thousand years old.'

'Oh! Was that when Queen Cleopatra was alive?'

'Close enough.'

'Goodness. It might have been a gift to her from Julius Caesar.'

He smiled at the awe in her voice.

'I don't think he would have been allowed past the first portal with such a modest gift. She was probably accustomed to her admirers presenting her with far more substantial offerings.'

'Size isn't all that matters,' she replied with suspicious

demureness, before adding, 'Though it is, of course, important.'

Kit was saved from replying to this suggestive comment by his grandmother, signalling that it was time for the women to withdraw. Lady Sarah impressed him further by showing no sign of regretting the interruption, but he had little doubt this had only been her first sally.

As the men stood he met Julian's gaze and his cousin raised his glass slightly.

Kit wasn't certain if his lopsided smile was mocking or commiserating.

'Damn the boy. He's disappeared again.'

Genny didn't even have to guess who Lady Westford was referring to. She'd noticed Kit absconding not ten minutes into the game of charades that was currently holding the guests rapt in laughing attention as Lady Calista and Serena tried to depict Hannibal's crossing of the Alps, elephants and all.

'He shall probably return soon,' she replied lightly, not in the least convinced that he would.

This wasn't the first time he'd slipped away from the after-dinner entertainments these past few days. He'd behaved admirably during the first week, but this second week she'd often had to run him to ground, either in the library or in the garden.

The first two times she'd been sympathetic. The coy picking over of his bones that society engaged in behind his back and sometimes not very far away was enough to put a strain on anyone's composure. But *she* was just as exhausted, and *she* did not allow herself to go and put her feet up in the library and read a book while the house was full to bursting with *his* guests.

'"*Probably*" won't cut it. The dancing will begin in half

an hour and he'd better be here,' Lady Westford replied. 'Tell Julian to fetch him.'

Tell him yourself, Genny thought mulishly, but kept silent. Just as she'd kept silent throughout most of this hellishly long fortnight.

'I don't wish to interrupt his flirtation with Lady Sarah. I'll go,' she replied.

Lady Westford gave a short snorting laugh. 'That little minx is making headway with both of them, eh? Good for her. You go, then. And have a word with my grandson. He listens to you. Society might have taken him to its bosom for the moment, but it's fickle and they're watching him. One misstep and they'll roast him over an open fire.'

Genny raised her brows at this image. 'I think we have a little more leeway than that. Lord Westford's entertainments have become the talk of the season.'

'For the moment. Title and wealth and a damned pretty face are excellent shields, but they aren't impenetrable, Genevieve Maitland, and his flaws run deep. Now, go and fetch the rogue.'

Genny did as she was told, happy to get away. But she knew Lady Westford spoke the truth.

It was true that *everyone* wanted to be invited to Lord Westford's entertainments.

Everyone spoke of how tasteful they were…how they married the right touch of intellectual interest with excellent food, wine, and music.

Everyone was now enamoured of this new jewel in society's crown.

Everyone wanted to see Lord Westford.

Lady Westford's now all too frequent 'At Home' hours had become a parade of ambitious matrons angling for invitations. Genny sat through them with a smile pasted to her face as she listened to the fruit of her labours being extolled by those hopeful mamas.

'What a fascinating man Lord Westford is.'
'So cultured.'
'Such good taste.'
'Such surprisingly fine manners.'
'And so, so much more handsome than Lord Byron.'

And on and on and on—until Genny felt queasy and found some excuse to leave the room before she let slip that, far from being as enchanted with them as they were with him, the handsome and charming Lord Westford was counting the days until he could escape.

All too often—like now—he had a tendency to disappear from his own festivities and had to be coaxed back like a skittish filly. And then, damn him, he had the audacity to look at her as if she was forcing him to do Latin declensions, when all he had to do was charm a bevy of beautiful women—an action which evidently came as naturally to him as breathing.

No wonder Julian envied and resented him. She envied and resented him herself.

The transition from light and laughter to dark silence as she stepped out through the library door into the garden was a blessing. For a moment she just stood there, soaking in the night. The quiet. The pleasure of being utterly alone. She walked to the end of the patio, where darkness hid the gardens, and leant her palms on the stone balustrade, breathing in the cool night air overlaid with the city smells of smoke and refuse, coming through the green scents of the garden.

Carrington House was set at the edge of town, its face to ever more tightly packed buildings, while its back still clung to the illusion of country, with a lush garden and trees beyond. From upstairs she could see the lights of houses in a very different part of London, to the south of them, but from here she could for a moment imagine she was back at the Hall in Dorset, with its far more impressive garden leading to open cliff faces and the bay.

Just the thought of walking down to the bay and sinking her feet into the cool damp sand where the waves kissed the shore calmed her jangling nerves.

She stood listening to the music from the house for a moment. Mozart sounded softer here, slipping beneath the gurgle of the fountain. Suddenly all the noise she'd left inside seemed brassy and discordant.

She gave a sigh of relief—and then almost fell off the patio as a dark form appeared beside her out of nowhere.

'Kit! You walk like a cat,' she admonished, her heart in full gallop.

'You scratch like one, so we're even. Have you come to herd me back inside?'

Even his smile looked feline in the dark, and his eyes caught the faint glimmer from the windows farther away in the house.

'Lady Westford wanted to send Julian, but I didn't want to interrupt his flirtation with Lady Sarah.'

She tried to gauge his response to that, but he merely leaned against the balustrade, his back to the darkness.

'They were making too much noise. I couldn't hear the music. Listen.'

The quartet of players were keeping to their instructions to be unobtrusive until called upon to play dance music, and so had chosen a slow, soothing tempo. But Mozart's genius defeated their aim—the violin sang in such sweet sorrow it was impossible not to be drawn in.

They stood side by side, listening, and when the tune slipped into another, warmer piece, she gave a little sigh, reluctant to let the pleasure of that moment go.

He shifted a little beside her, his voice a low murmur. 'Remember Los Dos?'

Genny gave a gasp of surprised memory. They'd been

two Spanish liaison officers who had served with her grandfather for several months and travelled with beautifully crafted guitars. They would play in the evenings as they sat in courtyards or on boxes beside tents. She could almost see the flicker of campfire and smell the dust, wood fire, and jasmine.

'Ramirez *y* Ramirez,' she murmured, smiling. The two men had been unrelated but had borne the same name, and had soon come to be called Los Dos. 'I missed their music when they left. I missed those evenings.'

'I miss music all the time—especially when we're sailing. I have some music boxes and my bosun plays the guitar, but not as well. I shall have to find some musically talented sailors before my next voyage.'

'Will you be leaving directly after the wedding?' she asked, keeping her voice light.

'Yes. I have to sail the *Hesperus* to Portsmouth for some repairs, but she should be ready by then. My grandmother will be relieved to see the back of me. Julian too.'

She didn't bother denying this. 'The Ton will be disappointed.'

He gave a low laugh. 'I daresay they will. Toddlers never like to have their toys snatched from them. But I prefer not to linger until they become bored and decide to toss me out of their perambulators.'

'I didn't realise you saw yourself as a baby's rattle.'

'I thought that was *your* opinion of me, Miss Maitland,' he said, and smiled, turning to look at her. 'All flash, no substance.'

'Now you are fishing for compliments. You know that is not in the least my opinion of you.'

'I admit I am not at all certain *what* your opinion of me is.'

'Does it matter?'

'Indulge me.'

'It strikes me that you have been indulged enough. I prefer not to fall in line with the rest of the female species.'

'It isn't like you to evade giving an honest opinion. It must be bad, then.'

'It isn't—and you know it. I have, for the most part, recovered my grandfather's opinion of you. However, he might have had a few words to say about your tendency to wander off in the heat of battle and leave your subordinates to hold the line.'

He laughed again, folding his arms. 'You have it topsy-turvy, Genny. You're the General here. I'm merely the battalion to be brought in with drums and flutes to make a great show at one end of the battlefield while you are engaged in flanking action on the other. It's all bells and whistles here.'

'That is arrant nonsense. If you are trying to make me feel sorry for you, you are failing miserably. You are luckier than you deserve, Kit Carrington. You have a life to go to. A life you love.'

'And you don't.'

It wasn't a question.

She turned away but he touched her arm, stopping her. 'I shouldn't have been so blunt. Forgive me.'

'What for? It is the truth. I don't love it, but I am content. I am luckier than most.'

'Resigned isn't content. Why don't you find a way to leave? You are intelligent enough to do so.'

A slash of fear struck through her and she almost asked him—where to? But she pushed it aside and clung to the one important thing. 'I won't leave Serena. Not when she needs me.'

He sighed. 'It is a waste for someone like you to set her life aside for another. And have you considered that Serena might not want this particular form of salvation? You cannot save people against their will, love.'

She squirmed at the casual endearment. It wasn't in the least complimentary. More pitying.

'I can do my damnedest,' she snapped.

He held up his hands. 'It wasn't my intention to upset you. Certainly not when I owe you so much.'

'No, you don't. What I do, I do for myself.'

Guilt joined the bubbling cauldron inside her. He wouldn't be quite so grateful if he knew of her pact with Lady Westford.

Suddenly it felt horribly wrong.

What would he do if she told him…everything?

She opened her mouth and raised her eyes to his. He was looking at her with that intent look she sometimes saw on his face when she caught him watching her—as if he was trying to decipher some runic inscription.

It felt invasive…dangerous.

'We should rejoin the others,' she said, her words rushed. 'The dancing will begin soon.'

'In a moment, little shepherdess. From the sound of those squeals they are still in the middle of one of those awful games. I have a few more moments of reprieve, and so do you. Your brief is to ensure I perform, so help me practise my quadrille.'

He took her hand and bowed over it, and as if on cue the musicians slipped away from Mozart and into a tune she did not recognise.

'What a talented quartet to anticipate my needs,' he murmured. 'This has the distinct flavour of a waltz to it. Come, let us see if we can't do better than our last attempt.'

Before she realised what he was doing, he slipped an arm about her waist.

'We can't dance here,' she whispered, even as her feet slipped into the rhythm.

'Shh…' he replied, and he guided her down the stairs onto the grass without losing the rhythm of the music.

The warmth of his body was a sharp contrast with the night air and the cool, springy grass beneath her soft shoes. All her objections gathered for a grand resistance and then fizzled as he guided her deeper and deeper into the darkness.

She had the strange sensation of dancing off the edge of the earth into an inky stillness populated only by them and the music. The scents of the night were joined by his—a deep, warm musk and a hint of something cool and distant.

'Damn, you dance like a dream, Genny. It's like dancing with a summer breeze scented with orange blossoms.'

It was such a lovely, whimsical thing to say that her panic faded and she smiled up at him. For the first time his steps faltered. Then slowed and stopped.

'No, don't stop smiling,' he murmured, and there was a strange urgency in his voice. 'You have no idea how dangerous that smile is, do you?'

She shook her head. His face was a pale chiaroscuro composition above her, the darkness both muting and highlighting his beauty.

'You smiled just like that in the theatre, when you were lost to the world,' he said, his fingers brushing the corner of her mouth, setting it tingling, as if the stars had sprinkled down on her. 'All those layers, Genny... No matter how many I peel away, there seem to be more. What would it take to lay you bare, I wonder?'

This is as bare as I've ever been.

His fingers moved over her face in a soft, feathery exploration that was lighting fire after fire. They skimmed down her cheek to trace the swell of her lower lip, and without thought she licked the tingle left behind by his thumb. He made a sound, muted but harsh, and it jarred through her body, bringing to life an answering urgency.

He breathed out slowly, shifting away from her. 'We should return.'

She didn't want to. It might be wise, but it felt unfair—
ungentlemanly, even—for him to set a fire alight and then
slither away. But it was precisely what he did, she realised.
He'd charm some pretty young woman or other, or engage
a guest in conversation, and then be off, leaving them tan-
talised but with no foundation to build on. It was as if he
was playing out his life's pattern—sailing from port to port
and settling in none. Always ready to leave.

She moved away from him, striding into the darkness.
He caught her arm, slipping his hand down to capture hers
and stopping her.

'It's the other way,' he murmured, his breath warm
against her ear.

She turned, and somehow in the darkness found herself
pressed full-length against him, her hand on his chest. He
made the same sound, deeper this time, and his arm moved
around her. But not like in the waltz.

She didn't wait to see what he would do; she leaned in,
rising on tiptoe to find his mouth with hers.

She stayed like that, her mouth fitted against his, his
breath filling her with a midnight promise that had nothing to do with the reality of day. It was like being filled
with life, slowly, with the darkness melting into her, melting her against him.

She'd never felt anything so…right.

Then his mouth moved, his hand sank into her hair,
and his lips brushed over hers in soft coaxing sweeps that
forced her to follow, like a teasing breeze on an unbearably hot day. She heard herself exhale a soft moan as her
lips parted and his body shivered against hers, his tongue
tracing that parting.

That simple touch shattered the dreamy beauty with a
surge of heat. It swept through her, expanding her, making her hands wrap around his back and tighten on the

warm fabric of his waistcoat as they pressed into the rigid muscles of his back.

'Yes…' he whispered against her mouth. 'Take what you want…'

She kissed him, not thinking, just opening, her tongue tasting the firm line of his lower lip, retreating when his tongue came to meet hers, and then giving in to the need to explore, feel. He let her lead the kiss, encouraging her with warm, rumbling sounds of pleasure that were as addictive as his hands shaping her body. They swept down her back, curving over her backside as he raised her against him, their bodies swaying to the half-heard strains of the music.

But when one large hand brushed the side of her breast there was a strange burst of pain, almost as if she'd touched a voltaic cell.

It angled through her like an arrow, striking hard at her core, and she felt a welling of heat between her legs. It wasn't the tentative excitement that came from reading illicit books—this was molten, almost vicious.

Frightening.

She stiffened, suddenly afraid to move, and he stopped as well, his mouth still against hers but not moving. His hand was cradling her breast but nothing else.

Then he breathed in deeply and pulled away. She felt the draw of air cooling her burning lips.

'That went further than I planned,' he said lightly, but his voice was hoarse. 'I'm sorry.'

'Don't apologise.'

Was that her voice? In the darkness she sounded prim, like a governess reprimanding a child.

She cleared her throat. 'We should return.' She echoed his previous words, but this time she managed to head in the right direction.

He followed, but at the patio steps he stopped. 'You go first. I will follow in a moment.'

She didn't argue. If he disappeared again Lady Westford would have her head, but at the moment she didn't care. She couldn't feel much of anything through the chaos of sensations and the jumble of conflicting thoughts and the sheer burning haze of embarrassment.

'Where have you been?'

Genny jumped in alarm, pressing a hand to her chest.

'Julian! Must you sneak up on one?'

'I must if that "one" doesn't want anyone noticing that she looks like she's been dragged backwards through a hedge. You can't go in there looking like that—your hair is coming undone at the back.'

She flushed and reached up.

Julian all but shoved her into the library. 'Not here, where everyone can see you. They'll likely blame it on me and then we'd be in a fine fix, love. Here, let me do it. Turn around.'

She stood still and let Julian pull a couple of pins from her hair, too shaken to object. There was something comforting about his competent motions, and it struck her as both strange and rather depressing that Julian's touch felt as impersonal as her maid's. Her nerves weren't dancing or singing or doing anything they ought not to be doing.

She sighed. 'I think you're a lovely man, but I'm glad we never married,' she said abruptly, and winced a little as his fingers slipped and he poked her with a pin.

He said nothing until he'd secured the last pin and stood back. 'There, sweetheart. You look half presentable. And thank you for the compliment… I think. Now, will you tell me what happened?'

'No.'

'Did any of those bores try to take liberties? If they did…'

'No, Julian, really—they didn't. I doubt they even see me.'

He opened his mouth, closed it, and opened it again. 'Genny Maitland, for an intelligent woman you are shockingly stupid. If you gave the slightest sign of interest you'd have them lined up and down the hall, vying for your favours.'

She smiled at that nonsense and went to the mirror to inspect her hair. It did look presentable, but she didn't feel ready to return to the guests.

She sank onto a sofa and Julian joined her.

'You don't believe me, do you?'

'I believe you are kind as well as charming, Julian. I think I will sit here for a moment. You needn't stay with me.'

He took her hand. 'Listen to me, Genny—' He broke off as the door opened and a tall figure cast a long shadow into the room.

'What is going on here?'

With the light behind him Genny could not make out Kit's expression, but his tones were a mix between ice and acid.

'Close the door before someone sees you, man,' Julian remonstrated, waving his hand at Kit.

Kit shut it with a distinct snap. His gaze flicked over her and past her, settling on Julian, but she felt it like the snap of a whip.

'I know I suggested you conduct your flirtation at Carrington House, but I didn't mean while it was full of guests.'

The irony of his words after their interlude in the garden made Genny's jaw drop, and chased away both embarrassment and confusion. She sprang to her feet, but Julian spoke first.

'Then you should have been more explicit, Pretty Kitty. We'll know better next time.'

Genny had never seen Kit so furious before. He hadn't

moved, but something in his face had been transformed utterly.

Without thinking, she held out her hands, as if to put herself between the two men. Kit's eyes snapped to her, glittering like obsidian in the dark and she swallowed.

'I think you'd best return to the guests, Miss Maitland. Julian and I will continue this conversation alone.'

That woke her further.

'Don't be ridiculous. You two can't indulge in fisticuffs in the library while we are entertaining. If you must act like troglodytes, I suggest you prove your manhood at a boxing salon, or something with at least a pretension to respectability. And you, Julian, don't stand there grinning. I take back everything nice I said about you. You are not helping in the least.'

'Sorry, Gen,' Julian said. 'You're quite right. And you're way off the mark, Kit. I didn't do a thing to Genny but try to help her. Someone roughed her up and I was offering cousinly comfort.'

'Someone roughed—' Kit repeated, shock erasing the anger from his face.

'No one roughed me up,' Genny interjected hurriedly. 'Really, Julian, where do you learn these vulgar phrases? Julian was merely offering to help with my hair.'

Oh, God, she was making it worse. She had best leave before she began bawling and even more thoroughly disgraced herself.

She cast one last harassed glance at herself in the mirror and hurried out, back into the anonymous safety of the crowd.

Chapter Eleven

Kit stopped on the threshold of the library. Genny was half expecting him to excuse himself and leave, but he entered and shut the door. She remained seated on the sofa, her hands tight on the book she had been trying to read, unsure what she should do next.

'You are up early, Miss Maitland.'

'So are you, Lord Westford.'

'I don't sleep well here,' he said, moving restlessly towards the shelves.

Neither do I. Not since you arrived, she almost replied, but kept silent.

The library faced east, to the gardens, and light was streaming in, casting a golden light over him. Sometimes it struck her all over again how handsome he was. It was like coming across a painting and being caught by the skill of its creator.

'I am glad for the opportunity to speak to you before the others wake,' he continued. 'I wish to apologise. For last night. I know I should never have asked you to dance, let alone… You didn't object… But was what Julian said true? Did you feel I had…roughed you up?'

She could feel her cheeks become viciously hot. 'No! Of course not. That was Julian's supposition, because he noticed my hair and presumed one of the guests had… I told him it wasn't so, but naturally I couldn't tell him the truth…'

'I see… In any case, I must still apologise. I should not have taken such liberties.'

He looked and sounded as uncomfortable as she felt.

'You have nothing to apologise for, Lord Westford. Or rather we both do, for acting in a manner that might have caused concern had we been observed.'

'I think I bear a rather larger share of responsibility, Miss Maitland.'

'Nonsense.'

'I accosted you.'

'Clearly your memory is at fault. I kissed you first.'

'I…' He seemed to run aground, his cheeks darkening with either anger or embarrassment. 'That isn't how it works, Miss Maitland. Weren't you the one instructing me to act the gentleman? A gentleman assumes responsibility for such matters.'

'I don't think it very gentlemanly to paint me as a sad little flower with no power to reject unwanted advances or make advances of my own. I think it would be more honest merely to say you would prefer I didn't try to kiss you again.'

'Being honest and being a gentleman are evidently two vastly different things,' he snapped. 'And if we are being honest, I certainly wouldn't say that. However, I will say that I will be certain not do so again if I'm going to have my knuckles rapped like this while I'm trying to do what is right.'

She felt absurdly close to tears and she rubbed her forehead, pressing hard.

'The only thing I object to is the presumption that men can do as they will, but the moment a woman follows an… an impulse, something must be wrong—something must be rectified. Believe me, Lord Westford, had I objected you would have been well aware of the fact. You told me to take what I wanted, and I did. What is more, I did so on the presumption that you were mature enough to follow through on that offer without making precisely the kind of scene you are indulging in now.'

She was shaking a little at the end of her tirade and he seemed rather stricken himself. Then, to her further consternation, he gave a short, rueful laugh and shook his head.

'You are quite right, of course. My only excuse is that trying to play by the rules of this foreign world has skewed my sense of right and wrong. I meant no disrespect— either last night or now.'

She gave a huff of a breath. 'Good. We shall forget about it, then.'

'Must we?'

Her mind stuttered. 'I beg your pardon?'

'Since that kiss is one of my only pleasant memories since walking into Carrington House, I would rather *not* forget it. If you do not mind.'

'I… No… What I meant was… You *know* what I meant.'

'Yes, you meant that with good, *mature* Tonnish hypocrisy, having attained what you wanted, we are now to act as if it never happened.'

'That is not what I meant,' she said, aghast, a little shocked at finding herself in a corner.

'What *did* you mean, then?' he asked politely. 'Not being versed in these rules, I am not certain how to interpret your demand.'

'I am not *demanding* anything. I only meant to allay your fears that I…that you…'

Oh, God, this was going in an entirely wrong direction.

'That you might once again make demands upon me?' he suggested.

'No! That is…if you felt the need to…to make amends… drastic amends…that is…'

He settled on the sofa opposite her and crossed his arms, for all the world as if he was watching a rather choppy attempt at charades but was too polite to hurry her along. His expression was utterly bland, but she knew—she *knew*—he was laughing at her.

Well, she was grateful for it, because her temper finally rushed to her defence. 'Are you enjoying yourself, Lord Westford?'

'I am certainly feeling better than when I walked in here this morning,' he replied. 'I know I am once again betraying my ungentlemanly roots, but watching you flounder is rather…appealing.'

'I am so glad. Now, if you are finished watching me flounder, you may leave.'

He didn't move, and his voice had lost its smile when he spoke. 'Don't expect me to dance to your tune like the others, Genny. I won't do it.'

'I don't expect you, or anyone, to dance to my tune. I don't *have* a tune.'

'You certainly do. You've been playing it for the past two weeks, and all those fine gentlemen and ladies are capering along to it like a group of monkeys because it suits their purpose to do so.'

'That is not very respectful.'

'You have no more respect for the parasitical wastrels than I do. Possibly less, since I possess a far less excitable disposition than you.'

'Excitable!' she exclaimed.

Of all his facial expressions, she most disliked his ability to raise one dark brow without looking ridiculous. It was merely one more thing to list under *Unfair Advantages Possessed by Kit Carrington*.

'I am *not* excitable,' she said with deathly calm. 'Anyone will tell you I am dismally dull and devoid of all the normal female—' She'd been about to say *passions*, but that word felt far too close to the bone at the moment. 'Attributes.' That too had its pitfalls, but it would have to do.

'I find *"anyone"* to be an unreliable source of information,' he replied. 'I'm a Baconian at heart—I prefer to draw my own conclusions, from the evidence before me.'

'Well, so do I. And, putting today aside, I would say that you have proved far more temperamental than I!'

'Today and yesterday.'

'What?'

'If you wish to skew the evidence, you might as well do so thoroughly. Put aside today and yesterday evening from your observations.'

He was doing it again. Just when she'd managed to climb back on deck, he shoved her into the water once more. She *hated* floundering.

'I am not skewing the evidence,' she insisted, amending her approach. '*Even* taking into account today, *and* yesterday evening, you are more temperamental.'

'I wasn't measuring temperamentality…is that the noun? Never mind… I was discussing excitability. I may be more temperamental—though I would strongly debate that, especially given the new evidence before me—but I deny I am more excitable. You didn't see yourself all but swooning over Kean's performance.'

'I was *not*…'

'If you'd leaned forward any farther, you would have toppled into the pit.'

'That wasn't excitability.'

'What was it, then?'

What *was* it, then?

She hadn't even realised she'd been so obvious. The thought that he had watched her while she'd been unaware that she was showing her pleasure was not only embarrassing, but unsettling.

'It isn't kind of you to make fun at my expense, Lord Westford.' She'd meant to sound authoritative, but her voice wobbled.

He frowned and stood abruptly. 'I was not making fun at your expense. Enjoying something fully and honestly is nothing to be ashamed of.'

'It is embarrassing.'

'Only if you are embarrassed. You shouldn't be. Damn, it wasn't my intention to make you check yourself...you do that far too often already.'

As if on impulse, he came to sit beside her on the sofa.

'If you must know, watching you take pleasure in the play was another of the few times I have enjoyed myself since I stepped off the *Hesperus* in London. You made me forget how much I'd been dreading that evening, and you reminded me why my mother and my grandfather loved the theatre as much as they did.'

She was blushing again, in a completely foreign tug of war between pleasure and mortification. This whole conversation was utterly out of her control, and yet she did not want it to end.

Her curiosity rushed into the breach. 'Why *were* you dreading it? I remember you saying something to your grandmother about an incident that had occurred there...'

He smiled, but it was that careful, shielding smile. She wished she hadn't called it up again.

'What a memory you have. I don't know if it merits the name of "incident"...'

'It must, to have left such bitterness.'

He gave an impatient sigh. 'We went to see a play.'

'Which one?' she prompted.

'The Lives of Henry the Fifth.'

'Oh. That was one of our favourite plays as children.'

'It was one our favourites on the ship as well. My mother would play young King Henry, and Patton, our bosun at the time, made an excellent Falstaff.' He leaned forward, his gaze on the carpet. 'I saw the notice when we were in London, my second or third summer in England. I told Mary I wished to see it. She suggested it to my father, and it led to one of the rare battles between them. Certainly the first that she won.'

'What happened?'

'Nothing much. We all went—my grandparents as well. Perhaps they thought a show of familial solidarity at the theatre would put paid to the tattle about my father's first marriage. I remember entering the foyer... I was impatient because my grandmother had stopped to speak to a woman with a monstrous wig...and then I saw my grandfather. Not Lord Westford. My mother's father. Whom I had been told had died soon after my mother's death.'

Genny's breath caught. She'd had no idea about that lie. She could almost see the scene. A boy standing in the foreign but wondrous world of the theatre, that linked him to his mother and her family, feeling their loss. And then...

'Oh, God...' she whispered.

'That was close to my thoughts at the time. I believed I was seeing a ghost. He must have felt me staring, because he turned and froze...'

Genny watched in shock as hot colour spread over Kit's face, and without a thought she took his hand in hers. He looked down, but barely seemed to notice her transgression. He was present, yet miles and years away.

'I can still see his clothes...down to the embroidery on his waistcoat—intertwined grey and black and white lilies. My mother's favourite flower. He just stood there, staring at me. He looked...stricken. Miserable. It can't have been more than a few short moments, but I remember realising the magnitude of the lie. I knew it wasn't he who had perpetrated the deception, but them. I knew that he had wanted no part in it but had given in because they'd convinced him it would be best for me.'

'The poor man… I had no idea. What did you do?'

'I went to him. My father tried to stop me.' Kit rolled his shoulder, as if feeling the weight of a hand settling on it. 'They all did. My grandmother caught my arm and hissed something in my ear, Lord Westford had my other arm, and my father went and spoke to Nathan…my maternal grandfather. Nathan looked at me and said, *"I'm so sorry, Kit."* And left.'

The silence stretched again. While he'd talked she had unconsciously intertwined her fingers with his. His hand was much darker than hers and worn rough at the knuckles. Not a gentleman's hands.

'I ran away. Again. I had grand ideas of disappearing completely, but after spending a freezing night sleeping under a bridge I found my way back here. I was sent down to Dorset and then to school.'

'I'm so sorry, Kit,' she said. His hand tightened on hers and she realised she'd unconsciously mirrored his grandfather's words.

'Don't be. It was merely an interlude. I feel sorrier for Nathan. He lost his daughter and his grandson in one fell swoop.'

'I had no idea they severed your ties with him. That is unforgivable. I'm so glad you found him again, despite their efforts…'

He looked up with a frown. 'How did you know I found him again?'

She faltered. 'I… Mary must have mentioned something.'

'Did she? I daresay she is the only one who has ever mentioned his name.'

'How *did* you find him?' she asked hurriedly.

'I had a book he once gave me, and the publisher's name was written inside. He'd told me he often bound books for them, so I went there and some kind soul took me to his shop.'

He smiled, and Genny could see the echo of relief and happiness.

'He tried to convince me to return to the Hall, but not very hard. We compromised by sending a letter saying that a school friend had invited me to his home for the summer. He was a duke's heir, so they didn't object. My friend Rafe told his mother the same, and we both stayed at Nathan's house. The following winter Rafe ran away to the army, so I hadn't that excuse, but I went to Nathan's anyway.'

'Didn't your father mind?'

'If he did, he never said anything, and I think my grand-parents were relieved to be rid of me. I was the one blot on the Carrington landscape at the time. This was before Charlie's parents and sisters died in India, when it was still expected that there would be more sons, so I was definitely expendable. Until I joined the army myself I spent a good part of my time away from school with Nathan. He was a good man. Everything he had he'd earned himself, and he was never bothered by his lack of roots. He encouraged me to explore the world and not to let others decide what I was worth. It was the best possible advice.'

'He sounds a little like my grandfather.'

He smiled, turning her hand absently in his, his thumb brushing rhythmically over the heart of her palm.

'I thought the same when I met General Maitland. My grandfather had all the flamboyance of a man of the stage and letters, but his roots were practical and kind. Your grandfather was the same under his martial façade.'

The pain of memory and loss, of sitting by her grand-father and holding his hand as he faded away, was suddenly so vivid she untangled her hand and went to the window, fighting long-forgotten tears.

'I miss him,' she said to the clouds skimming by. 'Every day.'

She heard Kit rise from the sofa and move towards her. But she knew she was in no state for any more excitability.

She turned, planting her hands on her hips. 'This isn't working.'

He stopped. 'What isn't working?'

'My plan. It has been well over a fortnight and neither Mary nor Serena is showing signs of any interest, let alone attachment. Other than when she is forcibly seated next to someone at dinner, Mary finds every excuse to sit with Emily and Peter or his parents, and as for Serena... Well, no one would believe she was once one of the foremost flirts of the Peninsular Army. I might not be very well versed in such matters,' she said, thinking of Julian's comment, 'but it strikes me that the men will need a little more encouragement than they are being given if we are to make any headway.'

'Quite true. But, to use an inelegant phrase, we may have transformed Carrington House into a trough, but we cannot force your sister or my stepmother to drink.'

The lump in her throat thickened and she swallowed. 'So there is no point, is there? We should stop.'

Stop and put an end to this. You will go back to your ship and I will go back to my comfortable uncomfortable life and Mary and Serena will have to find their own paths in life.

It would be safer.

She didn't like excitability. She didn't *want* it.

Liar, said another voice. *You like it far too much. And therein lies the rub.*

'We should stop.'

Genny was right. He'd seen it as well. When not forced

into proximity with one of the men on their list during dinner, Mary invariably chose to sit with Emily. He might have hoped that at least one of the male guests would see her reticence as a challenge, but, as Genny had said, men needed *some* encouragement.

The sensible course of action would be to admit defeat and return to the *Hesperus* until the wedding. It would put an end to his grandmother's cutting remarks and Julian's snide asides. Not to mention put some much-needed distance between him and the source of his increasingly unsettled nights.

All excellent reasons to do precisely as Genny was suggesting. To say, *You are right; let's put an end to this.*

Genny was waiting. She looked as she had that day she'd walked into the library and issued her first set of commands: resolute and resigned. And cold. As if she hadn't moments ago been almost in tears over her grandfather and his.

She would return to her life acting as buffer in his grandmother's household. Julian might toy with her, might even care for her, but it was unlikely he would extract her from that life. They would all exit this interlude precisely as they had entered it.

It should have been a relief, but it felt horribly wrong.

'Perhaps you are being hasty,' he said.

'Hasty?' she asked.

'Your grandfather wouldn't approve of abandoning a blockade without reviewing what went wrong, would he?'

'What I did wrong was try to impose my own wishes upon two women who are their own mistresses,' she replied tartly. 'You said yourself that I cannot save them from bondage if they do not wish to be saved. It is hubris.'

'It may be hubris, but it is well-intentioned, and I think it is too soon to admit failure. What *we* did wrong was provide our prey with too many degrees of freedom. It isn't a siege if your adversary is allowed to wander about between assaults, sampling pies in neighbouring markets and wandering back when he pleases.'

Laughter chased some of the coldness from her eyes. 'It is very ungallant to liken your stepmother to a pie.'

'Don't split hairs. Still, if you wish to concede defeat…'

'Of course I don't, but…' She sank onto the sofa with a thump, her shoulders sagging. 'I don't know what to do. I keep hoping I shall see that spark of…of true happiness on Serena's face. You must remember it from Spain. She was always so…alight. And I know everyone thought Charlie was rather staid for her, but she *loved* him. And I wish… I wish I could help her find even a little of that again… But I don't know what else to do.'

Kit had never reckoned that confusion and pain could act as a sensual stimulant, but Genny confused and did odd things to his libido. His pulse was quickening again, and his body was remembering precisely how she'd felt in the garden—warm, soft, with all those luscious curves her very proper gown had failed to hide pressed against him, her inner warmth bursting its barriers, sweeping him along.

'I still think we should make one final push,' he said, ignoring his mind's suggestive take on the phrase. 'With modifications.'

'Modifications?'

'Yes. We remove the degrees of freedom. We need to tighten our blockade.'

Her mouth curved in and out of a smile. 'I think we are carrying this martial analogy too far.'

'You started it. And blockades are naval territory— my speciality.'

She straightened. 'Very well—how would we tighten our blockade? Are you suggesting we kidnap those poor men and put them on your ship with Mary and Serena?'

'I wouldn't do that my precious *Hesperus*. I have my limits. I was thinking of the Hall. In Dorset.'

'The Hall... A house party!' she said, her gaze growing intent.

The Generalissima was back in command, he noted, almost with regret.

'Once Emily and Peter remove to his grandparents' house in Hampshire we can invite a select group to the Hall,' he said. 'Away from the distractions of London. You offered me as bait before...'

'I didn't mean—'

'Yes, you did,' he interrupted. 'You laid me out like a leg of mutton for the foxes. Well, on board the *Hesperus* I have a few other legs of mutton for our antiquity lovers, and I could arrange to bring them to the Hall as lures for a select group of gentlemen. I have to sail the *Hesperus* to Portsmouth in any case, so we shan't be too far from the Hall. And, since Mary and I must be in Hampshire in less than a fortnight for Emily's wedding, we have the perfect excuse not to extend our invitation for more than a week. Any more and I will likely lock them in a cellar. Or myself.'

'You wouldn't need to bring anything from your ship,' she replied with enthusiasm, her eyes growing hazy with plotting again. 'I have told you the Hall is already crowded to bursting with your treasures.'

He tried not to smile at the sight of Genny, back at the helm. Perhaps it was the lack of sleep, but he wasn't as resistant as before to the thought of returning to the Hall for the first time since his father's death. In fact, he could kill two birds with one stone. As Genny had pointed out, the cursed Carringtons were his responsibility now. It was time he went to the family seat.

'My grandmother might not agree to be uprooted from

London so soon after coming here,' he said. 'She appears to be thriving.'

Genny waved a dismissive hand, her eyes intent on some inner calculation. 'Leave that to me.'

He pressed his mouth firmly down on a smile. 'Don't mind if I do.'

'Good. Do I have your permission to send out invitations?'

For a moment he considered the wisdom of spending a week in a house he hated with his witch of a grandmother, a group of men who, though worthy, were hardly scintillating company, and the woman he was aching to bed.

In fact, there was nothing to consider. It was clearly, categorically, unwise. If any of his friends heard of this, he would lose for ever his reputation for calculated caution.

'Faint heart ne'er won decent husband for fair stepmother,' he said resolutely.

'"Once more unto the breach", then, Lord Westford?'

'Once more.'

He held out his hand and she smiled and placed hers in it. It took every ounce of his will not to pull her towards him and kiss that smile into something entirely different.

Chapter Twelve

'And this is the Capità's cabin,' the first mate announced in a heavy Catalan accent, motioning the visitors inside with a flourish that would have been comical if the room had not completely justified it.

Emily gave a gasp of appreciation which Genny echoed silently. It was the loveliest room she'd ever seen on board a ship. Kit certainly knew how to surround himself with the good things in life.

It was larger even than her room at Carrington House, with a wooden table at its centre covered in maps and books, and many more books filling the shelves along one wall. The floors were covered with carpets in deep, earthy colours that contrasted with a trio of watercolours of birds and mist-shrouded mountains.

There was also a bunk.

She'd thought that the bunks in the cabins assigned to them on the *Hesperus* for the short voyage from London to Portsmouth were quite generous compared with other ships she'd sailed on with her grandfather, but this...

This bunk should not in all fairness be called a bunk at all. It was far longer and larger than most beds at the Hall, and made even more imposing by a deep wine-coloured silk covering and tasselled brocade cushions the colours of a sunset. The light from the windows made the fabric shimmer, as if at any moment they might dissolve into warm liquid and spill towards them.

It was a bed made for pleasure.

And it had probably served that purpose well and often.

She turned to look at the paintings instead. If Kit lay against those cushions these were what he would see—the slight, light, almost wistful lines of birds and mountains. The sybaritic setting should have overwhelmed their fragility, but they were powerful counterpoints to the sensuality of the bed and the earthy tones of the carpets and the heavy furniture.

It was a disorientating room in more ways than one.

Just like its owner.

'Well!' Emily announced. 'That is the last time I shall feel sorry for Kit when he is on a long voyage. I would love a room like this—wouldn't you, Peter?'

Peter looked rather less enthusiastic than Emily, but perhaps that was due to the rising motion of the ship as it slipped out of the Estuary and into the Channel.

Mary sat down heavily in a chair, her hands tight on the armrests.

'Mary…?' Genny asked and Mary gave a wan smile.

'Perhaps I should have travelled by carriage with Serena and Lady Westford, after all.'

'Oh, no, Mama,' Emily protested. 'You know we have been wanting to see Kit's ship for ever and ever. It is not a long voyage to Portsmouth. We shall be there tomorrow.'

Mary's smile wobbled and Genny glanced at the first mate.

'Perhaps some fresh air would be a good idea, Mr Fábregas?'

Mary smiled with relief and Emily hurried to take her mother's arm. Peter followed, a little unsteady himself, and Genny and the first mate brought up the rear.

'You are feeling well, Mees Maitland?' he asked solicitously, and she nodded.

'I was used to sailing often with my grandfather between England and the Continent. It seems I have not quite lost my sea legs, Senyor Fábregas.'

'You must call me Benja, please, miss. Many men on this ship have no family and no past, so it is agreed we use only our Christian names. Even the Captain.'

'Captain Kit?'

'Ah… When he was a boy, on his father's ship, he was Kit. But when he bought this ship, after the wars, he did not wish to speak of old times. He is not Kit the boy, not Captain Christopher Carrington of the army. To us, he is only Captain Chris—or Capità Krees in my terrible English.'

Genny laughed at the first mate's obvious self-deprecation, a little surprised that he was being so open with her, and wishing he would be a great deal more so. Kit had introduced him as one of the sailors who had served under his father on the original *Hesperus* and there was evident affection between them—the same quiet but solid respect that seemed the order of the day among the other sailors. Another sign that this ship was more than a mere trading vessel.

It was like being back in Spain—she knew these men were used to risking their lives for each other. She'd missed this. Even if she'd always been outside that inner circle of male camaraderie, she'd lived with it so long that it felt like coming home.

Once they were on deck, Kit came to guide Mary towards the bulwarks, moving between the sailors and ropes with fluid grace.

'You'll be better on deck,' he said comfortingly. 'Keep your eyes on the horizon if you can. Meanwhile, Benja will prepare his magical mint tea.'

'But there are *waves*!' Mary objected, her hands as tight on the bulwarks as they'd been on the chair.

'But isn't the view marvellous?' Emily replied, though her hands also clung rather tightly to the railing. 'We are moving so fast…' she added wonderingly.

Genny had noticed the same; once in the Channel, the ship had seemed to jump forward, all but leaping over the choppy waves.

'Perhaps it is merely that I have not sailed for many years, but this seems much faster than the ships I remember ferrying us between England and Spain with Grandfather.'

Kit smiled at her, his face alight with pleasure. He looked younger—another side of him still. He was in his element, and his pleasure was infectious, but Genny also felt a strange pinching in her chest…perhaps envy.

'It is definitely faster,' he replied. 'The *Hesperus* has the same hull design as the dreaded *USS Constitution*— American live oak between layers of white oak. Though it is heavy, it sits very lightly on the water and is almost impenetrable to cannon fire. You will be happy to hear that, aside from being very fast, she is very hard to sink.'

'I'm glad to hear that,' Emily said. 'It is a little wet, though.'

A gust of wind confirmed this assessment by gathering an armful of spray and tossing it up at them. Mary retreated, spluttering, and Emily turned into Peter's shoulder.

'Perhaps we ought to go inside after all, until the storm calms?' Peter asked, looking rather worriedly across the choppy sea.

Genny caught the rueful amusement in Kit's eyes as he nodded and took Mary's arm, guiding her back inside.

Genny remained, watching the waves slip by faster and faster. Another burst of spray engulfed her and she laughed in sheer pleasure. It had been years since she'd felt so… so free.

She looked around the damp deck at the sailors going about their work. For a group of men with dubious pasts they looked surprisingly civilised and amiable, and not in the least put out at having women on board.

Just then Benja appeared from the hold, carrying a tray with impressive balance. He motioned her towards a strange construct which stood in the centre of the deck. She walked around a wooden partition and stopped in delighted surprise. Three wooden walls created a protected gazebo, and inside there were two armchairs and a table nailed to the deck.

She had never seen anything like it. It reminded her of a royal barge she'd seen in an illustrated book. The thought of sitting there as the world slipped by, under the shade of the stretched sails, perhaps with a book...

'Mint tea, Miss Maitland. It keeps your heart warm and your stomach cool. The Captain will join you soon.'

'Thank you, Benja. You are very kind.'

'It is a pleasure, Miss Maitland.'

Emboldened, she reached for her memory of Catalan. *'El plaer és meu,* Benja.*'*

His dark eyes lit with pleasure. 'You speak Catalan!'

'Not much, I am afraid. I have forgotten most of the little I knew.'

'Miss Maitland was in Spain during the war,' Kit said, appearing in the entrance to the gazebo. 'I served under her grandfather for a year—General Maitland.'

'Ah, yes. I remember you spoke of him, *Capità.* A wise man, and good to his men.'

Pain prickled at the back of her eyes and a surge of yearning for that good, wise man washed over her. She needed him now more than ever.

'He was,' she said, her voice hoarse.

Benja smiled and melted away, but Kit remained standing in the opening.

She felt absurdly embarrassed and rose to her feet. 'How are they?'

'They will be fine…just finding their sea legs.'

'Perhaps I should sit with Mary…?'

'No. Stay.'

She hesitated. 'You think I shouldn't intrude on them?'

'I think you should do as you wish. Do you wish to go inside or stay here?'

Again there was that strange shift in energy, like a moment in a play that presaged some portentous action. She looked past him out to the choppy grey surface of the sea, stretching into a sky of scudding clouds, and then to the scrubbed wood of the deck and the whimsical little study at its heart.

'I wish to stay.'

'Then stay.'

The ship tipped and a cloud of spray ballooned over the side like a cool kiss, commending her for her audacity. She laughed, and he took her arm and guided her towards the armchair.

'But this is *your* seat,' she objected.

'Not today. This seat belongs to the one who needs it most. Today that is you, Genny.'

She sat, her behind sinking into the generously upholstered cushions. It was a little stiff with dried salt water, but she could easily doze in such a chair, lulled by the waves, a book on her lap… She sighed.

'I feel I ought to issue a command,' she said.

'Try me.' He poured out a cup of tea for her and then leaned back in the other chair, stretching out his long legs.

The ship kept shifting, sometimes a little jerkily, like a rug being tugged and shifted beneath her feet, though Kit didn't seem to notice at all. The wooden partitions protected them from the worst of the wind and spray, and gave a strange sense of the two of them sailing alone, with only the masts and a strip of the sea in sight.

'I can't think of anything I'd care to command at the moment. I'm too content. I shouldn't be, I know—not when they are unwell—but...this is so much more pleasant than travelling in a carriage. I wish...'

He waited, and somehow she spoke the words.

'I wish we could keep sailing.'

He looked away, out to sea. She felt the flush of embarrassment spread over her cheeks. After their rocky beginning she'd become far too comfortable sharing her thoughts with Kit Carrington. Somehow, after every time they clashed, they seemed to reach a greater degree of understanding. She kept telling him things without thinking them through. She supposed he was becoming a...a friend. Like Julian.

No, not like Julian.

She was comfortable with Julian; what she felt when she was with Kit was not *comfortable*. And Julian, in his own way, would always be there for her. As soon as Kit was finished with Emily's wedding he would be on his way again. For a brief moment he'd entered her cage, just as she now sat at the centre of his. But nothing had truly changed except inside her.

It was not his fault, but he had done her a disservice worse than any enemy—he'd made her want more from life...from herself.

She leaned her head back and closed her eyes, raising her face to the sun dancing in and out of the clouds.

His touch on her cheek was so light she might almost have mistaken it for the caress of the breeze, or the sweep of her escaping hair across her cheek.

She opened her eyes, wondering if she'd imagined it. He was leaning forward now, his face intent and hard. Not with anger, but something that sent her nerves into alert far more readily.

He touched her again…just skimmed the back of his fingers down her cheek. 'You're crying.'

She touched her own cheek, a little shocked to discover he was right. 'It's the wind,' she said, her voice hoarse.

He shook his head and shifted, raising her off the chair only to slip under her and place her on his lap. She sat there, utterly shocked at this strange manoeuvre, and even more so at the feel of his body under hers.

'What are you doing? I cannot sit on you!'

'I certainly can't sit on *you*. I'd crush you.'

His voice was warm against her temple, and he compounded it by putting his arm around her and settling her more comfortably against his chest.

'There. Now I can offer you a shoulder to cry on in earnest. No, don't hold yourself stiffly like that. You'll get a crick in your neck. Relax.'

She tried not to, still clinging to her outrage—more at herself for not getting up immediately than at him.

'Is this common practice in your gazebo?' she demanded.

'This is the first time—to my knowledge, at least—that this seat has been occupied by two individuals at once. I wonder it has never occurred to me before. It is quite comfortable. Or at least it would be if you unbent.'

'I don't think it is wise.'

He sighed. 'It is certainly not wise, Vivi,' he said. 'But we are now outside the boundaries of society and will all too soon be back inside them. If you wish me to return to the other chair I will. Your choice.'

Her choice.

Perhaps it was the way he called her Vivi. No one had ever called her that. It made her feel…daring. *Vivi* would undoubtedly choose to follow her heart—or at least her body.

She relaxed against him, tucking her head into the curve of his shoulder. He'd dispensed with his waistcoat and wore only a linen shirt under his jacket, and he was warm…more than warm. She could feel his chest against her arm, the hard pressure of his muscles.

She closed her eyes and breathed in his scent. Beneath the wood and salt air there was an indefinable, magical spice that was beginning to haunt her. Now she could breathe deeply of it.

She canted her head so that her forehead rested against the warm skin of his throat. She could feel his pulse against her temple—swift and clear.

'This is shockingly improper,' she said, but in a different way from before, and he laughed.

'Let us imagine we have for the moment sailed off the edge of the earth and into another sea entirely. Where neither the Ton nor my grandmother reign supreme.'

'Where neither the Ton nor *men* reign supreme,' Genny amended.

'Where men *and* women are measured on their merit. We are becoming very revolutionary.'

'Why is it that revolutions so often begin with such fine ideas and invariably disappoint?'

'Because ideas are ideas and people are people.'

She sighed. 'Nasty, brutish things, people.'

'You aren't,' he replied gently, brushing aside a lock of hair from her face and gently twining it about his finger.

She smiled and let her eyes drift shut as he ran his fingers through the unravelled hair. So this was what Milly and Barka felt when she stroked them. Except that it wasn't truly soothing. His pulse seemed to grow around her, echoing inside her, carrying through her blood as if it was bringing her to life.

'This *is* comfortable,' she murmured, settling more

deeply against him, resting her hand against his chest. 'Though you are not as soft as the chair.'

His arm tightened around her, his other hand abandoning her hair and capturing her hand, threading their fingers together in an abrupt motion.

'No. I'm definitely not soft,' he muttered, his voice no longer playful.

He slid her a little down his legs.

'Am I too heavy? Should I move?' She forgot she was Vivi and began to shift, but his arm tightened further.

'God, definitely don't move, Vivi. Oh, the hell with it!'

He shifted her back again, so that she was once again pressed against his chest, her behind settled against his slightly splayed thighs. Her slow mind finally registered the hardening pressure of his erection against her thigh. It would have been obvious to any woman with a smidgen of experience. Even *she* realised its import.

He desired her. At least right here, right now, he desired her.

Her body went up in flames.

It had been simmering for the past weeks, flaring at the worst possible moments, reaching boiling when she'd kissed him, but this conflagration went far beyond that. It *ached*, with a hard, burning ache right at her core, tightening her breasts, making her skin tingle from her head to her toes.

The urge to touch his skin made her hands twitch. She might not know much about sensuality, but she knew what she wanted right then as clearly as she knew anything— she wanted to raise her skirts and straddle him so that she could feel him, hot and hard against that ache. She wanted to taste his skin. She wanted him to kiss her back into oblivion.

It didn't matter that they were on the deck of his ship,

exposed to anyone who walked by. It didn't even matter at the moment that there was no future to this.

He had said that this chair belonged to the one who needed it most.

This moment it belonged to *her*.

She touched her lips to the pulse at the side of his throat, brushing it in time with the shortening rhythm of his breathing. Then she drew her tongue along that beating artery, gathering his unique addictive flavour. He breathed in and out, deeply. Other than that, and a strange muted sound deep in his chest, he didn't react. But she could feel his body straining against his control like the sails above them, taut in the wind of the elements.

She was the wind—far more powerful than a mere man-made construct. Perhaps she could even tear through his defences if she wished.

She brushed her lips against the softness of the lobe of his ear and a shudder coursed through him, ending in another of those muted groans. She rather liked that sound. It rang something deep inside her, dragging an answering echo. So she ran her tongue along that soft curve again, and then, on impulse, caught it lightly between her teeth.

She hadn't expected the sails to tear quite that easily.

'Genny…'

His fingers splayed over her nape into her hair, canting her back to capture her mouth with his. It wasn't like the soft, teasing kiss in the garden. This was possession. It was begging and demanding and bringing this new Vivi to life like a wizard's spell. His tongue tangled with hers, caressing it as his hands moved over her body, then drew back to taste her unbearably sensitised lips.

It wasn't only the kiss that was conjuring her into existence, releasing wave after wave of need. His hands were doing as much damage—even more so. He was still holding hers and he ran their joined hands up her waist, brushing the curve of her breast, and a harsh groan was wrung out of her, as if the ship itself was being torn open.

It felt doubly wanton to feel the heel of his palm shaping it, his thumb skimming the bared skin above her bodice and her own hand moving with his, skimming the smooth fabric and the weight of her breast beneath it. Her skin tightened, her breasts turning heavy and needy, and when he shifted their hands to brush them over the taut, tingling peak she moaned against his mouth, her teeth catching at his lip, her legs pressing tensely against him as she tried to turn into the sensation.

She should have held still, because his body bucked under hers and with a strangled groan he pulled back from the kiss. For a moment he didn't move, breathing deeply, and she waited for him to stand up. But then he wrapped his arms around her again. He was caging her, but she didn't feel caged. She could feel the tension of his inner sails being drawn taut again, the quivering of muscle and nerve as he pressed down on the heat that was trapped between them. It was viciously frustrating to feel it, and viciously satisfying to know he felt it too.

'Hell, this is madness, Vivi,' he said at last, his voice hoarse and raw. 'If I had the power, I'd banish every last person off this ship right now.'

'That sounds dangerous. Who would sail it?'

'I don't give a damn.'

He touched his lips to her hair briefly, as if by compulsion. His voice was light, but hoarse, and there was still that rigid tension singing through every inch of his body she could feel.

The temptation to test his control was so strong she was just gathering her resolve to throw caution to the winds when she found herself suddenly seated alone while he was on the other chair. She hadn't heard a thing, but then with a clearing of his throat Benja appeared.

He cast an apologetic smile at Genny and broke into a spate of Catalan. Genny's Portuguese and Spanish had always been excellent, but Catalan was beyond her.

Kit cursed and scrubbed his hands through his disordered hair. 'Mary is asking for you. I'll go…'

'No.' Genny stood and brushed down her skirts. 'If she is feeling ill, I think she might prefer a woman to hold the basin for her. And you have a ship to sail, Captain Chris.'

Chapter Thirteen

'I prepare a feast and no one is here to enjoy,' Benja said morosely.

Kit smiled distractedly at the display of roast fowl, pies, and an impressive pot of Benja's speciality, *paella*.

The choppy weather had held, preventing Mary, Emily and Peter from finding their sea legs. And, since his step-mother drew the line at having either him or his sailors hold a basin for her, poor Genny had been recruited to tend to the sick. Luckily Emily and Peter had not passed from queasiness to outright illness, but they remained in their cabin despite his attempts to convince them they'd do better on deck.

'Well, at least that is the last time Emily will beg me for a pleasure cruise,' he said, heaping some food on a plate. 'Take this to Miss Maitland's cabin and remind her to eat while she can. Mary is likely to throw something at me if I show my face. I'll take a plate to my cabin and the men can come in here and do justice to this bounty.'

Benja sighed as Kit took his plate and glass. He could have stayed and eaten with his men, as he usually did. He *ought* to stay with them and take the distraction they offered. A lonely dinner and a bottle of wine while his cock was aching for satisfaction was not a good prescription for a sound night's sleep.

He even tried to insert himself mentally into Mary's sickroom, in the hope that envisaging the familiar sight of the contents of upheaved stomachs would douse the pulsing need he'd foolishly unleashed on deck.

Instead he saw in his mind Genny leaning over a bed, her rounded backside shaping what looked more like a nightdress than the proper gown and pelisse that had separated them on deck. He turned her around. But now she was wearing that unfairly low-cut peach-toned gown she'd worn to the theatre. He stood there in his mind, as hard as a mast, and reached out to set loose her hair, watching the thick honey-brown waves unfurl over her shoulders, covering her beautiful breasts...

No, not covering her breasts—he wanted those bared to his imagination. He reached out and gently brushed her hair aside. God, he could almost feel it between his fingers. He'd only touched that heavy, warm silk twice, but it was imprinted on him more deeply than an inked tattoo on a sailor's skin.

Her hair was now cascading over her shoulders, and he was free to take her hand, as he had on deck. But this time she guided his to her breasts, their fingers linked as they cupped the heavy warmth that rested in his palms— heavy, soft... But he could feel the skin tightening against his hand, just as it was tightening over his erection...

He opened his eyes and pressed his palms together. This was *not* a good idea.

Once they were safely at the Hall it would be easier to stick to the rules. There would be lots of guests, lots of servants...

Lots of rooms.

All those corners where he could...

No.

He kept forgetting that even though Genny might be unconventional, their worlds were utterly different. He might have begun by thoroughly disliking Genny Maitland, but somehow he'd come not only to desire her but to…to care for her…as a friend. He would not wish to see her harmed simply because he couldn't keep his hands to himself. It was not worth it. A flirtation, even a kiss, was all well and good, but everything else would come at a high price for both of them.

Still, he wished too that they could keep on sailing. A little longer. And while he had her in his world, he'd make damn good use of the armchair…

His mind grabbed hold of that pleasant thought: his ground, his armchair…his woman.

No—he amended—not his woman.

Genny Maitland was her own territory. He was merely toying at her edges. He didn't *want* to conquer her; all he wanted was to bed her.

But, *hell*, he did want to bed her.

The knock on his door was hesitant. He was about to send whoever it was to the devil when the certainty struck him that it was Genny. He was at the door and opening it before he realised he was dressed only in his trousers.

She stared at his chest, opened her mouth, turned away, turned back, and frowned at the floor. Luckily, her eyes skimmed past the evidence of his lack of self-control.

She planted her legs a little wider, rushing into speech. 'I'm terribly sorry to intrude. I did ask Benja, and he assured me I would not be disturbing you.'

He would have to have a word with Benja about his sense of humour. To Genny he said, 'Has anything happened? Mary?'

'No, no. She is finally asleep. But I'm afraid she will wake again and I thought it best to have a book with me when she does, to take her mind off her stomach. Mr Fábregas told me the books are in your cabin. I did ask if he could…but he said he had to hurry on deck…something about sandbars? I didn't know there were any so far out.'

Neither did Kit. Nor were there. And Benja knew full well there was a shelf of perfectly suitable books in the map room.

Damn him.

Or bless him, depending on the state of Kit's fast-fraying morals.

He opened the door. 'Come in and choose.'

'I… Perhaps you should?'

'I wouldn't presume. I'll even put my shirt back on.'

'I… Don't on my account. Though…aren't you cold?'

She stepped into the room and he shut the door before she could reconsider.

'No. No, I'm not cold.'

He went to pick up his shirt and she moved cautiously towards the shelf of books, her brows rising as she moved along the shelf.

'You have a great many books.'

'There is a great deal of time to read on a ship.'

'True. Are you ever bored?'

'Sometimes. I don't mind, though. Boredom is a privilege. Some of my best ideas come to me when I'm bored.'

She gave a slight laugh and ran her finger down the spine of one of the books. It seemed to shiver down his spine as well, and his erection rose against the confines of his trousers.

'I remember often being bored when we were billeted in one place for a long time,' she said to the books. 'I wanted to be *doing* something. Not sitting with Serena and the other women and gossiping.'

He could well imagine that. Genny had never belonged in such a setting any more than he had. He felt a twinge of heat a couple of dozen inches north of his erection and rubbed at it. Empathy was not what he wanted to feel right now. He wanted her to ask him to fetch a book for her from the top shelf, while she stood very, very close.

'Take a book or two,' he suggested. 'It might be a long night.'

Damnably long.

'I don't think I shall have time...' She took a book and clutched it to her like a Quaker with her bible, her hair a tangle of waves over her shoulder, glinting gold and dark wine in the flickering of the lantern.

He reached past her to pull out a volume. *'As You like It.'*

'As I like...?' she echoed, her voice hollowing.

'It,' he completed. 'Shakespeare. Rosalind is my favourite of his heroines. *"I shall devise something."'*

'Oh.' She took the book and added it to her shield.

He reached to her right, nudging her aside very gently. 'No, not *A Midsummer Night's Dream*, I think. That will likely give you nightmares. *Measure for Measure*? A little dark, and there's a beheaded pirate there, so we shall pass on that. What of...?'

'These two shall do, thank you,' she said hurriedly.

They both fell silent.

'I didn't tell you before, but this is a lovely room,' she added.

'Thank you. I bought the *Hésperus* from an American privateer. He liked his comforts.'

'Like you. It is impressively neat too. Everything in its place.' Her eyes flickered up to his with a hint of laughter.

'I was born and raised on a ship. When you live at the mercy of the elements and with hardly any room of your own you come to appreciate the benefits of order and comfort.'

'I wasn't making fun of you, Kit.' She looked absurdly contrite.

'No?'

'No. It is merely nice to see your human side… Oh, Lord, that didn't sound right…'

'My human side? You find me cold, Genny?'

'That isn't what I meant and you know it. Shouldn't you don your shirt?'

'Should I? One of the benefits of being on *my* ship, in *my* cabin, is wearing what *I* want. Or, in this case, not wearing it. If my state of undress offends you so, you can, of course, choose to leave. Yet here you are.'

'The books…'

'You are holding two perfectly serviceable books— masterpieces, even. Yet you are still here. Could it be you are contemplating another…impulse?'

'Right now I'm contemplating your chest,' she blurted out.

He planted his hands flat on the shelves on either side of her. 'I would love to do the same. Must you cover the most spectacular masterpiece in this room with all those layers?'

A laugh bubbled out of her. 'Kit. This is *very* improper.'

'If you were *very* proper, you wouldn't have sat on my lap and kissed me on an open deck just a few short hours ago.'

'I didn't…'

'You most certainly did. I was there.'

'I *meant* I didn't mean to be so brazen.'

'You weren't brazen; you were honest. You asked for what you wanted; I asked for what I wanted. So if you wish to play on equal ground, this is how it is done. At any time, no matter what, you can walk out through this door. I would never stop you.'

She swallowed. 'That almost sounds like a threat.'

'Freedom is threatening. We're beasts that like boundaries. We feel safe inside them.'

'*You* don't.'

'I mistrust them because they are too often used against

me. I'd rather risk my fate outside them so long as I don't hurt people I care for. But that's my choice; you make yours.'

She took a couple of deep breaths, her eyes fixed somewhere in the area of his right shoulder. 'So...if I would like another kiss, I could ask you?'

His elbows threatened to give way and close the distance between them. He almost said, *You could ask me anything.*

He pulled his sagging mental faculties back into some semblance of intelligence and nodded. 'You could. That isn't to say I would agree. The same applies to you.'

'Of course.'

She shifted her eyes up to his. They were a deep, metallic grey now, the pupils dilated. He very much hoped that meant she was strongly considering being impulsive.

'I really should return to Mary,' she said, hefting her books higher against her bosom.

Ah, damn.

'But first...fair is fair. Hold these, please.'

She gave him the books and then untied her cape, draping it over his braced arm as if he was part of the furniture. Beneath she wore a demure cotton nightgown, secured with blue ribbons at the neck. The simple cream-coloured fabric clung to her curves as lovingly as he would happily have done. She wore a chemise beneath, but no stays, and even through the double layer he could see the tight pressure of her nipples beneath.

Then she drove home the knife with a slow tug at the laces and the fabric fell open, revealing the plump curves all the way to the dark hollow between them.

'What is it with men and bosoms?' she asked as she watched him, her voice caught between laughter and embarrassment and a tamped heat that echoed his.

'I don't know, Vivi, but it's deep. Especially when faced with such perfection.'

'They're hardly perfect.'

'Exquisite.'

He allowed his eyes to sweep over her, gathering images—the outline of her thigh under the cotton, the rise of her hip, the faint echoes of freckles across the bridge of her nose, the warm, generous curve of her mouth. And her eyes... Perhaps they were the most damaging to his sanity. They glistened like liquid mercury...mystical and dangerous.

'And not just them, Vivi. Every inch of you. Utterly exquisite.'

'Now you are being foolish. Mary and Serena are exquisite. I'm short and passable, with a bosom that seems to distract men and make them say silly things. It is nothing to be proud of.'

'Mary and Serena are pretty like a hundred other women are pretty. Like that vase on the table is pretty. I have absolutely no urge to populate my wicked waking dreams with *pretty*. They are thoroughly occupied with absolutely...utterly...exquisite.'

He allowed himself to gently brush his fingers over her shoulders and the soft skin at the side of her neck before he regretfully tied the ribbons again and draped her cloak about her shoulders.

'Once we're at the Hall we won't be able to...to flirt like this,' she said, her eyes skimming past him to the rumpled bed.

A spear of fire cleaved through him—fierce and demanding—but instead of pushing him over the edge, it held him back.

The thought of exploring Genny's excitability might be threatening his sanity, but it wasn't the hypocritical Carrington morals that stood in the way of taking what she was contemplating offering.

Genny deserved far, far better—and that was precisely what he couldn't give her.

No, to be fair, it was not that he couldn't—he wouldn't.

If there was one thing his father's two marriages had taught him, it was that marriage should either be entered into with all one's heart and soul and conscience, or not at all.

'No, we won't be able to,' he finally agreed.

Fantasy would have to remain fantasy.

She nodded and took the books, pressing them to her chest again. Then she rose on tiptoe and brushed her mouth over his, lingering for a moment. His arms were already rising when she sank back down and slipped past him and out through the door.

He stood there for a while longer, staring at the books on the shelf. The gilt lettering of *Love's Labour's Lost* twinkled in the candlelight, mocking him and the long night ahead.

He put on his shirt and boots and went up on deck. With any luck it would rain.

Chapter Fourteen

How strange.

He'd forgotten how lovely Carrington Hall was.

In his boyish memories the house had been dark, brooding, oppressive. Since their arrival yesterday he'd only seen part of it, but he'd yet to find a dark corner.

The house was a large grey stone affair in the classical style with two wings, set in a slight valley that protected it and the lush spring gardens from the worst of the sea winds.

It was a resolutely English sight, cheerful and even comforting, but the jewel in the crown was the horseshoe-shaped bay which nestled below rocky cliffs and was accessible by a narrow and seldom used cliff path.

Tomorrow he would indulge in the only happy memory he had of the Hall—swimming. The cold water would be useful.

He felt strangely cheated. He'd been nursing a boy's resentment for well over a dozen years and now it had fizzled like a wet candle wick.

He walked through the gardens, wondering if he could identify the place where he'd constructed the fort Julian had invaded when they were boys.

'Good morning, Lord Westford.'

He turned at Serena's voice. She was coming out of the rose garden, carrying a basket filled with fully blown roses and peonies.

'We've missed the best of the peonies already while in London,' she said with evident regret. 'They were Charlie's pride and joy.'

'They are still beautiful,' he said, and she smiled happily at the flowers. It was the first time he'd seen a true smile on her face since his return to England, and he realised with surprise that Genny's sister was still deeply in love with Charlie.

In Spain he'd thought her rather shallow, both in intelligence and emotion. He still had no idea about her intelligence, but he rather thought her emotions ran deep—and they ran in the river bed she'd forged with sweet, straightforward, and ultimately gullible Charlie.

He encouraged her to talk about his cousin, watching the joy pour out of her just as the peonies were threatening to tip out of her basket, and he wished once again that Charlie had survived and was here, where he ought to be, as husband to this grieving woman and as rightful head of the Carringtons.

'He liked you, you know,' Serena said after falling silent for a moment. 'Very much. He always felt he'd been caught between you and the others and never quite knew how to be. That was why he was so happy when you both found yourselves in the same regiment in Spain. He even thought of asking your advice when he realised how bad matters had become.'

'Why didn't he?'

'He didn't know where you were at the time. Mary said the last letter she'd had was from somewhere in the East Indies. In any case he felt…he felt he had to fix it himself. To prove to everyone that he was not…weak.'

'Goodness isn't a weakness, though it is sometimes preyed upon.'

'Yes,' she said earnestly. 'That is what I told him. But he wished he were like you or Marcus. Men who insisted on what they wanted. But he was a *good* man—the kindest I knew. That is why I love him...but he never valued himself as I did.'

'Then he was a very lucky man.'

'I was the lucky one. I only wish...' Her smile wavered and she stopped by the kitchen path.

'Would you like to go live in the Dower House again?' he asked impulsively, and her face lit.

'Do you mean with Genny?'

'If she wishes.'

'I... No, we could hardly leave Mary with Lady Westford, and I don't know if we could convince her to leave her on her own. Oh, it would never work.'

'It strikes me that my grandmother would be far happier in London in any case. Racketing around there seems to suit her far more than it does you and Mary.'

'Oh, it does. But then *we* would have to stay with her there...'

'Why? I'm sure we could unearth some worthy but impoverished Carrington cousin who could organise her whist parties. Charlie wouldn't have wanted you fetching and carrying for that old witch for the rest of her life.'

'No... Charlie wanted us to have a large family and to live on one of the smaller estates where he could grow—' Her voice cracked and she shrugged and smiled. 'I must go and place these in water before they fade. Thank you, Lord Westford.'

Kit watched as she hurried inside and then continued towards the library. He'd ask Mary about Carrington cousins, and the steward about the Dower House, and Genny about—

'Hello, cousin!'

Kit stopped abruptly in the library doorway at Julian's salutation. His cousin was lounging in an armchair, looking through some papers, and the look he directed at Kit was half-smug, half-wary.

'What the devil are you doing here?' Kit demanded.

'I thought the past two weeks had rubbed off some of your rough edges, but apparently I was mistaken. Is this how you plan to greet all your guests, Kitty?'

'Guests are invited. You aren't.'

'I beg to differ. I most assuredly am. Well, if you wish to split hairs, it wasn't strictly an invitation. More of a command.'

'Whose?' Kit's voice snapped like a whip, though he already knew the answer.

'Who issues commands in this household? Or rather, who issues commands I'm likely to obey? Darling Genny, of course.'

Kit went to the sideboard, where Howich had cleverly placed a decanter at the ready for the new master. It was early yet, but he felt the need for a glass. 'Wine?'

'One of your purchases? Or the vinegar Grandfather indulged in?'

'Mine.'

'Then I will, thank you. It's been a long two weeks so far, and likely to be a longer week still. I need all the support I can garner, Kitty.'

Kit considered taking offence at Julian's needling him with the hated nickname, but decided that would only encourage the bastard. He took his glass and paced along the shelves, as he had last night when he'd reacquainted himself with the one room in the house he remembered fondly.

It was a graveyard by means of books, with each Carrington ancestor possessed of their own plot of land. His grandfather's collection of medieval Books of Hours was shut safely into glass-fronted shelves, his father's antiquarian tomes and plates covered part of the north wall, and then came Charlie's shelf, dedicated to agricultural tomes…

He moved away from Charlie's dreams and stopped. A book was leaning tipsily into a gap in the middle shelf. He set the book straight, momentarily distracted from his vexation.

'Did you take some books from here, Julian?'

'I haven't touched a book in this house for years. Why? Are they valuable?' Julian asked.

'Not in the least.'

'Oh.' The disappointment was evident. 'Pity. I could have used the hunt for a book thief to enliven the next few days. What books?'

'Three books. One on the battle of Thermopylae, Herodotus's *Historias*, and Chamber's *Life of Thucydides*.'

Julian's mouth quirked, as if at some secret thought, but then he shrugged. 'They will probably turn up on a table somewhere.'

Kit surveyed the rest of the shelves but there were no other gaps. 'Not that it matters. It is merely…curious.'

'I'm taking some more of this excellent tonic,' Julian said, wandering over to the decanter. 'Would you care for some more, or are you determined to keep your wits about you to meet the onslaught?'

Kit held out his glass to be filled. 'I'd rather have them dulled. I never would have guessed I'd prefer a forced march across the Pyrenees to another week entertaining the Ton.'

'God, yes. They're insatiable. If we have to play charades one more time… Other than the excellent food and wine, I'm regretting the moment I convinced you to show your face in society. I never realised how boring people obsessed with antiquities can be. Why the devil couldn't you invite some guests with an interest in something useful? Even an interest in pork jelly would be a relief at this point. The way they went all spongey at the sight of the vase you brought out that last night in Town made me queasy.'

'You're a damned waste of a good education, Julian. That vase is over a thousand years old and probably worth more than your horse.'

'Since I don't own a horse, you're undoubtedly right. You'd best watch how you flaunt those baubles. I overheard Lord Ponsonby telling his daughter how much it was worth, and the lovely Lady Sarah's sapphire eyes lit like bonfires.'

'Thank you for your concern, but I don't think someone like Lady Sarah would enjoy giving up her Tonnish pursuits to become the wife of a scandalous merchant—even one with a title.'

'Who says she'd have to give up her pursuits? Her type would lord it in London while you were out on the high seas providing the dibs.'

'You don't like her, do you?'

'I'm not particularly fond of schemers. Remind me of my mother. Always scheming and never stopping to see who they've stepped on along the way.'

'You say you don't like schemers but you seem very fond of Genny, and she casts Lady Sarah's machinations into a deep shade.'

'You have a point. Genny's ambitions may not be mercenary, but she's happy to sacrifice the two of us to keep the old witch happy and off Mary's and Serena's backs,' Julian continued.

The uncharacteristic shade of bitterness in his voice caught Kit's attention as much as the words. 'What do you mean, sacrifice the two of us?'

Julian leaned his head back in the chair, his smile mocking. 'I would have thought it was obvious. In between her efforts to snatch one of those prosy gentlemen for Mary and Serena, she and dear Grandmama have us surrounded by a constant buzz of lovely ladies like bees around a honeypot. You didn't think that was chance, did you?'

'Neither Genny nor Grandmama had anything to do with my decision to come to the ball in the first place. *You* were the one who convinced me,' he said warily.

'*Mea culpa.* Genny forced my hand. I knew Marcus would prove damn elusive, and I didn't see why I had to suffer alone. I honestly never expected the chase to last so long—and certainly not to see it transposed from London to Dorset with your full approval. Which of the pretty and pedigreed parcels arriving today are you leaning towards?'

'Arriving today?' Kit echoed, still hoping he had misunderstood.

Julian raised a brow. 'Were you hoping for another day's reprieve? I saw the Cavershams stopping at the Green Giant in Guildford on my way here. The Ponsonbys were with them. I daresay the Ducal pack is not far behind. Your few days' rest is up, Cuz. The old witch would obviously prefer you pick one of the Burford girls, to please the old Duke, but I put my money on Lady Sarah. She's almost as cunning as Genny, and she and her ambitious papa have clearly decided you will do very well indeed for their purposes. If I were you I'd choose that sweet little Caversham lamb—pretty, quiet and outrageously wealthy, with an irreproachable name that goes all the way back to the dawn of time. She'll brighten your tarnished coat of arms and wait patiently at home while you do as you please. What more could a man want?'

Kit hardly even registered the slipping of Julian's urbane charm, revealing the angry bitterness he usually kept veiled. He was too occupied with realising what a complete blind fool he'd been. Why hadn't he asked who Genny was inviting? He'd left it to her and assumed...

He'd assumed a great deal about Genevieve Maitland. And in his lustful haze he'd forgotten precisely what she was.

Yet it still felt…wrong.

He made one last bid to redeem her. 'Why assume Genny orchestrated this and not Grandmother? You would think marrying us off would go against Genny's interests. She and Serena would be forced to leave the Hall and Carrington House.' He didn't mention his surmise that Genny had long been holding a candle for Julian himself.

'Well, that is what she wants, isn't it? Independence. Grandmama has her own funds, you know. And that is what she promised Genny in return for one of us walking up the aisle and signing the register. She'll pay Serena's debts and settle a generous sum on her. A very comfortable arrangement.'

'Who told you this?'

Julian's shrugged. 'What difference does it make?'

Kit wished he could dismiss this as a sign of Julian's malice, but it rang true. Such a pact would provide Genny with everything she wanted.

He should have told her that very first week that he had settled Charlie's debts and arranged annuities for Serena and Mary. He'd been tempted to tell her but he'd held back, afraid she'd think he was doing it as much to please her as out of duty.

Which was true as well.

Idiot.

But he shouldn't be angry with her. Genny Maitland was simply doing what she did best—surviving.

He wasn't angry.

He was *furious*.

At her, at his grandmother, and at Mary and Serena for allowing those two Machiavellian women to control their lives… No, for practically forcing them to do so by the sheer force of their passivity.

He was furious at Julian as well. Not for his part in the subterfuge, but for seeing more clearly what he himself should have seen from the moment he'd walked into Carrington House. He *had* seen it. He'd just allowed his suspicions to be lulled, allowed himself to believe that in joining forces with him Genny had somehow set her other alliances aside—his grandmother, Julian…

Unbelievably gullible.

'Kit? Where are you going?'

Kit didn't answer as he strode out of the library.

First he would set his grandmother straight. And then…

Chapter Fifteen

'Lady Westford has sent for you, miss,' Susan announced.

Genny looked up from her writing and sighed.

Susan's mouth hovered near a smile. 'Yes, miss.'

'Very well, Susan. Are my sister and Mrs Mary still resting?'

'Mrs Mary is, but your sister is out in the garden with His Lordship.'

'With Lord Westford?' Genny tried to mask her surprise.

'Yes, miss. Bess said as she just saw her and Lord Westford there, miss.'

'Thank you, Susan.'

Genny closed her books and went to the window. She had a clear view of the gardens and the path leading back to the house. As Bess had reported, two figures stood by the entrance to the rose garden. Kit was smiling down at her sister and Serena was laughing, her face bright with pleasure, her hands moving animatedly.

She looked years younger, like she had in Spain, full of joy and flirtatious light. Genny hadn't seen that expression on her face in a long, long time. They looked perfect together, both tall and beautiful, dark and light. Genny's heart gave a painful squeeze compounded of pleasure at seeing her sister as she had once been, and sharp, undeniable jealousy.

She had resolved to accept whatever fate dictated, but if fate dictated that something should evolve between Kit and Serena...

Nonsense. They don't suit at all. Serena needs someone sedate and stable and cheerful, like Charlie. There is no reason to worry simply because Kit is making her laugh... and look happier than she has since...

She turned away from the sight and left her study, her hand pressed hard to her stomach as she made her way to Lady Westford's room, where she took a few moments to compose herself before knocking on the door.

She had barely crossed the threshold when Lady Westford's voice snapped out at her.

'I'm not happy with you, Genevieve Maitland.'

Genny took a deep breath and went to sit by the bed, where Lady Westford lay still in her dressing gown and lace cap. Carmine's cage was partly covered by an embroidered cloth, and his beady eyes glimmered accusingly from the shadows. She'd forgotten to bring seeds, and most likely Carmine was about to make her pay for her lapse.

'It's been over a fortnight and we've nothing to show for it,' Lady Westford continued, reaching for her cane where it lay on the coverlet beside her.

'A fortnight is not a very long period,' Genny replied, feeling the lie. This fortnight had felt very, very long indeed.

'It's enough to see that he spreads himself about but won't encourage any of them. I don't see what difference this week will make.'

'He has spent a great deal of time with Lady Sarah, during the past week in particular.'

'Aye, she sees to that! But sinking her claws into him is a sure way of making him bolt. At our last dinner in

London he flirted with Burford's youngest instead—the one who wants him to carry her off on his ship like Scheherazade, or some other foolish female.'

Genny didn't bother correcting Lady Westford's literary allusions. She'd noticed the same, and so had Lady Sarah, who had very wisely stepped back and spent the evening flirting with Julian.

She wondered what Lady Westford would say had she seen Kit and Serena just now. Serena had barely been considered good enough for Charlie when they'd thought her able to provide an heir. Lord Westford marrying his cousin's barren widow would likely give Lady Westford an apoplexy.

'Yet you must admit he has behaved exceptionally well—'

Genny cut herself off, realising she was following Lady Westford's lead in speaking of Kit as if of a child invited to join the adults at the dinner table. If she didn't need Lady Westford's co-operation and goodwill, she would be tempted to tell her precisely what she thought of her treatment of her grandson.

She gathered her scattering resolve and continued. 'Playing hot and cold at this juncture is probably his way of reminding Lady Sarah who is in command, Lady Westford. He knows quite a bit more about seduction than you...' She trailed off that sentence and took a deep breath. 'I, for one, think we are doing quite well. You shall have to be patient. The more you press, the more resistance you arouse.'

'In you as well, eh?' Lady Westford cackled and Carmine followed suit, hopping about excitedly.

'Yes,' Genny snapped. 'In me as well.'

Lady Westford's eyes widened in surprise and she looked far more human. 'What's eating you, child? Worried about Serena? You'd think the gel would be sensible enough to cast out some lures to Caversham. He might be tempted into the parson's mousetrap by a pretty face and soft ways if she but exerts herself. Can't have her mooning about Charles for ever or she'll lose her bloom. Best have a word with her.'

'I will *not* have a word with her. She is old enough to make her own decisions and mistakes.'

Genny felt an absurd need to cry and hurried to the door. She'd had her fair measure of being tested for the moment. For the year.

As she opened it Lady Westford's cane rapped against the chair, but lightly.

'Wishing me at Hades, aren't you, Genny?'

'There is a great deal to prepare and I'm tired, Lady Westford,' Genny replied.

Her answer seemed to upset Lady Westford, as if she'd somehow been snubbed.

'I can see that. Go and do what you need to do. But make sure you keep your eye on the *rouleaux*, Genevieve Maitland. We have a deal, you and I. Don't think I won't hold you to your part of it. Remember what's in it for you.'

'I remember, Lady Westford.'

'Yes, I daresay you do. Don't forget—it was your scheme to begin with, but it's my money you won't see a penny of if you don't deliver results.'

Genny didn't bother responding, just stepped out into the corridor.

And straight into Lord Westford.

Her heart gave an almost audible squeak as his hands closed on her arms, steadying her. She was about to apologise when she caught the expression in his sea-blue eyes. His gaze held hers for a moment, then shifted past her to the still-open door.

He reached past her and slowly closed it. The faint *thunk* of wood on wood sounded very loud.

She waited for him to say something. Anything. She knew without a doubt that he had heard her last exchange with Lady Westford. She was not quite certain how it had sounded to him, but by the absolutely blank look on his face it was bad. He just stood there, saying nothing, his face so leeched of expression she might as well have been boxed in by a statue.

'Excuse me, Lord Westford,' she said, her voice a shade too high.

'For what, Miss Maitland?'

Good point. She was tempted to point out that people who eavesdropped rarely heard anything to their advantage, but thought better of it.

'Mrs Pritchard is waiting for me. To discuss tomorrow's menus.'

'Mrs Pritchard is proving endlessly useful to you, Genny Maitland, isn't she? By all means, run along. I shall find you after I have a word with my grandmother.'

With that ominous promise he set her aside and entered Lady Westford's room.

Genny did not wish to admit even to herself that she had found every excuse to remain in Mrs Pritchard's neat little parlour far longer than their business merited. They'd reviewed the linen inventory, the references of a new housemaid, and everything else that had been piling up in the busyness of opening the Hall to guests after almost two years of mourning.

By the time she returned to her rooms she hoped Lord Westford had calmed sufficiently and would leave her be.

That hope died abruptly when she saw him on the sill of her parlour.

The menu lists she'd taken to review for the rest of the week slipped from her hand and fluttered to the carpet.

Lord Westford turned at the sound of the door opening

and leaned down to pick up one of the sheets of paper that had settled by his boot.

Her surprise was transformed into alarm and she calmed only slightly as she realised she'd put her private notes in the drawer out of force of habit before leaving the room.

'This parlour has been set aside for my use and Serena's, my lord.'

'I'm aware of that—which is precisely why I am here. You took your time hiding in Mrs Pritchard's lair.'

Her stomach tightened at his clipped tones. He looked much as he had during those first days in London, before they'd forged their tentative truce and tested the boundaries of propriety with their flirtation.

He certainly looked nothing like he had on board the *Hesperus*.

She waited for the attack, but to her surprise he placed one hand on the stack of books on her table.

'I was wondering where these had gone.'

A shiver of alarm ran through her, but her voice was steady when she answered.

'I apologise. I did not know anyone was looking for them. I shall return them.'

'No need. Now I know where they are...'

He raised the book he had been holding. A different kind of tension caught her.

'I didn't know your grandfather had written a book,' he continued.

'It is a volume of essays first published in the *London Magazine*.' She swallowed and tried to smile, adding a little impulsively, 'I have several copies if you wish to take one.'

He considered her, but there was no lightening of his expression. She'd begun to forget how unfairly handsome he was. When he was aloof like this it was hard to ignore the sheer beauty of his face and physique. Every time she was reminded, the differences between them slammed down like a drawbridge clanging into place.

'Thank you.' His words were cold and something turned inside her—a flicker of welcome anger to press back at the confused heat.

'You are welcome. Now, if you do not mind, I must review the week's menus.' She waved the handwritten sheets she'd collected from the floor and scooted around him to sit at the writing table, pulling the inkwell towards her.

'An excuse, Genny?'

Far from leaving, he came to stand by the desk, picking up one of the entwined jade dragons and weighing it in his palm. She felt a tremor shimmer down her spine. It wasn't fear—it was that damnable awareness, made all the worse now it was backed by experience.

'It is no excuse, my lord, merely a care for details. It might have escaped your notice, but a house party is a nightmare of logistics,' she said with dignity, keeping her eyes on the menus but seeing very little.

'Not at all. I'm impressed by your skills, Madam Quartermaster. Even more so having seen you in mid-campaign. What were you and my grandmother discussing just now?'

That answered her question about whether he'd overheard. Her stomach sank to somewhere below her ankles. Which was suitable—she truly felt a heel.

'Lady Westford is naturally unsettled by the house being invaded. I merely reassured her I shall do my best to keep everything in order.'

He planted his hand on the menu she was trying to read. It was a very large hand, splayed wide on the white paper. She swallowed again as another potent memory arose— that same hand, entwined with hers, his calluses rough against her palm. She felt the warmth of his body as he leaned over the desk but she didn't look up. Not that staring at his hand was any better.

'Someone who lies as often as you should do a better job of it, sweetheart.'

His voice was as soft as silk and as menacing as a coiled snake.

'I'm not—'

'I am serious,' he interrupted. 'Whatever you and the old witch are concocting, I hope… I very much hope…it has nothing to do with me.'

She tried to tug the paper from under his hand, but achieved nothing more than a ripped corner.

'I told you I do not care to be loomed over, Lord Westford. If you are in a foul mood, please exorcise it elsewhere.'

'I'm in "a foul mood", Genny, because I don't like being manipulated. If you put so many pokers in the fire, don't be surprised when one burns you.'

A flush of sheer, brutal heat swept over her. She bent further over her lists, but he caught her chin, angling up her face.

'What are you two plotting?'

His voice had dropped into a hoarse, coaxing rumble. He wasn't exerting any pressure on her skin, but she felt his touch deep inside her, as if it was setting roots and spreading.

'I'm not *plotting* anything,' she said, a little desperately.

His fingers traced the line of her jaw, feathering the hollow below her ear. 'So what do you call it, then? Merely doing what needs to be done to *"get through the day"*?'

She realised he was using her own words from that day in the stables. They sounded all wrong like that. She shook her head, but that only made his fingers graze the lobe of her ear and she couldn't stop the answering shudder that swept through her. He felt it, closing his hand on her nape. A deep sound, almost of pain, caught in his throat.

For a second she couldn't breathe. Her lungs just

stopped, waiting out the wave of scalding heat that swept through her, setting fire after fire—in her cheeks, her chest, and again at that unfamiliar core inside her.

He spoke first, his voice a sensual drag across her nerves.

'You don't like being out of control, do you? You're like a cat, clinging to the ceiling, afraid to sheathe your claws for fear of the fall.'

'Cats land on their feet. I don't.'

'But you do. Or rather you somehow arrange for one of us mortals to lay a mattress precisely where you need it.'

The mention of mattresses was not fortuitous. She thought of his wide rumpled bed on board the *Hesperus*, and of her own bed behind the door not two yards from him.

She couldn't think of anything intelligent to say so she kept silent, waiting for him to stop the assault and leave her be.

'What were you and my grandmother discussing?'

This question was a whisper of coaxing warmth, spilling like silk down her spine. She knew what he was doing, but it made no difference to her body.

It was *aching* to be seduced.

'I will find out, Genny.'

This time she heard frustration, determination—and, she thought, hurt. That surprised her, and she looked up. His eyes were in full storm, dilated. She didn't see any hurt in them, only concentrated fire. Goosebumps rose on her arms.

'It's dangerous, not giving quarter, Generalissima. You should know that,' he continued.

I do.

She almost spoke the words, but nothing came.

He smiled. 'Defiance by silence, darling? You're not the only one who can be stubborn.'

His thumb brushed the cleft of her chin, and then the soft pillow of her lip. His eyes followed, his lashes lowering to shield the deep blue eyes. She let her eyes drift to his mouth; she could feel it on her still, in the gentle, sensuous kiss in the garden, the wild, drugging kiss on the *Hesperus*, even the kiss that had been promised but never came in his cabin. Each was a different aspect of this man.

This time he was using his skill on her consciously. He might not use his weapons as lightly as Julian, but when he chose to do so he could clearly play a beautiful seduction scene. It might have been a little more believable if he hadn't been radiating anger.

There was none of the teasing warmth she'd begun to expect when they crossed swords, when the battles were almost a pleasure as they skirted around the heat they sparked off one another.

'Tell me.' His eyes were icy, his voice raw.

She shook her head, the friction of his fingers dancing deliciously over her mouth and adding fuel to the fire. 'You should know I don't respond well to threats, Kit.'

'I'm not threatening. I'm asking,' he murmured, his hand slipping into her hair, cupping her head, his fingers moving gently against her scalp.

She laid a hand against his chest to push him away but stayed there, feeling his heartbeat fast and hard against her palm.

'Why don't you trust me?' he asked.

'Why should I?'

He gave a small laugh. 'Damn you. No reason.'

'I'm not the only one who doesn't like being out of control, am I, Kit?' she asked impulsively.

He shook his head, lowering it inexorably. 'No. No, you're not…'

The last word was a whisper against her mouth. But he didn't kiss her. Not like before. This soft brushing of his lips over hers, sweeping like a willow branch on water, wasn't quite a kiss. It felt more like a dance…like that waltz on the patio as the music had wound about them and carried them deeper and deeper into darkness, swaying only for the sake of the lightest of frictions.

'Such sharp claws and such soft lips,' he murmured. 'What a chimera you are, Genevieve. I never know if you'll command, condemn or tantalise.'

'I never tantalise,' she protested in a whisper.

Shaking her head only increased the friction.

'Yes, you do.' He kissed her gently, mouth closed, just nudging her lips with his before whispering against her mouth, 'You use whatever tools you have at your disposal.'

'Not this.'

'You did in the garden. On the ship.'

'*You* did that,' she protested, drawing back a little.

He shook head again, his eyes narrowed and slumberous. '*We* did that. You know you could have told me to stop and I would have. You can tell me to stop now and I will. Admit it, Genny. You enjoy this. Another field to test your powers.'

A shiver ran through her. Damn him for being right. Perhaps it was best to think of it precisely like that?

'So what if I do? Me and the rest of humanity. It is nothing extraordinary.'

A flash of challenge turned his eyes near black. 'Isn't it?'

He leaned forward again, his mouth hovering below her ear, his breath slipping down the side of her neck and setting it alight. Slowly, slowly his lips approached the lobe of her ear. She could feel the ebb and surge of warmth as his breath came closer.

'Can't you feel it, Vivi? I'm on damn fire here and it feels wonderfully out of the ordinary. This is what people live for. Not society, not propriety…this. *This* is beautiful.'

His lips came to rest on the peach-soft flesh of her lobe and she couldn't hold back the moan that rose from the deepest part of her. It *was* beautiful.

But it doesn't mean anything, her mind insisted. *He probably uses the same tactics with whichever female sparks his interest. Or whenever he needs to prise secrets from credulous women.*

I don't give a damn, replied her body. *Right now, I am the one sparking it.*

She turned her head, making his lips skim her cheek, stopping when they reached the corner of her mouth. His breath stuttered against her skin before he withdrew, sending the tiny hairs on her cheeks shivering.

'Show me,' she goaded. 'Show me something extraordinary.'

There was a thundery echo of anger in his eyes in the moment before his head descended to hers once more. She waited for that anger to be reflected in his actions, but his mouth settled on hers as gently as a dandelion seed on a pond.

'Vivi...'

The word was a slow exhalation of smoke against her lips and they opened of their own accord, letting him brush the parting with his lower lip.

'I want to do this…everywhere. Every inch of you. I can close my eyes and see you on my bed, your hair tangled, your thighs bare, the silk sheet slipping between them, begging me to follow. I should have thrown scruples to the wind and accepted your invitation on the *Hesperus*. Have you any idea how much I wanted you at that moment?'

She shook her head, a little shocked by the urgency in his voice, and more than a little mistrustful.

Kit would tell her what she wanted to hear, what any woman wanted to hear—that she was desired, that her powers in some way overcame his. He'd warned her that he meant to make her tell him the truth. This was nothing more than another negotiation—wasn't it?

She didn't know what to do. This was not a game she knew how to play. This was not a *game*. Not to her. All she knew was that she wanted him.

He still held her hand pressed to his chest and his heart beat against her palm, against her own hurried, tumbling pulse. She wanted that beat against her bared body, not a stitch of fabric between them and only the cool slide of the silk sheet beneath.

'I didn't know. I *don't* know. Show me…'

'If I do I'll go up in flames, Vivi. Just your scent… You smell like the orange blossoms that bloom on Capri—the scent of paradise. And the taste… I've never tasted anything so exquisite, Vivi.'

His fingers slipped down, tracing the outline of her breast, tightening the muslin over her skin until it dragged against the tightened peak, the friction sending a shower of tingling need right down to her toes.

She wanted him to bare it, to touch her properly, and while he was at it to do something about the insistent discomfort that kept surging and ebbing between her legs. She'd thought she understood a great deal about the interplay between men and women—what she hadn't gleaned from Serena and Mary she'd learned from books or by asking an amused but co-operative Julian. But she realised now that in this domain reality was very, *very* different from theory. She was still as green as the greenest of virgins and she was tired of her ignorance; she wanted to *know* in the most biblical sense.

His lips explored hers in a series of light, almost playful kisses, like a butterfly flickering on and off a flower, except each contact was like a strike of flint on flint, teasing, making everything tighten unbearably. Then he raised her from the chair and onto the desk in one motion, drawing her towards him so that he could stand between her thighs.

She'd felt his erection before, on the ship, but now it was a thudding presence against the flame-hot pulse between her legs. Her moan was lost in his own low, guttural groan as he held her there, his mouth against hers, his skin warm on hers, the rasp of his stubble making her skin tingle, a tantalising contrast with the velvet of his lips, making her wonder what that contrast would feel like…elsewhere.

The sensations, so foreign and so right, and the vivid images conjuring themselves in her mind, were both frightening and wonderful. She wanted so much more. She wanted to press deeper, impossibly deeper against him. Until there was nothing at all that stood between them… until she was nothing but these unnameable sensations… until they went up in flames.

Then he spoke, his words a whisper against her temple. 'Why won't you tell me what you and my grandmother were discussing, Vivi?'

Sometimes Genny woke from a dream with a harsh thud, quite as if she'd rolled off the bed. His words struck her exactly like that. They cut through the haze of lust and finally set bells pealing.

She gathered every shred of her control, put her hands on his chest, and pushed. His hands tightened on her behind, then released her. He moved away, towards the window, tucking his shirt back into his buckskins. She hadn't even realised she'd pulled it out.

She truly must have lost her mind.

She slipped off the desk but remained leaning against it. 'If I tell you…'

He gave a short, bitter laugh.

'Ah, here it comes. Tit for tat.'

'*You* began this negotiation.'

'It isn't a negotiation, damn it.'

'An interrogation, then.'

He didn't answer, but nor did he deny it.

Then, 'So, what price *are* you demanding for your confession, then, *darling*?'

The word was a slap but she ignored it. 'Serena.'

He frowned. 'Serena?'

'Yes.' She took a deep breath and forced the words out. 'I don't want you making her fall in love with you.'

His eyes narrowed. 'Are we talking about *Serena*?'

'Yes. I saw the two of you coming up from the gardens. You were laughing together and she looked…alive again. Like she did before everything went wrong.'

Her voice faltered and she could feel the unfamiliar burn of tears in her throat, in her eyes; even her cheeks ached.

'And you thought…? Do you want to know what we were talking of, Miss Maitland?'

His sudden formality stung, but she shook her head.

'My brilliant strategy of seduction was to inveigle your sister into telling me of the time Charlie tried to win the prize for the largest turnip in the village fête. How he finally grew one larger than Squire Felston but the night before the fête his favourite sow… I think her name was Annie…found her way into the garden and ate it.'

He gave a harsh laugh at her expression.

'You are right about one thing, though, Miss Maitland. It was the first time I had seen her come to life since I returned to England. Whether you wish to face the truth or not, Serena is still in love with Charlie, and I think the last thing she wants to do is find herself another husband. All she wants from me is someone who will talk to her of Charlie and not pity her. She is not interested in me and I am not interested in her. And if this…' he swept the room with his hand, encompassing everything that had transpired there '…was an attempt to keep me away from your sister, you have truly outdone yourself, sweetheart. You are so bent on winning this game you're playing against life, I think you forget what you are playing for.'

He went to the door and stopped, his hand on the knob.

'Intelligence isn't maturity, Genny. You're long on one and sometimes frighteningly short on the other. That's a dangerous combination and one day it will burn you badly.'

Kit closed the door as quietly as the explosive mix of fury, lust, and hurt allowed him. It was the dignified thing to do, but he was almost tempted to open it again and slam it shut so hard it shook the whole of Carrington Hall. Shook it right into rubble.

He strode down the corridor, but stopped at the sound of voices in the hall below. The deep voice of the Duke of Burford and the higher chatter of his granddaughters intermingled with Lady Sarah's laughing tones. Beyond them he could hear the rumble of carriages on the drive.

Now he could remember why he hated this house. He could feel it shutting the cage door, pressing him deep into a corner. Except this time, he'd walked voluntarily into this cage. Invited it, even.

He wished he could leave. Ride back to Portsmouth and raise anchor on the *Hesperus* and leave.

He'd known this visit to England would be difficult. He hadn't realised it would be purgatorial.

Chapter Sixteen

'And what ring of hell are we entering today?' Kit asked Mary, and she glanced around swiftly to see if anyone had heard. But only the two Burford girls had yet come down to breakfast, and they were surveying the dishes set out on the sideboard.

'Hush, Kit. We have a quite unexceptionable activity arranged for today.'

'You said that the day before yesterday, when we spent the whole day traipsing around the house as if it was a damn—dashed museum, and then you said it again yesterday when we spent the day in Weymouth, following in old King George's footsteps along the promenade.'

'The Duke and your grandmama have many fond memories of the town and you must admit it is a rather lovely place. I only wish it had been warm enough to try the bathing machines.'

'I don't. I much prefer swimming on my own in the bay.'

'Hush. If only you would at least *try* and enjoy yourself.'

'I am on my absolute best behaviour, Mary. I have never in my life made such an effort to be pleasant so far against my will.'

'I know it, and I appreciate it, but I wish you would try and *enjoy* yourself.'

Kit refilled his coffee. He should be on the *Hesperus*'s deck now. This was his hour, after seeing to the morning rote, to go to his deck study with a book and a cup of Benja's strong, bitter coffee. Everyone knew he was not to be interrupted unless they had run aground or were about to be boarded.

God, he missed his freedom.

To think that people actually wanted this life.

He wanted none of it. So far it had brought him nothing but headaches. And cock aches.

At least he'd held firm to his determination to steer clear of the little Field Marshal these past two days. They'd hardly talked, and when they had it had been either with the most punctilious politeness or with the sharp biting jabs he had promised himself he would not succumb to and kept succumbing to nonetheless.

At least until yesterday morning, when by a stroke of bad luck they'd found themselves alone together in the breakfast room. It had been absurdly awkward. They'd sat there like two painfully shy greenhorns, trying to think of something unexceptionable to say. Since then, they'd stopped sniping and moved to ignoring. Genny clearly shared his wish to get through this week as swiftly and painlessly as possible and forget that anything at all had happened between them.

Eventually that was what would happen: the same fate that overtook everything—it faded.

His heart hitched, stumbled down a hill, and then slowed again. He was becoming accustomed to these anatomical anomalies, but he hated it. It was like a gammy leg—it served well, nine parts out of ten, but the tenth…

He dragged his mind back to the matter at hand. 'You still have not told me what is planned for today.'

'Why don't we let it be a surprise?'

'Good God, no. Out with it. What horror have you planned?'

'It is no horror. It should be quite enjoyable.'

'This is sounding more and more ominous.'

'Nonsense. It is merely a treasure hunt.'

'A *treasure* hunt! You are jesting!'

'Shh! It was Lady Calista's idea.'

'Of course it was. Why don't I just bury a chest full of jewels for her to find and be done with it?'

'Now, now… It shall be great fun. What a pity Emily isn't here. She would have enjoyed it mightily.'

Kit decided it was politic not to answer and concentrated on his coffee. He should have asked for it to be sent up to his rooms—but, besides it being impolite not to share breakfast with his guests, he was too restless. And he needed the distraction.

Just not a damned treasure hunt.

'What does this damn—dashing idea entail?' he asked in calmer tones. Forewarned was forearmed.

Mary greeted Lady Sarah and Lord Ponsonby, as they too entered the breakfast room and went over to the sideboard.

'It entails,' Mary answered, keeping her tones low, 'the guests being divided into two groups. Each must search for a hidden object by following a series of clues. We knew you would be difficult, so Genny did not include you. Unless you wish to be included. We shall say you have hidden the clues and so cannot in fairness take part. You need do nothing more than follow along.'

'Does that mean they shall be crawling all over the house again?'

'They shall be exploring and enjoying themselves. And you shall be polite.'

'Yes, Aunt Mary,' he replied obediently.

The door opened and he prepared his polite face again,

but it was only Genny and Serena. Genny's eyes met his for a moment and fell away, a faint flush touching her pale cheeks. Serena went to join the others at the sideboard, but Genny sat next to Mary and pulled the teapot to her.

'Is everything in place?' Mary asked cheerfully.

'Yes. You needn't worry.' Genny's tones were as flat as the sea in the doldrums.

Serena sat opposite, casting a peculiar glance at her sister. 'Are you feeling quite the thing, Genny?'

'Of course.'

'Oh, I'm so excited!' Lady Calista exclaimed as she bounced into the chair next to Serena, the abundant contents of her plate very nearly finding their way onto the pristine linen. 'I am quite certain our group shall be the first to solve all the clues.'

'I would not wager on that, Calista. I saw the lists in the hall. I am in the competing group,' Lady Sarah said as she sat beside her with rather more decorum.

Lady Calista's eyes sparkled. 'Perhaps we ought to lay a wager.'

'You shall do no such thing, young woman,' the Duke said as he entered the room, but he patted her affectionately on the shoulder as he passed.

'Oh, Grandpapa!'

'I said no. You shall have enough excitement, hunting for that treasure. Learn to be content with what you have, child.'

Lady Calista's pout lasted only for a moment. 'Never mind. It will be enough to know we've beaten you to flinders, Lady Sarah. We have Julian… Mr Carrington… on our side.'

Lady Sarah's mouth pinched but Julian, who had settled on Genny's other side, raised his cup in salute to his bubbly teammate.

'You may console yourself with that dream until it is

rudely shattered,' Lady Sarah retorted and smiled across at Mary. 'We have Lady Westford and Mrs Mary Carrington on our side, and when you are a little older you shall realise that women are far better at clues than men.'

Mary laughed, and despite his sour mood Kit couldn't help smiling.

'I didn't see everyone's names on the lists,' Lady Sophronia intervened, her eyes flickering in Kit's direction and then dancing away. 'Which side are you on, Miss Maitland?'

Genny set down her still-full cup and folded her hands in her lap. 'Neither, Lady Sophronia. Since I hid the clues, my role is merely to grant each group a hint if they are truly stymied.'

'I thought Lord Westford hid the clues?' Lady Calista said, throwing him a disappointed look.

'I'm afraid I am as much in the dark as you are, Lady Calista. Miss Maitland is the true mastermind here.'

Genny's chin rose, her mouth flattening, but she was clearly the only one who had heard anything questionable in his tone. Lady Calista laughed and clapped her hands.

'Why, that is marvellous. Then you *can* play. You must be on our team.'

'I think it wouldn't be fair play to have both Carrington cousins on one team. Since they grew up here, they have an advantage, don't they?' said Mr Caversham as he sat beside his daughter.

Since Miss Caversham was in Lady Sarah's group, his suggestion was a trifle transparent and his poor daughter turned an unfortunate beet-red. Kit, who'd had no intention of voluntarily joining the game, found himself smiling across at the young woman.

'You're quite right, Caversham. I value fair play above all else—it is so hard to come by. I shall add my name to the list. Unless you would rather do that, Miss Maitland?'

'No.'

Genny's answer was bald enough to breach even Lady Calista's bubbliness. She threw Genny a rather puzzled look, and Serena hurried to explain the rules of the game, drawing everyone's attention.

Kit missed most of it. He was too busy kicking himself for succumbing once again to pointless, petty sniping. Whatever Machiavellian schemes Genny engaged in, and however much he resented them—and her—he should not allow it to affect his own conduct. What he should do was play the game and count the hours until he left all this behind.

'*"Enlightened One by any other name."* What can it mean?' Lady Sarah smoothed out the strip of paper they'd discovered in the music chest, where their previous clue had led them.

Kit was about to speak when Miss Caversham cleared her throat nervously.

'Roses?'

The team turned to her and she shrank back a little.

He smiled encouragingly. 'What made you think of roses, Miss Caversham?'

'The quote. *"A rose by any other name would smell as sweet"*?'

She seemed to finish most of her sentences with a question.

'I think you are right. Shall we go to the rose garden?' He held out his arm and Mr Caversham beamed with pride, which only made his daughter's blush deepen.

'But what does *"Enlightened One"* mean?' asked Lady Sarah as she fell into step on his other side as they entered the garden. 'Is that the name of a rose?'

'Sounds like what you'd name a saint, or something,' Lord Lansdowne replied as he helped Mary down the steps. 'Maybe one of the roses is called Bishop or Cardinal or something. They have Mrs Serena Carrington on their team for all the horticultural questions, so we'd best ask Lady Westford.'

'It's not a rose,' Kit answered.

He had no wish to draw this out any longer than necessary. Lady Westford and the Duke had very early on abandoned their respective teams to offer their support from the comfort of the card room, where Genny sat in readiness to supply the teams with their one hint.

'Oh, you know what it is!' Lady Sarah exclaimed, with an enthusiasm that would have done Lady Calista proud. 'Why did you not say?'

'Fair play. I thought you ought at least to work for it. And Miss Caversham has proved I was right to trust your abilities.'

They entered the garden and he led them to its centre, where a small pedestal that had once housed a sundial now supported a stone statue of the Buddha he had sent Emily years ago. The roses were in full bloom and the garden bathed in an intoxicating rainbow of scents. Once again he was struck by the almost reluctant realisation that Carrington House was a place where someone could, and should, be very happy.

The Buddha certainly looked content with his setting. The group fanned around it.

'He doesn't look very enlightened,' said Lord Ponsonby. 'Saints usually look rather more serious. This fellow looks like he's contemplating a good joke. Either that or picking a thorn out of his finger.'

'This *fellow* is called Buddha. He lived well over two thousand years ago and was the founder of the religion of Buddhism. He is often called the Enlightened One or the Awakened One.'

'Well, I don't see how we were to know that. And he certainly looks more asleep than awake.'

'Papa!' Miss Caversham reproved as he and Lord Ponsonby laughed at the jest.

Lady Sarah went over to inspect the statue. 'Whatever the case, here is our last clue.'

The group clustered round her and Kit gave a silent sigh of relief.

'Almost over,' Mary whispered to him—just as there was a distinctive cry from the direction of the house.

They all turned as Lady Calista's high tones carried joyfully through the air. 'We won! We won! Oh, I do wish you had let me place a wager, Grandpapa.'

'Oh, dear,' said Lady Sarah with an uncharacteristic slipping of her mask as she balled up the strip of paper with the clue and tossed it back onto the pedestal. 'She is going to be more insufferable than ever now.'

'Julian was marvellous,' Lady Calista said as they all gathered in the conservatory, having completely discarded formalities in the excitement of the chase. 'We had already used our hint, and were convinced we were all done for, when suddenly he practically rode to the rescue on a great white steed when he remembered that marvellous portrait of the Fifth Earl in the hallway. Why, I must have seen it a dozen times since we arrived, but I never noticed there was the dog at his feet. And I certainly had never looked at the name on its collar.'

She cast Julian an adoring look as she took another grape from the fruit bowl.

'What can I say?' Julian smiled as he sat on the sofa next to Genny. 'I love animals. Of all kinds.'

Lady Sophronia actually tittered, but Lady Sarah's fine lips curled a little in distaste.

'I don't think "love" is quite the correct verb to employ in your case, Mr Carrington.'

Surprised silence followed this uncharacteristically blunt blow from Lady Sarah, and then her father rushed into speech.

'Hard to believe the week is almost over. You shall be leaving soon for your sister's wedding, won't you, Lord Westford?'

'Yes. In three days.'

'And then? Back here or to London?'

'To Portsmouth,' Kit replied. 'My ship is there.'

Again conversation floundered, and then Miss Caversham's sweet and seldom heard voice piped up.

'You are leaving England again?'

Kit knew the answer to that, but for a moment he couldn't seem to find it. He latched on to the one certainty—the *Hesperus* was waiting for him. The life he knew and trusted.

'Yes. Of course. We are sailing for France and then Italy.'

'I hope you will bring back some more of that marvellous Montepulciano,' Julian said with a mocking smile as he surveyed the guests' responses to this news.

They were varied, and swiftly hidden behind polite masks. But Kit could see disappointment, annoyance, distaste, and—touchingly—on Miss Caversham's face, regret.

Genny's face showed no expression at all. She was still looking as stiff as she had at breakfast.

Julian leaned towards her to ask her something, but she shook her head without answering. Her hands, Kit noted, were still folded in her lap, but they didn't look in the least restful. They were held tightly, her knuckles slightly pale. It struck him that she too was pale and had been since breakfast.

Not that it was any of his concern. His concern was to reach the quiet of his rooms and refresh his store of patience and good manners so he could survive three more days of this…

Howich entered, his gaze seeking Genny, and she stood stiffly and after a moment's hesitation went towards the butler.

With a word of excuse Kit rose to join them.

'Is something wrong?' he asked, and Howich gave a slight bow.

He seemed to expect Genny to answer, but when she remained silent he shook his head. 'No, my lord. I was merely enquiring whether we should set back dinner half an hour to give the guests time to rest, seeing as the treasure hunt took longer than expected. If so we had best decide now, so that Cook may adjust her timetable.'

Still Genny said nothing so Kit spoke.

'If Cook can manage it, then I think that is wise, Howich.'

Howich bowed and left, and as Genny turned back towards the others Kit touched her arm, stopping her, lowering his voice.

'If this silence is some form of punishment for what you imagine to be a slight against you, I should tell you I'm damned if I'm apologising, Genny. You were utterly at fault and you know it.'

'I have the headache,' she said, and he laughed, all the resentment he'd managed to tuck away during the day's activities filling his vessel to the brim.

'Surely you can do better than that threadbare excuse, sweetheart?'

'Don't call me that!' Her voice sounded as raw as his nerves.

'No, you're not very sweet, are you? You might smell like orange blossom but you have the bite and sting of a lemon. Are you certain it is a headache, or are you merely finding it hard to stomach Lady Calista winding her ivy around Julian?'

She finally looked at him. Her face was pale, but there were harsh spots of colour on her cheeks and the fury and loathing in her eyes were utterly unveiled.

'You say one more word to me today, Lord Westford, and I will...' She stopped, shoving a hand hard against her temple. 'Stay *away* from me.'

'With the utmost pleasure, Generalissima.'

Chapter Seventeen

'Genny? It's time to dress for dinner…'

Serena's voice, though low, shoved the hot steel nail in Genny's temple an inch deeper. She gave a faint protesting moan, but even that made it worse.

A soft hand rested for a moment on hers where it was fisted on the blanket, and then an even softer voice spoke somewhere above her.

'Rest.'

The curtains were blessedly pulled shut and the door closed. Genny gave a little mewl of relief and let go of consciousness.

'Is Miss Maitland not joining us this evening?' Lady Sarah enquired as she inspected the piano, running her fingers along the ivory keys.

'My sister has the headache,' Serena replied, not looking up from the music sheets she was inspecting with Miss Caversham. 'I cannot seem to find the Northern Garlands ballads you asked for, Grandmama.'

'What's that? A headache? Genevieve? Nonsense,' declared Lady Westford, putting down her cards and waving her cane in Howich's direction. 'Howich, go and see what is keeping the girl.'

'Let the poor gel rest, Amelia,' the Duke of Burford said soothingly, over his cards. 'It's no wonder she's feeling out of sorts; she's been run ragged these past weeks. Dashed competent girl.'

'Genevieve hasn't had a headache in her life,' protested Lady Westford. 'And she will know where the ballads are. Why can no one remember where everything is? Send one of the maids for her, Howich.'

'There will be no need for that, Howich,' Kit intervened. 'I am certain whatever music Serena has for the pianoforte will do.'

'I think perhaps the ballad sheets are in the cupboard in the blue drawing room. I shall go and see,' Serena said swiftly, and both she and Howich beat a hasty retreat.

Lady Westford's cheekbones were mottled with colour as she faced her grandson. He smiled slightly, wondering if she would manage to rein in her temper. Her cane hovered ominously a few inches off the floor. The conversations around them dipped in tone. Everyone was waiting.

He was spoiling for a fight after his clash with Genny, and it was high time his grandmother had her wings clipped. He was damned if he would have her ordering everyone about as if they were her serfs.

'If you wish, Lady Westford, I know several of the ballads by heart,' Lady Sarah interjected, her voice a soothing breeze in the heated atmosphere. 'I could play them while we wait for Mrs Carrington to find the music. There is no need to bother Miss Maitland.'

For a second longer Lady Westford's temper teetered. Then the Duke of Burford gave a slight, almost imperceptible *tsk*, and she lowered her cane, turning to Lady Sarah and Lord Ponsonby with a smile.

'What a dear, accomplished girl you are. You are to be commended in your daughter, Lord Ponsonby. Yes, do come and play something for me, my child. And perhaps dear Calista and Sophronia could sing for us. Such lovely clear voices.'

The Duke beamed at her and Kit leaned back, half-amused, half-wishing she'd picked up the gauntlet.

He watched Lady Sarah take a seat at the pianoforte. She and the vivacious Lady Calista and Lady Sophronia presented a lovely tableau: three English beauties polished to a high sheen of perfection.

All he had to do for Society to bestow upon him its seal of approval was choose one of them and lay her pedigree like a silken cloak over his tainted roots. *Unite with us and all will be, if not forgotten, then at least only whispered behind fans when we are bored or feeling more spiteful than usual.*

Lady Sarah laid her hands on the keys and glanced up, meeting his gaze, her lips softening in the slightest of smiles. If he'd been at all impressionable he'd have melted into a puddle by now.

He switched his gaze to Lady Sophronia as she began singing, her clear high voice bringing the ballad about a shepherdess and her lost flock to life. She too met his gaze but, not possessing Lady Sarah's poise, faltered for a moment, her cheeks warming.

He sank his chin into his cravat and turned his gaze to the second singer. Lady Calista twinkled with all the bravado of an eighteen-year-old accomplished flirt. He rather thought that by twenty she would either be ruined or, more likely, married to a pleasant, tame man who would let her run rings round him. She would probably live a long and happy life.

The thought cheered him a little, but then he caught sight of his grandmother's complacent smile, her hands rocking her cane.

'Three on a silver tray...take your pick,' Julian whispered as he settled on a chair beside him. 'At least they're musical. That's an advantage.'

Kit shifted in his seat, leaning his heel heavily on Julian's toes. His cousin grunted, but sank into silence.

At the end of the ballad Serena entered with a stack of music sheets and Julian went forward to help her. He was promptly dragooned by Lady Calista into turning the pages for them.

The three pretty blonde heads followed Julian like sunflowers turning to the sun. Kit watched his cousin smile and charm them, and might himself have been convinced that Julian was truly taken with their charms—except that he'd seen his cousin smile very differently at a far less beautiful woman. There was charm aplenty in his current smile, but not even a hint of the affection evident in his eyes when he spoke with or about Genny.

Affection, ease…intimacy. So much so that Julian was even willing to forgive her for trying to marry him off to another woman. Perhaps that was even what he wanted? A wealthy bride would give Julian a degree of freedom…

Kit shifted in his seat. It was damned uncomfortable. Why did they have to produce seats that made sitting for more than half an hour a penance? He missed his armchair on the *Hesperus*.

He missed the *Hesperus*.

No, he missed his uncomplicated life before he'd ventured onto the Carrington web.

He damned his cousin again for drawing him into this world. It was as brutal and competitive as navigating the Barbary Coast, and it had brought him nothing but headaches.

Not only him, apparently.

Did Genny truly have a headache? Or was she tired of facing him, knowing she'd been caught? She hated being in the wrong—he was certain of that. It didn't suit her vision of herself. She was probably up there, reassessing her campaign. Perhaps even planning how to turn this defeat to her advantage.

Probably.

The girl was relentless. If she'd been one of his men he'd probably be commending her determination and enterprise, not hating her for it. And she owed him no allegiance, so it wasn't even worthy of being called a betrayal.

But it felt like it.

It felt...vicious.

Chapter Eighteen

When Genny woke again she had no idea whether she'd been asleep for a day or a week. She shoved aside the blanket, but someone pulled it back up. Serena.

Her sister was dressed in her travelling pelisse, and Genny remembered the excursion planned to the Osmington White Horse. The thought of tramping through the countryside with the gaggle of young ladies while they made eyes at Kit made Genny groan, but she tried to put back the cover once more—only to have Serena stop her.

'You are not rising from this bed until you are well, Genny.'

'But the guests...'

'Will do perfectly well without you. Mary and I shall see to them. You have just come through a megrim, love. You are in no state to do anything but rest today.'

Genny slowly shifted onto her back and tested her forehead, then placed a hand over her right eye where the pain had been unbearable yesterday. A dull, faraway thud answered her with a Parthian shot—*I might be leaving but I'll be back when you need me least.*

She sighed. 'I thought I'd left these behind with childhood.'

'So did I,' Serena answered, sitting carefully on the bedside. 'Why did you not say anything? I wondered what was wrong yesterday, but a megrim didn't occur to me, not after so many years. What happened?'

I made a dreadful mistake and I'm tired. And scared. And hurting dreadfully.

She turned onto her side, her back to Serena. 'A megrim happened.'

'Well, you should have gone to rest the moment you felt the first sign, love. You have been doing far too much recently.' Serena sighed. 'I am glad to be back in Dorset, but I wish you hadn't begun this.'

Genny squeezed her eyes shut. *I am doing this for you.*

'I know you are doing this for me, and for Mary, but it has to stop, Genny,' Serena said softly.

Genny turned over cautiously. She hadn't spoken aloud, had she?

Serena smiled at her. 'You are so like Grandfather sometimes, but you don't always know best. I would rather live under Lady Westford's thumb than marry again. Thankfully, there is another option. Lord Westford has offered to let us return to the Dower House and I think it best we accept. I will ask Mary if she wishes to join us.'

Genny pressed her hands to her eyes—not because her head hurt but because this weakness was making her weepy. 'Is that enough, Reena?'

'It is for me, Genny. I still have hopes that you at least shall marry one day and provide me with nieces and nephews to spoil. If you would only lower your guard long enough to allow a man over it.'

Genny shook her head. The burning in her eyes was worse and her head was thumping again.

The bed creaked as Serena stood. 'Stay in bed today, love. We'll speak later.'

* * *

Lady Westford looked up from the card table with a smile. It disappeared promptly when she saw Kit standing in the doorway.

'I thought everyone had gone to Osmington,' she said a trifle sullenly.

'Almost everyone has,' he replied, closing the door behind him. 'The steward called me back just as we were leaving, with the excuse of urgent estate matters.'

Across the room the garden door was open, and he could see the absurdly named Milly—Militiades—spread like a furry rug on the lawn, no doubt missing his morning walk with Genny.

He'd been more than a little surprised when Genny had missed breakfast as well. It wasn't like her to hide. Still, she could not be very ill if both Mary and Serena had departed on the excursion to the Osmington White Horse and the Roman wells. It was probably merely that Genny wished to avoid him as much as possible. Had she known he planned to remain at the Hall, no doubt she would have gone with the others.

'You really must have a mind to your manners, Kit,' his grandmother said behind him. 'One would think you could manage a week without shirking your duties.'

He wrapped his hands around the back of one of the spindly gilded chairs she favoured. It wasn't much of an anchor, but it was better than nothing.

'You should be grateful, Grandmother. The reason I am shirking my duties is so that we can hold this discussion while everyone is out. I would prefer we are not overheard.'

Her back straightened. 'I don't see what we have to discuss. You made your disapproval clear when you stormed into my rooms the other day.'

'So I did. But today I would like us to establish some rules, Grandmother.'

The cane wobbled a little. Carmine peeped, but with a wave of Lady Westford's hand he fell silent.

'Rules, Christopher?'

'Rules. If you wish to remain at Carrington House in London, you are free to do so—on the understanding that you never again interfere in my private life.'

'Interfere!'

'Do you have another word for conspiring to manoeuvre me into marriage with one of your carefully chosen titbits?'

'I do indeed. *Duty.* My duty to the Carrington name. It should be yours too but as you are too lax in your morals to see that as clearly as I, I decided to act.'

'Putting my morals aside for the moment, I understood it was Miss Maitland's suggestion to auction us off.'

'Her suggestion was sparked by my concerns, and quite frankly I didn't put much stock in it. But if there was even but the smallest chance of success, I thought it worth pursuing. In any case it has kept her occupied and hopeful that she might yet secure Mary's and Serena's futures. Her efforts have been commendable—her results less so.'

Several epithets were burning on the tip of Kit's tongue, but he held them back. 'You don't appear very bothered by her failure,' he said.

'I did not say that, but since I hold the trump card I am resigned to playing it.'

'What trump card?' he asked with deep foreboding.

'My pact with Genny is that should she find a bride for one of you, I will secure Serena's and Mary's financial freedom. If she fails, she has offered to marry Julian herself.'

'She has *offered.*' He couldn't manage more than that.

His grandmother smiled. 'She did. In fact, after watching your rather dismal performance yesterday I spoke with Julian, and since he seems no more inclined than you to progress from his empty flirtations with the young women here to a more settled state, I told him I would settle a lump sum of ten thousand pounds on him if he weds Genny.'

She paused, searching Kit's face, but when he said nothing she continued.

'Since her lineage is not up to Carrington standards I opposed the idea when there was talk of them marrying some years ago, but I've come to believe someone like her is precisely what Julian needs. They certainly spend enough time in each other's pockets. They think no one notices them scurrying off together whenever he comes to the Hall, and that I don't know she went up to see him in London when she said she went to visit an old friend of the General last month. Well, I have noticed, and I don't like it. There will be a scandal and then where will we be? So, if all that comes from this rigmarole is that those two finally cease shilly-shallying and wed, then at least I shall know one of my grandsons has married a woman capable of securing the Carrington legacy.'

The chair creaked ominously beneath his hands. He'd never felt such an urge to throttle someone...not even a Carrington.

'You manipulative, conniving bi—'

'May I join you?'

The deep voice cut through Kit's and he turned. The Duke of Burford stood in the doorway, an uncharacteristic frown on his florid face.

Kit took a deep breath, dragging his temper down. 'If you don't mind, Your Grace, this is a private matter between Lady Westford and myself.'

'I gather as much, young man. And I shall not apologise for eavesdropping as I think it is best I join this discussion.'

'There is no need, Robert,' Lady Westford intervened, her voice softer than it had been up to that point. 'I do not need your protection. We can have our hand of whist later.'

'I think there *is* a need, Amelia. And I am not here to protect you; I happen to agree with Lord Westford.'

'Robert!'

'If what I have heard is true, you are sorely at fault, Amelia. I was under the impression we had been invited here in good faith—not as the result of some convoluted plot. A plot which would never have been necessary had Alfred made fair provision for the members of this family. I told him often enough that when you hold the reins too tight, the weak might buckle but the strong will bolt.'

He turned to Kit.

'If I have one complaint to place at your door, young man, it is that it was your duty to return and set matters right directly when you inherited the title and estate. You may not wish to shoulder the burden. You may—and rightly—resent your family's treatment of your mother and yourself. But to indulge in pique by continuing on your merry way as the others struggle to find their way out of the swamp left by your grandfather's mismanagement of his family's affairs should be beneath the man I have come to know these past weeks.'

Kit raised a brow at this softly spoken but sharply delivered reprimand. He waited, half-annoyed, half-amused, for his grandmother to let slip her dogs—or canaries—of war, but she merely sat there, twin spots of colour on her cheeks.

He gave a slight bow to the Duke. 'You are quite right, Your Grace. I have been remiss in my duties. However, since my return I have tried to make some amends. I have already settled Charlie's debts and arranged annuities for Serena and Mary. I will do the same for Julian…with no strings attached so he shall have no need to succumb to extortion. As for you, Grandmother, you may have the London house for your lifetime. I don't want it. I'm sure there is some Carrington relation who will be more than happy to stay with you if Mary…understandably…chooses not to.'

The Duke cleared his throat. 'As to that, I think Amelia will be better off with me and the grandchildren at Burford Manor rather than racketing about in that big house with no one but some poor relation to order about. Don't you think so, Amelia?'

It took Kit a moment to register the meaning of the blandly spoken words.

It took his grandmother even longer.

Then her eyes went wide as saucers, her cheeks pale, only a sharp streak of colour standing out across each cheekbone. 'Burford Manor?' she whispered.

'Indeed. I would not wish to show you or Alfred any disrespect, but he has been gone for over a year and I think it is high time I spoke. You and I have not many more years on this earth, Amelia. I think you enjoy my company as much as I enjoy yours—foul temper and managing ways notwithstanding,' he added with a smile. 'It would make me very happy if you would accept my hand in marriage. That would remove at least one of your concerns, wouldn't it, Westford?'

'It certainly would…if Lady Westford is agreeable.'

'Yes, that is the crux of the matter. And *are* you agreeable, Amelia?'

Kit didn't wait to hear the outcome of the Duke's proposal, not even for the pleasure of watching his grandmother rendered speechless. He shut the door and stood for a moment in the hall, until Julian's voice dragged him out of his stupor.

'You look as if you have just witnessed a murder, cousin.'

'No—a proposal.'

Julian's face was suddenly wiped clean of expression. 'Congratulations. Who is the unlucky lady?'

'Our grandmother, you idiot. We cannot speak here.

Come into the library. I need a brandy. This family is driving me to drink.'

'What do you mean, our grandmother?' Julian demanded as he closed the door behind them.

'Burford has proposed to her.'

'Good God! Bless the fellow. Please tell me she accepted.'

'I rather think she will. What are you doing back so early?' Kit asked suspiciously.

'It doesn't feel early. They stopped for refreshments at Falworth and I realised that I preferred not to spend another two hours evading that little minx Calista. So I got on my horse…sorry, *your* horse…and rode across the fields back to Carrington. I haven't had such a good ride in years. Do try and flirt with her a little so she returns her allegiance to you, Cuz.'

'No, thank you. I'm quite happy having her enthusiasm directed elsewhere.'

'Yes, you have your own fish to fry, don't you?'

'What does that mean?' Kit paused in the act of pouring two glasses of brandy.

But Julian shrugged, looking a little sullen. 'Nothing.' He took one of the glasses and raised it. 'Here's to gullible dukes. Cheers.'

'I don't think he is in the least bit gullible. Amazingly, he appears to know precisely what deal he is brokering. To each their own.'

'Well, well… I wonder if Genny planned this too. It does solve quite a few of her problems in one fell swoop.'

'You seem to credit her with omnipotence,' Kit snapped.

'No, merely superior tactical skills.'

'Yes. That deal is off the table, by the way.'

'What deal?'

'Ten thousand pounds if you marry her.'

'It…it is?'

'It is. I'm making you another offer. If you accept it, when you leave Carrington Hall with the rest of the guests you don't come back.'

Julian set down his glass. There was danger on his face, but Kit didn't care. He was beyond caring about much at the moment. If they wanted him to play head of the household and set them all to rights, he damn well would.

'Twenty thousand pounds and you will never receive another penny from the estate. Unless, of course, fate favours you and Marcus and someone does away with me. Then you can touch up Marcus for more. You will also stop whatever game it is you are playing with Miss Maitland. While she lives under my roof she is under my protection. No more furtive meetings in town, in theatres—anywhere.'

Julian shoved his fisted hands deep in his pockets.

Kit wished, ardently, that his cousin would take a swing at him. Playing by the rules meant he could hardly attack the man while in his home, but he was so tempted to he could practically taste blood.

'So…' Julian drawled. 'Grandmother offered me ten thousand to wed Genny and you are offering me twenty thousand not to?'

'I am offering you twenty thousand to go away and stop moaning about being treated unfairly. Burford said Grandfather enjoyed keeping everyone on short strings and he was right. It cost my father his happiness, it drove Charlie into debt and an early grave, and it has turned you into a resentful malcontent. Take the damned Carrington money and do something with it.'

'So… I can have the money and Genny too?'

Kit's blow took both of them by surprise.

Julian stumbled back against the door and they stood for a moment, glaring at each other.

Then Julian wiped his mouth, smearing blood on chin. '*Damn*, I've been spoiling for this, Pretty Kitty.'

'So have I, you petulant brat. Let's see if you're more than talk.'

Julian snarled and launched himself at Kit. He had clearly spent a good many hours at Jackson's boxing salon. He had good science and was quick, blocking the worst of Kit's blows—at least in the beginning.

But Kit was stronger, all those years of sailing and swimming giving him an advantage, and it wasn't long before he got a blow over Julian's guard, sending Julian crashing into a delicate table that held a figurine of a mother and baby elephant connected trunk to tail.

The figurine flew up and Kit made a grab for it, but missed. It hit the floor, splitting in two, with the babe's grey trunk still wrapped about its mother's tail.

'Was that expensive?' Julian asked, his hands on his knees as he drew panting breaths.

'No, but it was one of the first gifts I ever sent Emily, damn you.'

'Sorry,' Julian said, abashed.

'What the devil do you care?' Kit snarled, wiping away a trickle of blood from his temple. 'Do you want the money or don't you?'

'Yes, damn you!' Julian snarled back, all contrition gone. 'And, for your information, I don't know what that old witch told you, but she doesn't know everything.'

'She said Genny has been to see you in your rooms in London. Do you truly wish to see her ruined?'

'Blast you—of course not. I told Genny that was a mistake. We usually… Look, this isn't what you think, but it's not my place to tell. Why don't you ask her? You seem to have everyone telling you their business anyway.'

They glared at each other until finally Julian shrugged and glanced down at his bruised knuckles.

'This wasn't as satisfying as I'd hoped.'

'No,' Kit agreed, the fight going out of him as well.

Everything seemed to have gone out of him. Like an empty ship's hold—dark, dank, empty.

'We're too old for this.'

'Speak for yourself, old man.' Julian's mouth quirked, then flattened again. 'It feels wrong, taking money from you.'

'Well, too bad. It should have been Charlie's in any case. If it makes you feel any better, I'll offer the same to Marcus. I don't need it.'

Julian grinned and winced, gingerly touching his split lip. 'I'd pay to see Marcus's face when you make that offer. In fact, I could probably raise a crowd to watch the fight. You have a mean left hook, man. The benefits of life on board a ship, I daresay. I ought to try it.'

'I would be only too happy to put you on a vessel to the Antipodes, cousin.'

'No, thank you. I'll make good use of the funds right here.' He hesitated. 'Genny told me years ago that Marcus and I were fools to blame you for Grandfather packing our parents off to India. I have to concede she was probably right. My mother made her own choice when she took advantage of your father's melancholy, and we shouldn't have blamed you for crying bloody murder when she slipped into his bedroom that night. But it was easier than admitting one's mother was an arrant flirt who enjoyed taunting my father with her conquests.'

Kit took a deep breath. 'Grandfather blamed me as well, so I don't see why you should have been any different. He told me outright that a true Carrington would have known better than to air family mistakes in public. Another lesson on how you Carringtons were superior to dregs such as my mother and myself.'

Julian winced. 'Charming fellow. Almost as bad as dear Grandmama. I pity poor Burford. Well, I'd better be off, before I start liking you. I'm definitely not ready to do that.' He paused by the door. 'And do remember that although the old she-devil sees much, she understands little. Try not to emulate her, old man.'

He gave a slight salute and left before Kit could give in to temptation and demand an explanation his cousin was highly unlikely to provide.

Chapter Nineteen

Kit could do with a less honest mirror in his dressing room. His hair was damp and spiky with perspiration, reddish rivulets from the cut on his temple streaked his cheek, and his poor cravat looked as if he'd tied it underwater.

He wondered what his men would have thought, had they witnessed his behaviour these past few weeks. He wished Benja or Rafe were here. Anyone who knew him as a sensible individual. Reliable, detached, unflappable…

He pulled off his shirt and sluiced his face and neck with water from the basin. He had just put on a new shirt when he heard a tapping coming from his study. He debated ignoring it, but then it came again, a little louder, and he strode through to open the door.

'What—?' His teeth snapped shut on the word. For a moment his mind went blank as he stared at Genny.

'Lord Westford? Howich said you might be in your study and I thought… I thought it would be best for us to speak…in private…before everyone returns.'

Her voice was hardly above a whisper and her warm-toned skin was sallow and leeched of colour, as if she'd been cupped by an over-enthusiastic surgeon. She looked nothing like Managing Miss Maitland.

An unfamiliar shiver of fear was followed swiftly by

remorse. He'd truly thought she was shamming, but she looked fragile, almost waxen. 'You *are* ill.'

She shook her head and a thick tress of hair slipped from the ribbon that held it back and fell over her cheek. She tucked it behind her ear and winced. His fingers twitched. Surely anyone with a headache would be more comfortable with their hair released from its bondage, spread out...

He quashed that thought. Whether she had a headache or not should make absolutely no difference to the magnitude of her betrayal.

As the silence stretched, her cheeks began to suffuse with colour, but it merely made her look wearier...and more miserable.

He stood in the doorway, damning both of them. If this was another ploy, it was working. The anger he'd been nursing skulked away in shame, ignoring his attempt to grab it by the scruff of the neck and shove it back to the front line.

'You don't look recovered yet, Miss Maitland. You should be resting. In your room,' he added pointedly.

'It was only a megrim. I am better now.'

'Well, I'm glad you are better, but I'm in no mood for any more...games.'

She raised her hands, rushing into speech. 'I won't stay. I thought you had gone with the others to the wells, but then Susan mentioned you were here and I thought... I thought it best not to wait...to make my apology. I should have done so right away, but... You were right. It was foolish...ch-childish.'

She stumbled over the word, and when she shoved the thick tress of hair behind her ear again he noted her hand was trembling.

He struggled for a moment with common sense and then, with a quick glance up the corridor, he stepped back. The worst that could happen was that he would solve most of Genny's problems in one fell swoop. And cause quite a few others.

'We cannot talk like this. Come inside.'

'I don't… I think…'

'Don't think. Or, if you must, don't do it in the corridor. That is inviting trouble.'

Her flush deepened but she stepped inside, flattening herself against the wall as he closed the door. He moved away to the other side of the room, leaning back against the writing desk and crossing his arms. She took a deep breath and plunged into speech, her eyes on the carpet as if her tale were woven into the blue and brown geometric design.

'You are right. About me. I struck a bargain with your grandmother before you even came to Carrington House. It wasn't… I am not making excuses… Well, yes, I am, but…'

She floundered and glanced at him, but when he kept silent she continued.

'Since your grandfather died Lady Westford has become obsessed with an heir for the Carrington line. But instead of taking you men to task she has been flaying my sister and Mary, making them feel like…like failures as women, with no regard to their own pain—especially Serena's.'

She stopped for a moment, rubbing her cheeks as if she'd only just come in from the cold, but she did not look up.

'My sister lost three children to stillbirth. It shattered her and it shattered Charlie and I think it drove him even more deeply into those foolish ventures. Your grandmother never says so outright, but it is clear she holds Serena accountable for Charlie's debts and his death. The worst is that poor Serena has come to believe it herself, and it is…it is destroying her. I couldn't bear it any longer, so I promised Lady Westford I would do everything I could to ensure one of her grandsons married in exchange for Serena's and Mary's freedom. If either of you became betrothed, she would pay Charlie's debts and settle funds on Mary and Serena.'

There was nothing he did not know here. It should not make any difference. But the impotent, wounded anger he'd felt was melting faster than ice in an Egyptian summer. He wanted to keep hold of it, but it was useless in the face of the raw pain in her husky voice. The best he could do was remain silent.

Her eyes flickered up to his and fell again. There was no guile there, no calculation, only a brief, rather desperate appeal for clemency. She looked far younger than her years now—far more like the little Genny Maitland of Spain, held together by nine measures of determination and one measure of cunning.

'I also told her that if I failed I would marry Julian,' she burst out, as if determined to make a clean breast of all her sins.

His anger fired again, in a visceral resistance as old as childhood. He managed to ride that out in silence too— which was just as well, for she continued.

'I didn't mean it, of course.'

'Why suggest it if you didn't mean it?'

'I wanted her to feel there was always something to fall back on.'

'Would he have agreed?'

'Not unless there was some serious monetary—' She broke off at his expression. 'It isn't that he is mercenary… merely…' She stalled again.

'Merely that he needs the funds,' he completed dryly.

She sighed. 'He has his reasons. And I had mine. Which brings me to my other admission.'

God, he didn't know if he could take any more admissions.

'This.' She held out a copy of her grandfather's book. 'It isn't truly my grandfather's, though he had a hand in it. I had trouble sleeping for years after my parents died, so every night, after Serena fell asleep, my grandfather would tell me about battles.'

'Battles as bedtime stories?'

'He didn't know any other tales. We would read from his books together and wonder what went through the mind of a Trojan soldier who woke from his sleep to shouts that the Greeks had penetrated the impenetrable city. How he must have felt when only the evening before he'd celebrated victory after years and years of suffering under siege.'

She paused, her eyes searching his.

'When Grandfather died, and I came to live with Serena, I began writing the stories down. One day Julian found one and read it. After I had torn strips off him for reading other people's private writing, he convinced me to send it to an acquaintance of his at the *London Magazine*. They asked for more. So Julian oversaw the correspondence and we split the proceeds. At some point Julian suggested compiling them into a book, and this is the first of them. There are two others, and I am working on a fourth at the moment—which is why I took those books from the library. No one else knows of it—not even Serena and Mary—so I would appreciate you not...'

She shrugged and held out the book. He had to force himself to move and take it. Strange that this revelation affected him more than her deal with the devil.

The book felt heavier than when he'd taken it from her table yesterday. He brushed his hand over the cover. The binding was marbled, the words *A Soldier's Tales* and *Maitland* engraved on the spine. He opened it and looked again at the frontispiece.

*A Soldier's Tales or
A Collection of Tales of Historic Battles
as Told by a Common Soldier
By Gen. Maitland*

He'd naturally presumed it was *General* Maitland. Here too Genevieve Maitland had hidden herself in plain sight.

Then his eyes caught the publisher's name at the bottom of the page—and the year. As far as coincidences went, this was…strange.

Genny noted the placing of his finger and took it as a question.

'Julian and I didn't know any publishers, but Mary had once mentioned your grandfather's name, and that he had a bookbinding shop in Cheapside. So when I was in London I asked a hackney driver to take me there. He was a lovely man, your grandfather. He arranged matters with a printer and oversaw those bindings personally. This is the very first copy he printed for me. I would like you to have it.'

Her voice was becoming choppy again.

His own insides were far choppier.

'Did he know you were connected to the Carringtons?' His voice was harsher than he'd meant, and her now empty hands were clasped together so tightly her knuckles gleamed a pale yellow.

'I didn't tell him. I didn't want him to feel obligated in any way. But, you see, he recognised my name, or rather Grandpapa's name, from your letters. When he asked me if I was any relation I realised there was little point in subterfuge. He was so proud of you… I enjoyed my visits with him—he was like a version of my own grandfather, only with a sense of humour and…and easier in his skin.'

She smiled, her gaze now inward, and it took him a great effort not to move towards her. Then she focused, and the hesitation returned, and her hands resumed twisting into each other.

'I had hoped to earn enough to settle Charlie's debts and set up house for Serena and Mary. But I'm afraid I shall likely never earn enough merely with my books, and every year Serena remains... I am not making excuses... Well, I am. In any case, I owe you an apology. You were right about me. Sometimes I think I'm older than anyone here, and sometimes I feel like I'm still the same as when Grandfather came to fetch us when our parents died. I cannot seem to find the in between.'

Her voice hitched and caught and he set aside the book and took her tense hands in his. They were shockingly cold.

'You're frozen.'

'No, my hands are always cold after a megrim, and when I'm nervous.'

Her voice was as rough as gravel, but she didn't pull her hands away. He took her towards an armchair and went to find a blanket.

He'd never credited confessions could be seductive... One learned something new every day.

But she was unwell and vulnerable... Hell, *he* was vulnerable. He would not take advantage of either of them at the moment. All he would do was warm her, calm her, and send her on her way.

He repeated this to himself, just to be absolutely clear. *Warm, calm, send away...*

He brought the blanket and crossed the line a little by smoothing it over her primly pressed together knees, then he stepped back behind the line and went to sit in the armchair opposite.

'If you wish to make amends, you can sign the book you gifted me. Not Gen. Maitland. Your full name.'

She opened her mouth, did some more damage to his

resolve by licking her plump lower lip, and then gave a nervous smile.

'My full name? Genevieve Elisabeth Calpurnia Maitland?'

'Calpurnia? Good Lord. Genevieve Maitland will do. You shouldn't hide behind your grandfather's name.'

'I cannot write under my own.'

'Why not?'

'Why *not*? That should be obvious.'

'Not to me. These are your books, not his. You can dedicate them to him, but they are yours.'

'No one would read a book about battles written by a female.'

'It might be a trifle difficult at first, but you might actually gain some readers due to the novelty—in particular female readers. I read the first two essays while I was waiting for you to exhaust your Mrs Pritchard excuse. They are far more than dry accounts of battles; they are deeply wrought human tales.'

'I don't *want* anyone knowing I write books. Other than your grandfather, and Julian who sees to all the interactions with the publishers, no one knows.'

Her mouth had flattened completely. Stubborn Genny was back. Genny the General might pen part of these stories, but the rest was by the young girl who'd sat up into the night spinning tales with her only anchor of safety.

He set aside the issue for the moment. It did not matter now. The only problem was he wasn't quite certain what did. Not any more.

Two weeks ago he'd known full well what mattered. His list of responsibilities had been quite clear—his sister and her mother, his friends, his men, his ship. The Carrington title and responsibilities had been nothing but irksome duties, imposed upon him by a family he despised and which despised him, to be evaded for as long as possible. Perhaps he had even believed what his so-called family had always seemed to convey—that in time either he or they would conveniently fade away.

Nothing had truly changed since his return. He might play at being Lord Westford, but he wasn't. A proper Lord Westford would wed Lady Sarah Ponsonby and do his best to obliterate the tarnished stain of his birth and occupation.

His guests might enjoy his wine and admire his art collection, but they couldn't completely hide their distaste. He was a novelty, and he was tolerated, but not accepted. Nor did he wish to be. He would never sit comfortably in Lord Westford's life. This…this performance was a temporary illusion—a what-might-have-been-but-will-not-be. Because at heart he didn't wish it to be. Soon he and Mary would attend Emily's wedding and then he would join the *Hesperus* and be on his way again.

That plan had not changed simply because he'd found himself temporarily entangled in Genny Maitland's web. Neither her plots nor this confusing, unfamiliar, sometimes painfully aggravating pull she exercised on him should make any permanent change to the trajectory of his life. It would not be wise for either of them.

Genny gave a sigh, her knees sinking a little from their rigidity. But her hands were still tangled in the blanket.

'Are your hands warmer?' he asked, resisting the urge to test for himself.

She touched them to her cheeks and his own tingled.

'Yes. Thank you. I was so nervous.'

'I'm not an ogre.'

'You were furious. Rightly so.'

'Upset,' he corrected. He didn't add hurt.

'Upset and furious,' she corrected.

'Do you wish for me to apologise?'

'No, of *course* not. I was merely explaining why I was… why I *am* nervous.'

'Still?'

'Are you still…upset?'

'I'm absorbing everything you have told me. I'm not angry.'

Bruised, battered, confused…but not angry. Not with her, anyway.

She smiled. 'I promise no more plotting. It isn't working, anyway. What you said earlier, about Serena… You are right. She isn't ready. I think… I think I've known all along that she is still in love with Charlie, but I hoped perhaps… And Mary… I don't think there is anyone here she fancies, either. Perhaps she too is still…' She stopped and sighed again.

'Still in love with my father?' he continued. 'I hope not. I think Serena's affection for Charlie was far truer and more grounded than what Mary thinks she felt for my father. Unlike Serena she was very young and untried when she married him—and unlike Serena she never had the experience of being loved. I'm hoping that when she finds someone who feels love for her she will see the difference and be drawn to it. This house party might yet do her some good. With Emily away she cannot cluck about her like a mother hen, so she is being forced to enjoy herself all on her own. If that is all that comes of this week, then it is well worth it.'

Her smile grew. 'Thank you for rescuing that ember from the ashes of my ambitions.'

'You're welcome, Genevieve Maitland. Thank *you* for fighting for her. As for the rest… Well, I should perhaps have taken everyone into my confidence earlier about my actions, but quite frankly I planned to leave it until after I departed, so there would not be unnecessary discussion around it. I've already settled Charlie's debts, as well as set up funds for Serena and Mary. If you three decide to continue to live together at the Dower House, that will be your choice—*your* choice.'

Her smile fell away, her hands twisting back into the fabric of the blanket. 'I didn't tell you this to force you... This isn't...'

He pulled his chair closer and closed his hand over hers. Her hands were warmer, but only just.

'This has nothing to do with you, Genny. I realise it will take you a while to cut yourself loose from the moorings of responsibility, but you didn't create my duties and you are certainly not forcing me to honour them. The only thing you did was draw my attention to them. If in a rather convoluted and uncomfortable manner.'

She was still looking a little stunned. 'What of your grandmother?'

'Are you guilty at how happy you feel to be shot of her?'

'A little.'

'Well, don't be. She is about to become a duchess. Burford proposed.'

Her mouth spread slowly into her lovely smile. 'Oh! I am so *happy*. He is so very right for her.'

'You don't seem very surprised.'

'I am not surprised that he cares for her. I wasn't certain she cared for him—though I was hopeful, since he is the only person she seems to wish to please.'

'I saw as much today. I feel a blind fool not to have realised that before.'

'You have been...distracted.'

'True...' He took a deep breath and placed his last card on the table. 'I am giving a substantial amount to Julian as well. Grandfather ought to have done that long ago.'

Her smile faded and her hands dug deeper into the blanket. 'I hope he took it. I'm afraid it will make him resent you even more, though.'

'He took it. As for resentment—that is his problem, not mine.'

He only hoped Julian didn't tell her either of their grand-mother's offer or his own stipulations.

She nodded, her teeth sinking into her lower lip. It set his own lips tingling and he wished he had something to sink his fingers into as well...preferably warm and soft.

Without the defensive barrier of anger, lust was seeping through the cracks. Not that she would notice. She was still looking dazed, and there was certainly nothing on her face to indicate that his proximity was affecting her as hers was affecting him.

Perhaps, as he'd suspected, whatever impulses he sparked in her were more the product of circumstance and curiosity than anything deep and lasting. It was probably eminently better that way. In a couple days he would leave for Hampshire and then join the *Hesperus* and be on his way to France within a week. All this would be behind him.

'That's the lot of them, isn't it?' he prodded, trying for lightness. 'Unless there are some bequests for the servants you wish me to make? No? The dogs, perhaps? Carmine the canary?'

She smiled and shook her head, her eyes warming from pale grey to liquid mercury, driving up his temperature with it. He gave in to temptation and took her hands in his, untangling them from the blanket and rubbing them in a pretence of warming them as he spoke.

'So now you'll have to find some other strays to succour—or, better yet, don't. Think of all the energy you could expend on your writing if you had nothing to think about but Thermopylae. Which side are you writing, by the way? Persians or Spartans?'

'Both...' she said dreamily.

She looked as if the concept of being unmoored from

the anchors which had held her in his family's port for so long was both tantalising and terrifying. His heart gave another of the annoying squeezes it had become prone to recently.

He kept his mind firmly on other battles. 'I have never read any records from Xerxes' side of the battle. Are there any?'

'I only know of Herodotus's account.' Her gaze focused back and she was Genny the General, surveying her troops with a critical eye. 'It may be the fashion to revile the veracity of his reports, and compare him unfavourably with Thucydides, but I think he is sorely maligned. He may be more colourful than Thucydides, and less objective, but he is no less valuable as a recorder of history.'

'I never said he wasn't,' Kit said meekly, still gently rubbing her hands between his, despite her increasing agitation as she spoke. 'I happen to enjoy reading them both. Two of the books you purloined from the library are mine, you know. I'd only just put them there the day we arrived, which was why I was surprised to see them gone. The Greek copy of Herodotus was given to me by a woman named Laskarina Bouboulina—one of the leaders of the Greek war of independence. Now, there's a tale for you to write about—although most people would find it too fantastic to be true. She's an Albanian widow with seven grandchildren and eight ships to her name.'

Genny's eyes lit like a kitten with a stretch of yarn dangled above it. 'You were there?'

'I didn't take part in it, if that is what you are asking. Unlike Laskarina, many of the *klefth*—the warlords—are little more than pirates themselves, and I don't deal with their kind, however much Lady Calista might be disappointed to hear that. Not that they wanted me there. They were afraid I might be part of the English Navy's attempt to replace the Turks. But I did bring arms and provisions to her on Spetses, and I was also there when she took Monemvasia.'

'Oh, how I wish I could speak with someone like her myself.'

Her hands had warmed and softened in his as he spoke, her eyes turning dreamy again. If he could have produced Laskarina at that very moment, he would have. But it was a very bad sign if he was contemplating outrageously unrealistic chivalric gestures...

'I could write her story,' she murmured, the dreaminess gathering into purpose. 'What it must be like for a woman to take those risks—her family, her possessions, everything at stake. It would be different than for a man. There is no distance...'

He didn't answer, merely watched the thoughts and ideas chase across her face. Was this how she wrote her tales? Boarded her mind's ship and sailed into those other worlds?

There had been that same intimacy and presence in the essays he'd read. She might as well have been standing by Tiberius Longus's side as he watched Hannibal's monstrous-seeming elephants charge the plain along the Trebbia River and destroy three-quarters of the Roman army. It was a sign of his addled mind that he was beginning to believe that Genevieve Maitland would have found some clever way of routing Hannibal's enormous army without harming a single elephant in the process.

She smiled at him, her eyes focusing. That now familiar, near-unbearable surge of energy gripped him, demanding action, outlet—something.

He sat this out as well.

He was glad to have cleared the air between them, but it had not resolved the real problem—Genny Maitland was disastrous for his equilibrium.

This was new territory for him. It wasn't the first time

he'd been attracted to the wrong woman, but he'd always been able to solve those situations quite readily, merely either by distance or by finding more convivial company to soothe his libido and his pride.

Those reliable solutions no longer felt practicable.

There was one potentially practicable solution, of course—he could offer marriage.

His hands tightened on hers, his hunger threatening to spill over.

'Never go to the market hungry,' his mother had used to tell him when they'd dock at a new port and he'd want to run ahead and see what treasures awaited them. *'Shopping with your stomach is the best path to indigestion.'*

A breeze twitched the curtains and with it entered the distinct sound of carriages coming up the drive. Genny glanced down at her hands in his and with a slight shiver withdrew them, lighting each nerve-end in him.

'They have returned,' she said, her voice muted. 'Mrs Pritchard has arranged for an early dinner as they will be tired. I'd best go.'

'Of course.' He rose and went to the window. 'You needn't come down to dinner if you are still unwell, Genny.'

'I'm not...' She stood hurriedly, the armchair grunting a little as it was shoved back. 'Of course. Goodbye. Thank you.'

'I didn't mean you *shouldn't* come down...'

But she was already out through the door.

Blast the girl—he couldn't do a damn thing right around her.

Chapter Twenty

Genny woke in the dark, but immediately knew that it was almost dawn. The birdsong had a clear, faraway sound, carving the air into crystal notes. She lay on her side, listening to their avian conversation for a long while, postponing the moment when she must think.

At least her head was clear of the last remnants of pain. She hoped another dozen years passed before another such assault.

A dozen years...

She lay on her back, staring at the blank ceiling. She'd always been careful not to think of the future. She had her writing, her sister, her friends, a home...of sorts. It had always felt enough.

Now it felt like a chasm. No...a desert. A great, empty, parched expanse. Nowhere to stop, no one to talk with, no one to hold her hand or kiss.

She covered her burning eyes with both hands.

She'd never felt this before, and she rather feared that it was a sign of something very bad. If this...all of this...was love, then it was horrid. And stupid. It made one maudlin and weak and unable to think clearly except of deserts and loneliness and other foolishness. No wonder some poets wrote such pap.

Yes, but most of those foolish poets weren't really writing about love, but about lust. They made a great show of feeling desperation and loneliness, but they hardly seemed to know the objects of their desires beyond having seen them in the village square or across a dance floor. One could probably exchange their particular maiden with another and they would hardly know the difference.

Perhaps that was all this was—her first encounter with lust. After all, he was so damnably beautiful, and he kept walking around in nothing but a shirt, and on the ship not even a shirt, and…

She turned over and shoved her face into her pillow.

It was definitely, unequivocally lust.

But what frightened her most was that it was more. Far too much more.

He mattered.

She shoved her face deeper into her pillow but it was no good. The list kept growing.

His opinion mattered, his wellbeing mattered, his presence calmed something deep inside her even as it sent other parts into chaotic confusion. He'd brought her to life when she hadn't even realised she'd been hibernating.

She fisted the soft linen of the pillowcase against her burning eyes. Her head didn't hurt but she felt exhausted and battered. She wished her grandfather was alive. She needed him to tell her that all would be well. That she was strong, that she needed no one but herself, that life would still be good and full when he left.

He's only passing through, Genny. You've never been a dreamer…don't start now.

She sat up abruptly and tossed away the blanket. She needed to clear her head, and there was one place on the Carrington estate that always did that for her.

Outside, Milly came dancing along the path at her whistle, delighted that his mistress had finally come to her senses and resumed her early morning walks.

The breeze was blowing in from the sea, bringing salt-water promises, the sun still too low to soothe away the chill of dawn. The ground too was wet with dew, weighing down her hems, but they would likely soon be even wetter with sea water so it hardly mattered.

She passed through the gate in the garden wall and the wind welcomed her with a burst of tangy exuberance. She loved the extreme transition between the lush abundance of the garden and the bare clifftops, kissed with hardy clumps of sea pink and nothing beyond but endless shades of blue and cloud.

At the bottom of the cliff path she removed her shoes while Milly sniffed at a clump of seaweed before prancing off in search of something more rewarding.

Genny sighed with pleasure as her bare feet settled on the cool, gritty sand. She hitched up her skirts, securing them into a knot about her waist with her hair ribbon, and set out across the sand.

The first contact with the lapping waves made her whole body curl in shocked resistance, but within moments she was striding happily along that magic line between water and land. By the time she reached the edge of the bay her internal cloud had lifted a little, and she gave a happy sigh and ran her hands through her hair. Whatever pain yet awaited her, it could not take away all pleasure. Even if all else in the world was ill, *this* was good.

She gazed out over the gentle waves and gave a slight gasp as she saw an arm rise from the water… Her heart slammed to a halt and then stuttered on.

Someone was swimming.

Someone was swimming very well.

He was far out, but his strokes were long and he was heading directly for the bay. She looked along the horizon for a boat but there was none. She could make out a head now—dark hair—and arms glistening in the rising sun.

Muscled arms, brown from the sun.

Kit.

She realised far too late that at any moment now he would reach the shallows. She'd already seen him shirtless, but he might be rather more than shirtless...

The thought of Lord Westford rising from the water as naked as Adam...

She had enough of a challenge with memories of him in a state of partial undress. She did not think surveying him naked was a prescription for battling lust.

There was no time to reach the cliff path, so she whistled to Milly and climbed over the boulders to where a natural ledge was shaded by the overhanging cliffs. Milly leapt from boulder to boulder, very pleased with this new game, and settled beside her, panting happily as he surveyed the shore below.

Genny did the same, realising that the shadowed ledge might protect her from being seen, but it did nothing to block her view of the man rising from the water like a god being formed from the foam of the sea.

Though a divine being would not be wearing breeches.

Well, she was surely a hypocrite. All this effort not to view him naked and all she could feel was disappointment that he wasn't. Not that the short, light-coloured breeches hid much. His skin had the warm, honeyed tone of a man accustomed to sun and sky. It was glistening with the water that ran down over his shoulders and chest. He shoved his dark hair back and began drying himself with a length of towelling he'd picked up from a boulder. He stretched, his arms high, his abdomen hollowing and the muscles of his chest gathering.

The urge to walk over and lean against him, capture

the cool dampness of his skin, the hard length of his body against hers…

Goosebumps spread over her skin as she watched, knowing it was a sore mistake to knowingly add fuel to this fire. She shifted deeper into the shadow and waited for what seemed like an eternity. Finally, she risked a peep, and the stab of disappointment at the sight of the now empty shoreline damned her for a besotted fool.

She began her descent, wondering why climbing down was always so much more treacherous than climbing up. It certainly required more concentration—which was probably why she had no forewarning.

'Genevieve Maitland. I should have known you'd come to plague me here as well.'

The shock hit her with the force of a gale.

She might have regained her balance if Milly hadn't chosen that moment to leap onto Genny's boulder and shove past her in his attempt to reach the new master, who always scratched precisely the right spot behind his ears. Genny felt her sandy feet slip, and with a cry of warning she went over.

If Kit meant to catch her, he failed. If he meant to break her fall, then it might be considered a success—though a rather more painful one for him than for her.

She lay winded for a moment, staring at the sky. She was half on him, half on the sand, his arm tight around her waist. Then the sky was blocked by Milly's panting grin and waving tail. Kit nudged him aside and raised himself onto his elbow with something between a croak and a grunt, his eyes the shade of deep, unsettled water.

'Are you hurt?'

She shook her head, taking stock of her almost-saviour. To her disappointment he was now wearing a plain linen shirt and buckskins, instead of the wet breeches. His hand was still on her waist, but he didn't seem to notice.

'I am sorry I fell on you,' she whispered. Her lungs felt as if they dropped from the cliff and bounced on every boulder along the way.

'I'm sorry I didn't do a more elegant job of catching you,' he replied, brushing sand from his hair. 'But you know my chivalric skills leave much to be desired.'

'Perhaps you should practise.'

'You would like to attempt that again?'

'I don't think so. You could practise on Milly. I'll watch.'

Milly, hearing his name, shook himself vigorously, spraying them with wet sand.

Kit cursed. 'Go away, you canine catapult. You've done enough damage.'

'He is usually better behaved,' Genny said.

'That's because he spends more than half the day snoring in the sun. I'm also very well behaved when I'm asleep.'

Genny's mind went inexorably to the silk-covered, cushion-festooned bed on the *Hesperus*. She would dearly love to check that assertion for herself. What would Kit look like asleep?

'No retort, Genny?'

His hand softened on her waist. His gaze moved down the length of her and then, more slowly, back up.

He smiled. 'I seem to find you in a some very… interesting circumstances, Genevieve Maitland. I wonder why that is.'

'I don't know,' she answered foolishly.

'Hmmm… You're covered in sand,' he said, and brushed at the fabric of her dress. She could feel the grains of sand shiver off…thought she could even hear the scrape of tiny crystals against cotton. She felt a slight pinch at her waist as he raised a piece of dark green seaweed and flicked it onto the sand.

'I think that it is best these skirts earn their keep now,'

he continued, his voice pitched somewhere below the waves.

There was another, more definite tug. The knotted ribbon slithered free with a hiss of friction as he pulled it away. Then he slowly lowered the ribbon so that it spooled into a damp coil on her abdomen. She watched as if it was a venomous snake rather than a strip of cloth. It felt far heavier than it ought, and suddenly it was hard to breathe again.

His hand slipped over the warm curve of her hip, raising her a little to release her bunched skirts. For a moment his fingers sank into the warm fullness of her flesh as he gathered the hem of her gown. Then he drew it down her legs with excruciating slowness.

She could feel everything: the weight of the fabric shifting against her, the way it sent sand cascading off her bare skin... And then his fingers slipped under the softness of her inner knee and stopped.

Her whole body clenched. Her toes pressed into the sand. It was the same thing all over again—her body taking control, shunting her to the baggage train and riding into battle, drums beating.

A sound between a moan and a mewl formed deep inside her. She tried to stifle it, but he heard, tightening his fingers, his own breath hitching. Then his hand skimmed upwards, his palm riding up her thigh, tightening on the damp fabric even as he bent over her.

His mouth settled on hers and she sighed, half in relief that it was finally happening, and half in anticipation. His lips were cool, as she'd known they would be, and she couldn't resist the urge to test her other hypothesis by gently tasting the curve of his lower lip.

Yes, sea salt and the ineffable, addictive flavour of Kit Carrington.

She pulled his lower lip between hers, tasting it, laving

it with her tongue and slipping past it. The tip of her tongue encountered his and a jolt of lightning coursed through her. Without thinking she wove her fingers through his hair, pulling him towards her. She wanted that dance again; she wanted him to make good on his wish to taste every inch of her. She wanted to do the same.

A raw, feral growl swept through him and his body covered her, pressing her into the sand, his chest heavy against her breasts, his leg sliding up between hers to press against that agonising heat. She abandoned all control of the embrace, meeting the demand of his kiss with more of her own. She wanted *more*.

So, apparently, did he. His mouth became almost savage in its intensity as it plundered hers. This wasn't careful, civilised Kit. His raw exploration of her mouth and body was nothing like his previous kisses. He dragged up her skirts with no finesse this time, his hand curving around her thigh and raising it to cradle the hard pressure of his hip. Without thinking she hooked her leg about his, her hips rising against the pressure of his erection.

God, she loved that groan, coming from that same deep well as all this heat inside her. She rose again, reaching for it.

His teeth nipped and licked her lower lip, sparking fire wheels of pleasure as his hand eased the bodice from her breast, his palm, rough with sand, brushing against the sensitised peak. The combination was more of a shock than her tumble off the boulder. Her whole body arched towards him with a cry of need, her nails pressing into his back…

She had no idea what might have happened if Milly hadn't returned and tried to join this new game. With a happy bark he sank down on his front paws and stuck his muzzle into the fray, panting in pleasure and expectation.

They pulled apart and Kit let loose a curse she hadn't heard since Spain as he rolled off her and into a sitting position, hooking his arms about his knees. She rose rather more slowly, brushing sand from her hands and wondering how she kept making the same mistakes over and over.

'I keep forgetting how dangerous you are, Genny,' he said to the cliffs, and she almost laughed at the absurdity of that.

'I'm not dangerous.'

If anyone is dangerous it is you, Kit Carrington. Not merely dangerous—utterly, catastrophically, calamitous.

'*I'm not dangerous.*'

The fates were clearly toying with him. Dropping the half-dressed object of his erotic dreams on top of him was an act of Greek retribution. Having her then proclaim herself 'not dangerous' was a double affront.

God, help him, he was in trouble.

'That wasn't wise,' he said, trying for cool common sense. 'Anyone on the cliff might have seen us. I know I said you could indulge your impulses, but doing so on an open beach is…risky.'

'You kissed me first this time,' she replied primly as she rose and headed towards the cliff path.

He shoved himself to his feet and followed, feeling like a reprimanded schoolboy. 'I might have kissed you first, but you kissed me into oblivion.'

'I did no such thing. I wouldn't know how.'

'Coyness doesn't suit you, Genny. I don't know where or from whom you learnt to kiss like that, but I take my hat off to them.'

It was a petty thing to say, but it was out of him before he could stop it.

'You may do so next time you look in the mirror, then,' she said tartly as she extracted her shoes from behind a stone.

He stared down at her in shock. 'What does that mean?'

'You are an intelligent man. Sometimes. I am certain you can decipher the puzzle.'

'You expect me to believe you have never kissed anyone before…before me?'

She shrugged and began pulling on her stockings but he was too shocked to appreciate the show.

'You had *never* kissed anyone before that night in the garden?'

'No,' she replied baldly, cheeks flaming.

He stood silent for a moment, too stunned to move. Somehow he'd assumed…

He had no idea why. Genny's age…her competence and cool responses both to his and Julian's flirtations… and then that utterly, inexplicably explosive conflagration just now…

He'd expected… He didn't know what he'd expected.

'You're looking at me as if I've grown two spare heads at least,' she snapped as she straightened and headed up the path.

'I was only… You were…' He cleared his throat and followed, searching for solid ground in this sudden marsh and finding not an inch of it.

He couldn't possibly have misread her enthusiasm after that hesitant beginning in the garden. Unfortunately, he remembered every second of it. And now in the bay… She'd opened to him, her body arching against his with that deep, almost lost moan he could still feel singing through him, twisting him into knots of frustrated lust.

He'd presumed…

Taking that presumption out of the equation, his behaviour had not merely been ungentlemanly, it had been wrong.

The realisation doused the remaining embers of the firestorm. He'd never, *ever* taken something from a woman— not even a kiss—without the rules being absolutely clear.

'I never should have—' he began, but she cut him off impatiently.

'Please. We have already held this conversation, if I recall correctly. Let us not make a drama of it. I daresay it was high time I finally kissed someone.'

It was a welcome splash of cold water and he tried to feel grateful for it—but mostly he was still trying to assimilate the revelation.

'All those years surrounded by soldiers…how did you manage to avoid being kissed…?'

God, he should keep his mouth shut before she pushed him off the cliff path. But she smiled over her shoulder, surprising him.

'I never said I hadn't been kissed. Only that I had never kissed anyone back. There is a difference.'

He definitely should not have this conversation while his cock was still cocked. A mix of physical jealousy and protective instincts rose like a snarl through him, and he had to stop himself from demanding name, rank and regiment. A choking suspicion reared its head, and though he knew he should keep quiet the words kept coming.

'They didn't…harm you?'

'Goodness, no, of course not. I think they were mostly curious. Except for the last one. He was drunk and mistook me for Serena, because I'd borrowed her cloak. I mostly found it annoying and rather unpleasant, and couldn't in the least understand why Serena made such a great deal of it. No doubt I was too young to appreciate it—or perhaps they just weren't very skilled. Perhaps both. And since I've come to the Hall there hasn't been anyone even to be curious about.'

They passed through the gate to the gardens, where the wind dropped and the air was full of the scent of roses. He knew he should not keep prodding this open wound, but he touched her arm, stopping her.

'But…what of Julian? I thought you two had almost been betrothed?'

'Yes, but that does not mean I wished him to kiss me.'

'That does not make any sense. Why would you consider marrying him if you didn't wish for any…intimacy?'

'I didn't think it was important. Many women marry without wishing for intimacy. And still many more do wish for it, but don't receive it. It strikes me that it is a seriously problematic area in relations between men and women.'

Kit was saved from stepping into the quagmire attendant on that philosophical observation by a burst of frenetic barking from Milly, who had stopped by the fountain, his front paws braced on the rim as he addressed the lily pads with full-throated woofs.

'What do you see, Milly?' Genny asked, scanning the water. 'Oh, no!'

'What is it?' Kit fully expected to see a kitten flailing in the pond, at the very least, but there seemed to be nothing there but sedate lilies.

'He's fallen into the water.'

'He…?'

'If I could only reach…' She tugged a branch from a shrub beside the fountain and sank to her knees on the rim, bending over the water.

He caught her waist as she teetered, pulling her back. 'Careful! What the devil is in there?'

She settled back with a frustrated cry. 'A bee. My arm is too short. Here—you try.'

'A bee?'

'A bee. He is drowning.'

Now he could see it. Floating in an indentation on the calm surface, wings outspread, was a bee. Kit's nerves, strained to snapping, gave way to amusement, but one look at Genny convinced him that laughter was not politic at the moment.

'It's probably already drowned, love.'

'No, he hasn't. He was moving, and he tried to climb onto that lily before he floated farther away.'

She began unlacing her sand-speckled shoes.

'You cannot mean to go in after it?'

'If you cannot reach him, then of course. Bees are important.'

He sighed and took the branch, leaning out over the water. His size was a distinct advantage for bee-rescuing, and he soon managed to scoop a leaf under the prone bee and draw it towards the shore.

'Put him amongst those flowers by the wall. He can dry himself there in safety.'

'Yes, ma'am.' Kit did as he was told. 'When I suggested you find other strays to tend to, I didn't think you would start with Apidae. I wouldn't be doing this for a wasp, you know.' He laid the branch between the flowers, with the bee clinging to the side of the leaf, its rump and wings glistening. 'There. Let's hope he dries before the birds find him.'

'*He* might be a *she*,' she said, kneeling on the grass to arrange some flowers to provide cover for her near-drowned victim.

'Even better if it is. I feel very gallant now. I probably saved you from a dunking too. I think I have earned my breakfast. Shall we…?'

He held out his hand to help her up, but she looked about the trees around them with a slight frown at the chattering birds.

'Perhaps I should wait until he…she…is dry.'

He conceded defeat and joined her on the grass. The bee hadn't moved. If he…she…hadn't been clinging so decisively to the leaf Kit might have suspected their rescue had come too late. He wondered how long they would have to wait to discover if the insect was alive or dead. He had no intention of testing the fates by prodding it.

'How long does a bee usually live?' he asked.

'Oh, two months or so.'

He wrapped his arms around his knees. 'We might be here awhile, then.'

She threw him a grin that did more to dispel his embarrassment at his behaviour than her assurances.

'You needn't stay, Kit. You must be hungry after your swim.'

'You saw me swimming?'

She nodded, her eyes back on the bee. He watched her profile, the strong line of her chin and nose and that lush pout of her lower lip. His mouth watered.

He wasn't hungry; he was *ravenous*. He'd come down to swim precisely to counter this plaguing hunger, only to have the fates drop its cause on top of him. And now he was engaged in a bee-watching vigil with his tormentor while imagining her beside him in the water, their bodies hot against each other in the cold bite of the sea. He would stretch her out on top of him, the cool sand at his back, her warm, firm thighs encasing his, her breasts glistening from the sea...

'Do you know how to swim?' he asked, trying to prise his mind from that image.

'Yes. Grandfather's batman taught us when we were in Portugal. I am quite good. Not as good as you, of course.'

She gave him another quick, sidelong smile. Half-shy, half-teasing. He tightened his hold around his knees.

Milly, realising his masters were going nowhere for a while, plumped down between them. He stretched to the full extent of his wolfish frame, then gave a contented sigh and panted into canine abandon.

This was how he could be, Kit thought. If they were married. Keeping vigil over near-drowned bees with a woman who could write as if she'd walked through history and manage people as if she'd taken lessons from Napoleon. A woman who was fiercely loyal, who cared for people far more than she wished to, and whose body was a source of agony for him in a way he had never experienced.

And who had chosen him for her first kiss.

That shouldn't matter in the grand scheme of things, but it did. It was like a hand reaching through fog. The urge to clasp it and let it guide him was almost overpowering.

He'd been from one end of the known world to the other and he'd never felt...*this*. He was more content to sit with her in silence, watching over a bee, than going to explore the world in search of his next treasure.

He had no idea if this was what his parents had shared or what poets went on about. It felt outside the bounds of the known. A mix of dark and light and deep, deep water.

He was afraid it was here to stay and that scared the hell out of him.

It scared him even more that he had no idea what she felt.

For all he'd come to know her, she still kept rooms and rooms of her fortress carefully under lock and key. She'd explained her tie with Julian, but that was only on the surface. Underneath she was passionate, excitable, and she was fighting every one of those tendencies—had probably been doing so for years.

It would be something of a miracle if Julian—who cared for her, no matter what he might say—hadn't sparked some answering emotion. For all he knew, the two of them, equally defensive and defiant, frightened of the future and themselves, were a hair's breadth away from that tipping point that might bring them together.

And he had just given Julian the means to explore that possibility.

He shouldn't have.

He tried to focus on the rhythm of Milly's puffing breath, on the chatter of the birds that was becoming less energetic as the sun rose in the sky. On anything but the chaos the silent woman next to him kept unleashing.

It would be madness to allow this strange sinking to continue. Seductive and dangerous. It was time to kick his way back to the surface, fill his lungs with fresh air, and assess the situation in a rational light.

He couldn't do that around her. Whatever this was— rampant lust, love, a reaction to finding himself wallowing in the cursed Carrington swamp—he needed distance.

'Oh, look!' she exclaimed, pointing to the bee.

The furry, tubby little thing was flicking its wings.

'There,' she said, her voice rich with contentment, her lips parted in a smile. 'I told you she was alive. She merely needed to recover her strength.' Milly buffed her hand and she smiled down at the dog. 'Yes, you're a good dog. You have more than atoned for knocking me onto your master, haven't you, love?' she cooed, her voice pouring warm honey over both of them.

Kit gave a silent groan and sank his head onto his knees.

Genny watched Kit bowing his head and thought of the last time he'd caught her cooing, over little Leo back in London. It felt so strange that they were the same people. If someone had told her that love could transform her, she would have scoffed.

But she felt different.

Happy.

She knew it was about to end…that tomorrow the guests would leave and so would Mary and Kit and that the clock was ticking down to heartbreak. But right here, right now—she was happy.

Her throat tightened. The sun was burning her eyes.

She gave Milly one last pat and stood up. 'I'll have

Cook give you a fine bone, Milly. And you've earned your breakfast too, Lord Westford.'

He stood as well, stretching, his eyes glinting in the sun. 'Thank you, Generalissima.'

That stung a little—she hadn't meant to sound high-handed.

'I wish you would stop calling me that.'

'I meant it purely as a compliment this time, Genny. It is a tribute.'

'It doesn't feel like that.'

He shook his head. 'I don't understand why you are ashamed of being brilliant. You won't tell anyone you've written some of the most wonderful tales I've read in a long while. You roll into a ball like a hedgehog the minute I pay tribute to your considerable skills…'

'Scheming skills are hardly something to be commended for.'

'Of course they are. Politicians and generals are commended for them all the time. If you were a man you wouldn't be hiding your light under a bushel. The only reason you couldn't give Napoleon a run for his money is because you're too compassionate. Believe me, he wouldn't have stopped to pull a bee from a pond.'

Embarrassment and curiosity warred with a strange sense of hurt. She didn't want him to admire her. She wanted him to love her.

Quite desperately.

He should have known praising her intelligence would send her running. She was beet-red now, and looked ready to kick something in embarrassment. She was already shrugging off all the pleasure of the moments they'd shared, tucking herself away.

Except he wasn't ready to let this moment slide. He wasn't ready to let *them* slide. Because there was a *them*.

Where they were heading he didn't know, but there was, for the first time in his life a *them...us*.

He should let her go, but instead he crowded her against the garden wall and cupped her cheek, angling her face so that she had to look at him. Her eyes were shadowed, wary, but there it was—that wistful need that was always there. Carefully hidden, but there. That was the bridge that would either let him in or keep him out.

'Genny Maitland is smart,' he half sang, his eyes holding hers. They were defiant, but he could see the hurt beyond the defiance and didn't stand down. *'"What is it to be wise? 'tis but to know how little can be known, To see all others' faults, and feel our own."'*

She blinked, and he saw curiosity warring with hurt. 'Who wrote that?'

'Pope, sweetheart.'

'Well, it is not accurate at all.'

'Of course not. You are a model of arrogance and selfishness, employing all your considerable powers for evil ends. I daresay you only rescued that poor bee so he could help you infiltrate the hive and secure all the honey for your nefarious purposes.'

'Oh, the bee...' she said worriedly, trying to move past him, but he caught her waist, stopping her.

'She flew off while you were busy claiming how evil you are. Another plot foiled.'

Her mouth flickered into a smile. 'You must be dreadfully bored if you are resorting to flirting with me again, Lord Westford.'

He knew very well what flirting felt like—and seduction, and lust. This felt like all and none of those. He wished it did. He didn't want to accept the implications of it being something else entirely.

'I'm not bored in the least, Genny,' he said in all honesty.

Terrified, but not bored.

He bent his head, just grazing her cheek with his mouth.

Not smart, not smart, sang the voice of caution—and was tossed into the pond.

She shivered against him, and her voice was breathy when she spoke, but her words were pure Miss Genevieve Maitland.

'I don't think this is wise, Lord Westford. If any of your guests were to wake and glance out of the window you might provide them with rather more entertainment than you wish.'

He glanced over his shoulder at the row of windows twinkling in the sun. He was tempted to throw caution to the winds. More than that, he wanted *her* to want to throw caution to the winds and surrender to impulse. He wanted some sign that she was as confused, overwhelmed, and entangled as he.

But Genny, with her cautious eyes on the windows and her cautious mind on consequences, was not that.

He sighed and stood back. Sailing into the wind required a great deal of tacking. And patience.

'Come. Breakfast. I feel I've earned it twice.'

Chapter Twenty-One

'That morning walk certainly did you good, miss,' Susan said as she secured another pin in Genny's thick hair. 'You're looking much more the thing, if you don't mind my saying so. Now, hold still while I fasten your gown.'

Genny sat obediently, staring at the tell-tale colour in her cheeks. It had been flowing and ebbing all morning. As had her mood.

The morning had turned out to be quite, quite different from her expectation. She wasn't quite certain what to make of Kit Carrington's attitude to her, but she knew, as clearly as she could feel her heart thumping away, that she was in love with him.

He'd saved a bee for her.

She ought to be more affected by his actions on Serena's and Mary's behalf. Well, she *was*. By freeing them, he'd freed her. But he'd saved a bee for her and sat with her while it dried. And in that calm, companionable silence her heart had ceded its last plate of armour.

She loved Kit Carrington. It was no longer avoidable, negotiable, deniable. It just was.

He'd been good to Julian, though she was quite certain Julian had done his usual best to be annoying.

He thought she was smart, and not merely in a devious way.

He'd even found some merit in her devious ways.

He was, quite simply, marvellous.

And she was a fool.

She wished she were far more devious. Then she wouldn't have drawn his attention to the perilousness of their position in the garden. She would have kissed him in full view of whoever cared to glance out of their window on a beautiful sunny morning.

It would have been quite a scandal, and Kit, being Kit, would have offered to marry her. Poor Lady Sarah would have had to roll up her tents and cannon and depart the field.

Society would have been sorely disappointed, of course. Probably even vindictive. Charlie's impeccable birth had balanced out Serena's indifferent Maitland lineage, but that lineage would do nothing to help Kit's standing in society. He might believe he did not care, but he might yet change his mind. Especially if there were…if there were children.

She'd never indulged in the thought of children. But now the idea caught her by the throat with yearning and terror. She didn't want *any* children—she wanted children with *him*.

He would be a good father. She'd never been on any other ship where the men didn't merely respect their captain, but love him. Kit would know what to do when she was weakest. He would love their children when she was afraid to. He would check her when she tried to rule them for their own good.

But they very well might look like her, not him, and they too would have to negotiate the shoals of society. While his and Lady Sarah's children would sail through the eye of a needle with their perfect looks, and their wealth, and their much-mended pedigree. Lady Sarah would be another perfect piece for his collection. The jewel in the Carrington crown.

'There you are, miss. As pretty as a picture.' Susan stood back, pleased.

Genny eyed herself, thinking that there were all kinds of pictures, not all of them pretty. But she thanked Susan and hurried downstairs towards the breakfast room.

She wanted and did not want to see him again so soon. She…

'Good morning, Miss Maitland.'

Genny closed her eyes briefly before turning, donning a smile as she did so. Lady Sarah even descended the stairs like a work of art.

'Good morning, Lady Sarah. Did you enjoy the excursion yesterday?'

'We did indeed. Though you were missed. As was Lord Westford. I trust nothing serious occurred to keep him here?'

'I don't know, Lady Sarah. I spent the day in my rooms,' she lied.

'Ah, of course. I do hope you are recovered?'

'It was merely a megrim. Nothing serious.'

'But not pleasant.'

'No.'

Lady Sarah paused two steps from the bottom and did not seem inclined to proceed. 'I was wondering if I might ask your advice, Miss Maitland.'

No.

The word jumped into Genny's mind and she very much hoped it did not show on her face.

'I was about to go in to breakfast.'

'It will only take a moment.'

'Very well. This way.'

Inside the library, she stood by the door while Lady Sarah wandered along the shelves.

'Papa said you were raised in Spain. With all the soldiers.'

'My sister and I lived with my grandfather when we were young, that is true.'

'It doesn't show in the least on your sister.'

Genny didn't know whether to smile or spit. She opted for the smile. 'Thank you.'

Lady Sarah turned and smiled back—a surprisingly warm smile. 'I like you better.'

Genny blinked.

'I like it when I don't know what people think. It's boring otherwise. You're only a few years older than I, but you are…different. You do not seem to need anyone. I wish I was like that. Maybe if I'd grown up like you I would be.'

Well, this was a turn-up for the books.

'I don't think you would have enjoyed that, Lady Sarah.'

'You have no idea what I would enjoy.'

'At the moment, I think you would enjoy becoming Lady Westford.'

The words were out of her before she could check them.

Lady Sarah's eyes widened. 'You *are* direct. Yes, you're quite right. I don't think life with Lord Westford would be boring.'

'It might be when he returns to sea and leaves you here.'

'Not at all. I rather fancy having such a lovely house to myself, to rule as I see fit. Papa has very definite ideas about his household, and one reason I am still unwed is because I do too. I won't exchange my father's house for another cage. When I leave it, I want to go somewhere I can breathe. You can understand that, can't you?'

God, yes, she could.

'Wouldn't you worry about what he was doing while he was away?' she asked.

'You mean other women?'

Genny prayed the thump of heat she felt in her chest

wouldn't bloom into a blush. She had actually been referring to the danger of Kit's enterprises but, as Lady Sarah had supposed, it was probably the women that would occupy her mind.

Lady Sarah frowned at the tip of her pink silk shoe. 'I think I might—a little. But men always have mistresses, don't they? Papa does. His current one is quite nice... certainly nicer than Mama ever was. I feel sorry for her, though. She isn't his first and she won't be his last. That is the wife's advantage.'

'True.'

'Are you Lord Westford's mistress?'

'I beg your pardon?' Genny said, her voice a little hoarse.

'I saw the two of you this morning. In the garden.'

Oh.

'Have...have you told anyone?'

'It is hardly in my interest to do so, is it? He would have to marry you—which isn't in his interest either. If it were he would have done so already. I noticed it from the start. We were in the garden, and you were carrying a basket of flowers, and he took it from you and...smiled. He has a different smile for you. So does Julian Carrington. I learned to watch for those signs from Mama. She was good at spotting those things. I daresay it came from watching Papa all those years.'

A confused mix of anger, guilt and the sharp piercing pain of hope shoved through Genny's heart.

'Why are you telling me all this?' Genny managed.

'I don't even know...' There was a strange cadence to the younger woman's voice. 'Papa says Lord Westford wishes to contract a marriage of convenience or he would not have invited all these families with their daughters. When I told him what I thought about you he said that your birth, though respectable, won't balance out Lord

Westford's own parentage. That he needs someone from a family of the first order of respectability. Like one of the Burford girls. Or myself. I think I suit him better than Sophronia, and certainly better than that minx Calista. Don't you agree?'

The best Genny could do was nod. The girl's gaze was relentless.

'Papa said the best outcome is that Lord Westford marries me and takes you as his mistress until he tires of you. Papa says one must always be looking ahead and not be trapped by details. By "looking ahead" he means thinking of title and wealth, and by "details" he means loyalty and morality. They are for the vulgar, apparently.'

Genny held herself still through this barrage. She felt like a mouse trapped under the floorboards while a cat's paw groped through the cracks, swiping closer and closer. She no longer liked Lady Sarah. What she felt was very close to revulsion.

No—it was pain. The truth hurt.

'If you believe this…if you really believe this about Lord Westford…that he would do what you so despise in your father…you should not marry him,' Genny said.

'Why not, if every other man in our class would do the same?'

'Because even if that were true—and I don't believe it to be true—there are some men…worthy men…who wouldn't. Don't you wish for a man who would not dream of doing that? Not even because he respected you, but because he did not wish to hurt you.'

Lady Sarah's usually cool complexion mottled with sudden harsh colour. Unlike Genny, with her Mediterranean skin, blushing was not Lady Sarah's friend. Her eyes too had reddened, and Genny's sympathy sparked again. Lady Sarah and she were not that different. Both were a little lost in their search for safety.

'You ought not to marry Lord Westford, Lady Sarah,' she said.

'I'd be a fool not to. If he offered.'

'You wouldn't be happy.'

'I would be happier than remaining in Papa's home for ever and ever.'

'I don't know... There is something that happens to a person when hope and choice are removed from the table. Even if Lord Westford is not like your father, I'm afraid you would become more like your mother than you would wish if you married him without love. I hope that doesn't happen to you.'

'You're saying this because you want him for yourself.'

'That is not why I am saying this. But it is true that I don't wish to see him hurt, and I'm afraid you would both suffer if you married him for the wrong reasons.'

'You aren't denying that you want him.'

'I think we've gone beyond that with all this honesty. But I don't think he will marry anyone—not yet. I think he will return to his ship and his old life the moment his sister weds. He is comfortable there.'

'Lucky him.'

'Yes. Now, we should go in to breakfast. I do wish you well, Lady Sarah.'

Lady Sarah gave a slight, unhappy laugh, but did not follow Genny.

At the entrance to the breakfast room the sound of Kit's low, warm laugh reached her from inside and Genny stopped short.

'Miss?' Howich said from behind her in surprise, a large teapot in his hand.

Genny moved out of his way. 'I have forgotten some... letters I must write, Howich.'

She didn't wait for him to comment. She needed to escape before anyone saw her looking as shattered as Lady

Sarah. She needed to think—alone. Today the guests departed, and tomorrow Kit would leave for Hampshire. After the wedding he would leave altogether, and it might be years and years before she saw him again.

Pain lurched through her like a poorly thrust spear, and she pressed a hand to her sternum. The pain would probably fade. It must—like all pain. And she should be grateful to him for giving her so many memories to hoard. She *was* grateful.

She just wanted more.

Chapter Twenty-Two

Kit watched until the ducal carriage was swallowed by the shadow of the beeches and then let the curtain fall back into place with a sigh of relief.

It was finally over.

Except that now the real challenge awaited him.

He was halfway across the library when the door opened and Genny slipped inside, closing it behind her.

'The Duke and your grandmother have departed for London.'

'About time. I was afraid he might toss her out of the carriage at the last minute. Please tell me they took Carmine with them?'

She nodded, her dimples appearing and disappearing just as quickly. She was staring at the floor, the crease between her brows warning him that all was not well.

'What is it, Genny? I don't think I can bear any surprises at the moment.'

Her chin went up and she shook her head. 'It is nothing. Merely... Never mind.'

He reached her before she slipped out, easing her back into the room and closing the door again. 'I didn't mean to be abrupt. Tell me what it is.'

She was as tense as a topsail in a gale and his heart, already rocky, picked up speed. It was something serious.

'Is it Julian?'

The words were out of him without thought and she frowned, finally looking up at him.

'Julian?'

'Has he…? He's left, hasn't he?'

'Yes, he left this morning.' She gave a slight, distracted smile. 'With your letter to the Carrington solicitors in his breast pocket. I don't know if he thanked you properly, and he probably never will, but he is grateful.'

He didn't give a damn about Julian's gratitude or lack thereof, but her tone reassured him. Whatever this was, it wasn't either a proposal from Julian or her concern about him.

'Then what? Your sister?'

'No, no… She is already happily planning our removal to the Dower House.' She looked around the library, her frown returning. 'May I still come to the library for books sometimes?'

His much-maligned heart dropped with a wet splat onto the wooden floor. 'Of course. Whenever you wish. Is that what is bothering you?'

She shook her head, her gaze sliding to the floor again. 'No. It isn't bothering me precisely… That is to say, it is… But not… The thing is…' She took a deep breath. 'The thing is, I have a request to make.'

'What request?' he asked, without much enthusiasm.

'After Hampshire will you join the *Hesperus*?'

It was close enough to the truth, so he nodded.

She nodded as well, just once.

'Where are you sailing?'

'France and then Italy. Why?' he ventured.

She raised her chin. 'I would like to request something of you, Lord Westford.'

'I'll make a pact with you, Genny. I shall stop calling you Generalissima if you cease with all this Lord Westford nonsense.'

Her mouth curved and she looked up. 'Captain Carrington?'

'Kit. Say it. It rhymes with kiss, in case you were wondering how to pronounce it,' he said, a trifle testily.

'It does not rhyme,' she replied with that swift smile he loved, making his insides clench in confused yearning.

'If the first word is cut off by the second it does. Shall I demonstrate?'

She swallowed and leaned back against the door, as if the hordes of hell were beating down the other side. As far as he was concerned the hordes were right inside the room, engaged in pitched battle inside him.

'Pray stop distracting me, Kit. This is important.'

He didn't like the sound of that, but he shrugged and motioned for her to continue.

She gave a sharp huff of resolution and fixed her gaze on the floor once more. 'Before you sail, I would like to… to spend the night on the *Hesperus*, Kit. If it is possible. I could make my way to Portsmouth and after the wedding… before you sail…if it is agreeable with you, of course…' She stopped and then added a little explosively as he remained silent, 'You said it was honest to ask.'

'Honest…?' He woke from his stupor. 'Yes, it is very honest to ask. But just so I understand… You wish to spend the night on the *Hesperus* before I sail?'

'Yes. In your bed.'

'In my bed? With me?'

'Yes.'

'Not sleeping, I presume?'

'Precisely.' She was now a hot, dusky red, but her expression was as stern as ever.

'This is rather more than an impulse, Genny.'

'I am aware of that. But I trust you, and this is some-thing I wish to do. I think… I think you are attracted to me…'

'You *know* I am attracted to you.'

She shook her head, as if that was one of life's myster-ies. 'Then it wouldn't be distasteful to you.'

He rubbed his hand over his mouth. He'd wanted Genny to throw caution to the winds and this, in inimitable Genny fashion, was as caution-throwing as it came. It just wasn't enough. Genny discovering her considerable sexuality with him was an intoxicating fantasy on its own. But he wanted…he *needed*…to know she cared. He wanted her need to be as overpowering as the need he could no lon-ger deny he felt for her.

He wanted her to love him.

That was a rather more serious request than hers, and one neither had any control over in the end. But he could do his damnedest to try and ensure she did.

Genny hurried to fill the silence. 'I… I didn't say this for you to feel obliged.'

'This is not something I would ever do out of obliga-tion, Genny.'

'Oh, devil take it—I never should have said anything.'

She groped for the doorknob but he flattened his hand against the door. She wasn't going anywhere yet.

They both started at the jerk of the knob on the other side.

'Kit?'

Genny was halfway across the room by the time Mary opened the door.

'*There* you are, Kit. Where is your jacket? The car-riage is waiting. We must leave now if we are to reach them in time for dinner. Oh, Genny—you are here.' She came forward and enveloped Genny in a hug. 'I do wish you and Serena could come. It is a sad pity that Peter's grandparents' house is so small and his family so big. We should have—'

'It is quite all right, Mary,' Genny reassured her.

Mary gave her another hug and picked up Kit's jacket from where it was slung over the back of a chair.

'Come along, Kit.'

Kit took the jacket and ushered Mary towards the door. 'I shall be out directly. Wait for me in the carriage.'

'But—'

He shut the door on his stepmother. Now it was his turn to lean back against the door, his hand on the knob. Genny stood with her hands clasped before her like a prisoner in the dock.

'That wasn't very chivalrous,' she said, her voice wobbling a little.

'No. You do choose your moments, Genny Maitland. Unfortunately, we shall have to wait until I return to discuss your request in more detail.'

'Return…? I thought you were going directly to the *Hesperus*?'

He didn't tell her that that plan had flown away with her rescued bee.

'And leave Mary to travel home on her own after seeing her only child wed and dragged off to the wilds of Leicestershire? That would be even more unchivalrous than shutting the door in her face.'

She finally smiled. There was definitely relief there.

'So, will you consider my proposal while you are away?'

Every waking moment, most likely, he thought. *And probably quite a few unconscious moments as well.*

Aloud he said, 'I will. Will you?'

Her dimples flickered. 'I already have. Hence my request.'

'Come here.'

She stepped forward. Stopped. 'Does that mean you are interested?'

'That means the carriage is waiting and I require some more material for consideration.'

It was lucky he had the door behind him as support. Genny wrapped her arm about his nape without hesitation, went up on tiptoe and kissed him until they were both breathless. He held her against him, wishing against fate that he could consign Hampshire to hell. Words were burning inside him, but even more than that was the need to hear something from her.

'Now this is not only going to be a hellishly long drive, but a damned uncomfortable one,' he muttered against her hair, breathing in orange blossoms.

'I'm sorry,' she murmured against his chest, but her hands caressing his back were utterly unrepentant.

'Liar.'

'Kit!'

Mary's peremptory cry penetrated the door and Genny moved towards the window, straightening her dress.

'Godspeed, Kit. Give my love to Emily.'

I'd rather keep it for myself, he thought, but nodded, opening the door.

'Do try not to fall onto anyone or rescue a wounded tiger while I am gone, Genevieve Elisabeth Calpurnia Maitland.'

Chapter Twenty-Three

Surely she was seeing things?

No. It was *definitely* a longboat coming around the edge of the bay.

Genny stood and shaded her eyes to watch the apparition as it turned into the bay.

Her heart set off at a run. She knew that dark head, that broad back. She had no idea where Kit was coming from, but at the moment that didn't matter. He was coming.

The boat finally rode up onto the shallow sand and Kit jumped out and strode towards her.

'Well, this is convenient. You've saved me a climb.'

'I was walking,' she said foolishly. And then, equally foolishly, 'You and Mary weren't expected back until tonight. Where did you come from?'

He pointed towards the eastern cliff. 'The *Hesperus* is anchored in the deep waters around the head. I'm surprised you didn't see it from the cliff.'

'I've been down here awhile,' she said. She didn't add that she'd been so caught in a brown study she'd likely have missed a hot air balloon landing on Carrington Hall.

'Hmmm… Brimble?' Kit turned to one of the sailors who'd stepped out onto the shore with him and handed him the thick sheaf of folded papers he'd pulled from his pocket. 'Take this up to the house and present it to Howich. When he takes you to Mrs Serena Carrington, inform her that her sister is quite safe with me.'

He held out his hand to Genny.

'Come.'

She stared at it. At him. At the longboat. 'Now?'

'Now. It won't take long.'

Oh. That didn't bode well. Well, they would see about that.

He took her arm. 'I'd best carry you over the surf. Not that I object to seeing what happens to that pretty dress in water, but I'd rather not return you all salt-encrusted when we're done.' He picked her up with a cheerful grunt. 'You are more of a handful than you look, Genny Maitland.'

'That isn't a very nice thing to say,' she objected, and his arms tightened as he walked into the surf.

'It's a very nice thing. I happen to enjoy handfuls. In you go.' He settled her on the bench and hauled himself in, taking her hand as he sat beside her.

The grinning men in the longboat began their rhythmic rowing and she watched the bay recede, the waves hurrying away from them as they rose and fell, the water turning darker. She was out of her depth in so many more ways than one.

The *Hesperus* came into view, its sails vivid against the cerulean sky. Perhaps one of her daydreams had become rather too vivid. Perhaps it was the sun…

The longboat pulled up alongside the Jacob's ladder and Kit helped her to her feet.

'There is yet time to turn back,' he murmured. 'Once aboard you are in my domain once more and must accept the consequences.'

His tone was playful, but she felt the tension beneath it.

'*Would* you take me back?'

He paused, her hands in his. 'Of course. I told you—it is always your choice.'

She nodded and took hold of the Jacob's ladder. 'A gentleman would look away while I climb.'

There was relief in his smile. 'What if you need help?'

'Then I shall ask for it.'

She did not look back to see if her wishes were being obeyed. Some things were best assumed.

When Kit joined her on deck he looked suspiciously angelic. 'Come,' he said again.

This time she didn't object, but placed her hand in his and followed.

His cabin looked different. Or perhaps *she* had changed.

A tray with wine and fruit sat on the table. There was also a small wooden box she had not seen before, with painted panels of flowering gardens and a cover inlaid with mother of pearl.

'Oh, how beautiful!' she exclaimed, reaching out to touch it.

But he placed a hand on it. 'Sit down.'

She sat, feeling all at sea. His lightness had flown and he looked distant and rather stern. This definitely did not bode well. But if all he wanted to do was reject her advances, he could have done that on the shore.

'Did you consider?' she asked, annoyed at how feeble her voice sounded.

She picked up her glass and set it down again. He did the same.

'I did.'

'And what is your answer?'

'That depends.'

'On what?

'I am considering two courses of action at the moment,' he began, swirling his wine. 'I could accept your proposal and then leave with the *Hesperus* for France tomorrow...'

She clutched her hands together. Her heart was thudding so hard her ribs ached. 'And the second possibility?'

'I could go home.'

'Home?'

'Carrington Hall. It is not quite home. But it could be. I am considering staying. For a month. Maybe longer. It depends.' He took a deep breath, turning the wooden box round and round in a parade of luscious gardens: butterflies and roses, palms and honeysuckle, peonies and willows, orange blossoms and a single red-breasted robin, wings spread.

'For a month?' Her voice was calm, which was a miracle, because she was shaking like blancmange inside.

Oh, please. Please, please, please.

'It depends,' he said once more.

'What…what does it depend upon?'

There was a faint knock at the door and Benja's apologetic voice. 'Sorry, Captain. We need you for a moment.'

Kit's jaw tightened. 'Blast. Wait here, Genny… No, best come with me.'

Genny followed him, still feeling completely at sea. Which proved to be far more than a figure of speech—because the moment she stepped onto the deck, she realised the truth.

'We're sailing!'

'Took you long enough to realise that, Gen.' He looked up at the sails. 'Pretty strong against the current, Benja. We'll need to come around.'

'Yes. But it will take longer, *Capità*.'

Kit finally smiled. 'We have time. Do it.'

For a moment Genny felt a strange welling inside her, almost like grief, but then she realised what it was—joy. It made no more sense than what was happening, but still… The thought that he was taking her away, just the two of them…

But Managing Genny Maitland knew better. 'Why?'

'Maybe I'm kidnapping you,' he said, watching as Benja issued orders to the men.

'Depositing me on a desert island so I will cease my pernicious meddling with your family?' she asked.

'Hmmm…' he murmured, his eyes on the sails as they wavered and pulled.

Her voice also wavered when she spoke. 'I don't understand.'

He glanced across at her, his face turning serious again. 'Come, we'll leave the men to it,' he said abruptly. 'It's hard work, sailing into this kind of wind.'

He took her hand again, and this time she felt he hardly noticed he was doing it. She thought of that strange conversation with Lady Sarah. Of her sharp, bitter eyes, catching the tell-tale signs of intimacy.

'Where are we sailing?' she asked, her voice hurried.

He stopped and let go her hand. 'A little south…a little west. Why? In a hurry to return?'

She shook her head. 'No. I was thinking.'

'What were you thinking about?' he asked.

And she shut her eyes and threw herself overboard. 'I was thinking of that beautiful bed.'

Silence.

Waves splashed, gulls cried, sails flapped and wood creaked—but what she heard was that silence.

She kept her eyes shut.

His hand, warm and rough, took hers.

'Come. I want to talk with you.'

Talk.

She didn't want to talk. Talk was sensible. And sensible was what she'd been for so, so long. She wanted to *live*.

Inside the cabin he pressed her back into a chair and refilled her glass. She drank, grateful for the billow of warmth that filled her icy insides.

'If amethyst and gold had a flavour, this would be it,' she murmured. 'With blackberries too.'

He smiled and touched his glass to hers before he drank. Then he sat and pulled the wooden box towards him, turning it idly in his hands once more as he watched her.

'This is harder than I thought, Genevieve Maitland. You are a difficult woman to read. Here you are on my ship, and we are sailing, and other than your interest in my bed I am not certain what you feel. That places me in a quandary.'

'What…what kind of quandary?'

'My options. If the sum of your interest is in my bed, in theory we could resolve that during this voyage and then you can send me off to France.'

'But… I… You said you might yet remain at Carrington Hall a month.'

'Yes. I did. I was thinking… These last weeks have been eventful, to say the least. Quite a great deal has happened… God, this is hard.' He sank his head into his hands, shoving his fingers into his hair.

She clasped her hands together to stop herself from following suit. Her leg was bouncing from nerves.

He dropped his hands and said, almost explosively, 'Would you like me to stay at the Hall?'

Like?

Her wide-eyed silence seemed to exasperate him.

'Do you even like me, beyond your interest in my damn bed?'

'Of course…of *course* I do. You *must* know I like you. I would never have mentioned your bed if I didn't.'

'Forget the damned bed.'

'*You* mentioned it just now.'

'Very well—as of this moment, and for the next quarter-hour on the clock, there will be no mention of beds.' He shoved himself to his feet. 'What I am trying to say— extremely poorly—is that if you are agreeable I would like to spend the next month at Carrington Hall so that we may become better acquainted. Without my grandmother making mischief and without half the Ton in attendance, trying to suck my Carrington blood. At the end of that month, if you agree, I would like to make you an offer of marriage.'

Genny's thoughts tumbled in their chase of this speech, trying to make sense of what he was saying.

Better acquainted?

Marriage?

'If, on the other hand, this prospect does not appeal to you,' he continued, still pacing, his voice still stilted, 'I shall see you safely back to the Hall and be on my way. I think we are both mature enough to...'

He faltered and stopped in front of a painting of a long-tailed bird sitting on a branch heavy with cherry blossom. She could hear her heart thumping. Great big thuds echoing in her ears.

Marriage.

It wasn't wrong to want that, was it? They were friends, could be lovers... And if he wasn't in love with her, as she was with him, it could still be good...for both of them. She could give him something he lacked—something she felt he needed. She knew he was not asking lightly, or out of consideration for honour, and yet...

She wanted so, *so* much more.

'I would like you to stay,' she blurted out.

He turned and she hurried on, stumbling over her thoughts and her words.

'I would like you to stay and for us to be able to explore our...our friendship. But I think it is wrong to establish in advance that it must lead to a...a marriage of convenience. The truth is...the truth is I don't want to marry you for propriety's sake, Kit. *You* shouldn't want a marriage on those terms.'

'I don't.' He turned back to address the painting and for a long while neither spoke.

Finally, she couldn't bear the silence. 'Where does that leave us?'

He shook his head without turning. 'I don't know.'

She swallowed. Any minute now he would put her back in that longboat and…

'This isn't something we can resolve right here, right now,' she said.

'No. Probably not,' he replied, still in the same empty voice.

'Will you stay at the Hall a little while longer, then? Or will you sail?'

She saw his jaw tense but still he didn't turn.

'Stay. I don't seem to have much choice in the matter.'

She didn't quite understand what was happening here, whether to be happy or scared, and so she settled on both.

She had been prepared for the worst, but now Kit was to stay a little longer, and she was precisely where she wanted to be—alone with him in his cabin. She would concentrate on that and on her objective.

If she'd known she was to be kidnapped she would have worn something far more appealing, but at least her morning gown was easy to remove. It took less than a minute to slip off her dress and her stays. Her chemise was sheer muslin, with two thin straps, and ended about her knees. She debated making away with that as well, but lost her nerve. She went to the bed and sat down. The silk was warm and viscous, almost liquid. She rested her hands on it.

'Now that we have settled that, do you wish to join me? Or shall I put my dress back on? Your choice.'

He finally turned, his blank gaze coming into startled focus. 'Genny, what are you doing?'

She spread her arms, a little confused by his confusion. 'You *agreed*.'

He stood dumbly for a moment, his gaze moving over her, but already she could see the heat entering his gaze as it lingered over her form, moving down to her feet and then back, slowing as it went.

He took a step closer and stopped. 'Definitely better than my imagination,' he murmured.

A hitched sigh of relief escaped her and his eyes rose to hers, intent now. He took her hand and turned it over to touch a light kiss to her palm.

'Your hand is cold,' he murmured against her, his tongue testing the ultrasensitive skin of her palm and sending silvered shocks down her arm and sparking over her breasts. 'Are you nervous?'

'Terrified.'

'Don't be. I won't hurt you.'

You will.

'I need you to warm me,' she moaned, and the words were smothered as he bent to fuse his mouth with hers, pressing her back against the cushions as he lay beside her.

'I've been on fire ever since you ordered me into the ballroom,' he said urgently, and that strange distance that had so confused her was completely gone now. 'I've dreamed of stripping you bare, spreading you out on my bed, tasting every inch of you...'

She shuddered at the image. The contrast between his words and the languorous progress of his fingers as they moved over her, tracing the sweep of her hips and thighs and rising to stop just short of her aching breasts, had her stretched tauter than piano wire, vibrating as she waited for another chord to be struck.

'I didn't think you would agree...to this...' she said.

'I can't seem to help myself...' His laugh was shaky and it spread heat over the swell of her breast as he slid

down the strap of her chemise, very gently exposing her
breast, like an archaeologist extracting a precious find. 'I
need to touch you…'

Cupping it in his large warm hand, he bent to brush the
swell with his lips in hot, feathery kisses, never settling.
Then his teeth scraped very gently over the sensitised peak
and a wave of heat surged through her. Even in the haze of
desire the intensity of her need scared her. But not enough
to stop. And not enough to keep her words safe inside her.

'Kit… I want you. I *need* you.'

He groaned, his erection surging against her thigh. He
caught her hip, holding her against him so she could feel
the full pulsing heat of him against her. His mouth hovered above her nipple, his breath teasing it, taunting her.

'Say that again.'

She drew breath, her chest rising to scrape her erect
nipple against his lower lip, but he didn't move.

'I want you…' she repeated obediently, and his indrawn
breath dragged cold air over her nipple, adding pain to
pleasure.

'I *need* you…' he prompted, pulling down the second
strap and raising her so that the chemise slipped to her
waist. He leaned back a little, his hand gathering her breast
and brushing the tense peak with a feathering caress.

'Oh, God… *I need you...*' she breathed.

'I need you, *Kit*…' he coaxed, but his voice was hoarse.

He pulled away, abruptly discarding his own clothes and
then slipping back onto the bed, pulling the wine-coloured
silk over them as he gathered her full length against his
body with a broken groan.

His body was fire against hers, and his hands and mouth
were doing wonderful and dreadful things. She clung to
him, surrendering utterly to the storm he whipped up about
her, inside her. The whole universe was only this—nothing
else mattered.

'Tell me.'

His words were harsh, but even through the fog of pleasure she knew them for the plea they were.

'I need you, *Kit*.'

I love you.

She managed to keep those words to herself, but she thought them again and again as he continued his voyage over her body. Her hands tangled in his hair as he moved with infuriating slowness over her body. The air was cool against her heated flesh, and everywhere his mouth touched her skin leapt as if branded.

She floated in a haze of confused pleasure until his hand slipped between her thighs, easing them apart. Then her hands tightened in his hair, trying to pull him away.

He raised himself onto his elbow, his eyes warm and slumberous as he smiled at her. 'Freckles.'

'What?' she whispered hoarsely.

He trailed his fingers along her thigh. 'You have freckles here. I knew I'd find some.'

She laughed, embarrassed and strangely pleased. 'Were you looking for them?'

He shook his head, his fingers tracing up and down, just teasing the soft inner flesh and stopping short of the pulsing need between them.

'I'm not *looking* for anything. I'm exploring this wondrous new land where everything is beautiful, and lush and…' His fingers grazed the soft curls at the apex of her thighs and another flare of almost unbearable new sensation made her body clench and her knees press together. 'And very, very responsive,' he continued, his voice hoarse.

'I can't seem to stop it,' she said apologetically. 'It's like those frogs.'

'Frogs?'

'Emily took us to an exhibition about electricity once.

The man was making frogs' legs dance with a voltaic cell and… And I should be quiet now, shouldn't I?'

'No, don't stop.' He grinned down at her before sliding lower on the bed again. 'Do tell me all about electricity and frogs' legs while I continue counting freckles. Here is one,' he murmured, his mouth brushing the skin just above where he held her knee. 'And two more here…and another here…'

He worked his way up, slowly smoothing aside her legs with teasing licks and kisses. His hand was on her breast too, his thumb teasing the sensitive peak and adding to her agony.

She didn't continue her discourse on Galvanic impulses. She couldn't. She couldn't seem to do much of anything other than lie there, one hand anchored in the silk cover and the other biting into his shoulder as he drove her higher and higher on a wave of agony.

'You can touch me…you can touch yourself,' he murmured against her thigh. 'You can do anything you want, Vivi.'

Without thinking she released the silk sheet and tentatively touched his hand where it stroked her breast.

'Yes…' He breathed warmth against her. 'Show me what you like.'

'This. I like all this. Only more.'

He laughed, and his breath finally feathered over the centre of her heat. She pressed her head back against the cushions, trying to twist her hips away—or into the sensations he was unleashing. She'd never, ever imagined anything like this.

Her whole body rose in the shock of pleasure. It crashed through her body, connecting all his assaults like veined bolts of lightning. Suddenly it was unbearable, impossible, beautiful. She gave a long, tense cry and he rose to catch it against his mouth as she shattered inside.

* * *

Genny woke to the sensation of his fingers trailing slow circular patterns over her abdomen and she smiled without opening her eyes. She stretched, testing the strange new awareness of her body. He'd rearranged her...no, *they'd* rearranged her. It felt so much better...*truer.*

She finally opened her eyes to his smile.

She could become addicted to that smile...no, she already was.

'That was amazing, Kit.'

'It was.'

She frowned as her scattered senses gathered. 'But I don't think you... Did you?'

'Did I what?'

He was teasing her, but she didn't mind. Not when he looked at her like that.

'You know perfectly well what I mean. You didn't... have pleasure.' She cringed at how stilted she sounded, but he didn't seem to mind.

'You have no idea how much pleasure it gave me to see you like that, Genny. If I had to trade my pleasure for the privilege of watching yours I would do it without regret.'

She shook her head, embarrassed and pleased. 'That is a very gallant thing to say, Kit.'

He kissed the corner of her mouth and drew back, inspecting her. 'I knew you would look beautiful in my bed,' he murmured. 'These are the colours you should wear... all the shades of wine and warmth.' He drew the edge of the silk cover over her midriff, moulding it to her. 'Yes, we could make do with you wearing nothing more than this for a month at the very least.'

She smiled, brushing her fingertips over his exploring hand. 'I didn't realise mistresses were required to go about in nothing but sheets.'

'You aren't my mistress; you are my lover. That is a whole different matter.'

She warmed from head to toe. 'Is this what it is like? Having an affair?'

An affair.

The words caught Kit like the swipe of a cat's claws—sharp and stinging, scattering the slumberous satisfaction of bringing her to orgasm. She had such a casual ability to cause pain, and the worst thing was he never knew when it would strike, or how.

She looked so beautiful—her cheeks flushed from love-making and sleep, her hair a tangle of honey and wood. She looked beautiful. Vivid and utterly unique.

His Vivi.

It was time to make it perfectly clear what this was and what this wasn't.

'You said you aren't interested in a marriage of convenience, Vivi. Well, I am not interested in an affair.'

Her eyes widened, shot through with pain and dismay. 'I didn't mean to imply that you wished to do this again...'

He caught her, pinning her down with his arms and his body. He was done with having her slip away the moment she felt the ground pulled from under her.

'I wish to do this many, many times, in many, many places—but not like this. Not an affair. Not with you. Did you honestly believe I could contemplate that? Or a cold-blooded marriage of convenience?'

'But...'

'You are happy at the Hall, aren't you?'

'Yes, but...'

'And you enjoy...this...?'

His hand trailed up from her thigh, over the dip by her hipbone and across the warm softness of her abdomen to her beautiful, luscious breasts, lingering there. His erection hardened against her thigh. He couldn't resist leaning down and pressing a light kiss just above the dark areola. It gathered to a hard peak, and goosebumps rose along the arm that was trying to stop him.

He loved how responsive her body was, shifting towards him almost against her will as she tried to remain impassive. He wanted to reach the point with her where she would finally trust him enough to let slip that control. It would take work, and trust, and many, many days and nights, but it would be well worth it. If it took a lifetime it would be well worth it.

'You enjoy *this*,' he repeated with emphasis, holding her gaze. Her eyes were misty now, the hurt ceding to desire.

'Yes, you know I do,' she murmured, her leg rising against his. 'But you cannot…'

He trailed his hand down again, resting it on her hip, his thumb brushing the soft valley between her hip and navel,

'What can I not?'

'Marry me.'

'Not good enough for you?'

'Don't be ridiculous. You ought to marry someone like…like Lady Sarah. She wants to marry you, you know.'

'Huh… She told you, I suppose?'

'She did, actually.'

He pushed away a little, a slight smile on his mouth. 'People tell you everything, don't they? Why would she do that?'

'She wanted advice. And to determine if I was your mistress.'

The smile faded. 'Those two subjects strike me as contradictory. And why would she think you were my mistress?'

'She saw you take a basket of roses from me in the garden.'

'In the…?' He frowned, his eyes narrowing. 'I would have done the same for anyone.'

'She said you have a different smile for me. She learned to look for it from her mother. The woman apparently had an eye for philanderers.'

He shifted over her, nudging aside her legs to slide one of his much larger legs between them.

'Is that what I'm doing? Philandering? You do know the word means being fond of men?'

'I don't require a lesson in Greek right now. Lady Sarah—'

'Devil take Lady Sarah! Do you really believe I would be happy with someone like her?'

'I… You might. She's beautiful, and intelligent, and not unkind—and she would be the right kind of Lady Westford.'

'I don't like her. I like you. I don't stay awake at night hoping she will be on the shore when I come in from my swim. I don't wake up as hard as a damn mainmast and realise I have to make do with my own company because of her. I don't go searching that monstrosity of a house when I'm in a foul mood, hoping to run her to earth so I can be dragged out of whatever pit I've cornered myself in. I've never felt anything even close to this.'

He watched the expressions chase themselves across her expressive face—worry, want, and that awkward helplessness that was still little Genny Maitland.

He stroked her cheek gently. 'She doesn't truly wish to marry me. And I certainly don't wish to marry her. I have other plans. And if you don't wish to study Greek right now, we could try Italian. Do you speak Italian?'

'No, but…'

'Pity… But your Spanish is a good base. It won't take you long to learn if you set your agile mind to it.'

'Why…why would I learn Italian?'

'So you will know how to order everyone about when we sail there for our honeymoon. And quite a few of my men are Venetians. A good general knows how to communicate with his…sorry, *her* troops.'

'They aren't—'

'Yes, yes,' he interrupted. 'Say after me: *Mi chiamo* Genny. My name is Genny. Go ahead, say it.'

She sighed. *'Mi chiamo* Genny.'

'Beautiful. Your accent is a little on the Iberian side, but we'll soon change that. Now say, *Mi chiamo Genny e ti amo.*'

'Mi chiamo Genny e ti…'

Her breath left her, falling as dead as the wind on a hot day.

Genny fixed her eyes on his, sinking into that deep dark blue.

'It's j-just like Sp-Spanish,' she stuttered.

He nodded. 'Say it.'

His voice was a purr, almost menacing, but she heard something else in it and it made the world shrink to the space of their two bodies.

She swallowed and wet her lips. *'Mi chiamo* Genny and I love you.'

His lashes fluttered down to cover his eyes, his head lowered, and his forehead came to rest on hers very lightly. But there was tension in every inch of his body. It was endless, the wait—either for the trap to close or the world to open.

'Genny… God, Genny. You had better mean it.' He turned his head, his lips just touching her temple, his words low and raw. 'I need you to *mean* it.'

'I couldn't say it if I didn't mean it,' she whispered, laying her palms against his cheeks. She slid one hand down to press against the beat of his heart and touched her lips to his, felt them shiver. 'Kit. I *love* you.'

'Ah, sweetheart, don't cry,' he said, his voice hoarse and she realised she was. She brushed at her eyes but the tears kept slipping out, slow and inexorable.

'I'm sorry. I've been trying not to for weeks. I'm so sorry.'

'God, don't be sorry, love. Come here.'

'I'm already here. If I come any closer, I'll be inside you.'

'I'd rather be inside you. And now you have finally admitted you love me I will be inside you soon enough. You *can* come closer...here, like this.'

He sat, pulling her onto his lap and tucking her head under his chin. Then he tucked the silk blanket about them like a cocoon, one arm warm about her waist, one hand curling around her feet as he held her against him.

'It's very useful, you being this small.' He brushed a kiss over her hair, rubbing his mouth against it.

'I hate it. I always wanted to be tall and beautiful, like Serena.'

'You are far more beautiful than Serena.'

She rubbed her wet cheek against his chest. 'Your eyesight is fading; that cannot be good for the Captain of a ship.'

'My eyesight is excellent. I've told you before: your sister is the very definition of pretty, and I wish her well with it, but she isn't beautiful. Beauty is another thing entirely. Those paintings you like on the wall here—I bought them because I kept going back to look at them...they kept playing on my mind. I've never once looked at them and thought, *How nice*, or *How pretty*. Beautiful is what is vivid, alive, demanding. Everything *you* are, Genevieve Maitland—soon to be Genevieve Carrington and, God help you, Lady Westford.'

She shook her head. Her throat was too tight for her to answer and the tears kept leaking out of her.

'I think, love,' he continued, threading his fingers through hers, 'you should just let go and wail. It's long overdue. I'll survive.'

'I don't know if *I* will,' she croaked.

'Oh, you will. Trust me.' His arms tightened around her, his voice dropping. 'You *do* trust me, don't you?'

'With my life.'

'Good. Maybe one day you'll trust me with your heart too.'

Sometimes things could break in the strangest way. You could drop a glass a dozen times and it would just roll across the floor. Then one day you'd set it down on the table, just as you had a hundred times before, and it would shatter.

And just like that she shattered into a thousand sobbing pieces.

He murmured all kinds of wondrous things at her, just as she did to Leo and Milly and all the other strays she'd gathered. But mostly he held her, rocking her like a boat on a gentle swell…

'It is my birthday today,' Genny said, much later.

She'd wept her heart out and he'd put it back together with slow, gentle lovemaking that had almost driven her to tears all over again.

She'd expected pain, but there had been none, just a strange stretching as he filled her, a sense of finally growing to encompass her own body. The pleasure had been different too. She'd been carried higher and higher on a rising swell that had refused to let her loose, and pleasure had flowed through her like a wave within a wave, depositing her like a shaking mass of jelly on the other side.

He raised himself now, leaning over her, with the smile

she loved so much curving his lips. Then he stood, walking across to the table, his body caressed by lamplight.

'I know,' he said. 'Mary told me. I have something for you. Here.'

He brought the wooden box from the table and set it on the bed, before slipping back under the cover with her.

'It is beautiful,' she whispered, caressing the box.

'Open it.'

She opened the lid. On a bed of milky silk lay a delicate filigree gold ring with a deep, almost red amethyst surrounded by seed pearls.

'I bought this long ago in Naples. They said it had belonged to a princess, but I don't know if that's true. I just saw it and had to buy it. I had no idea that I would keep it, let alone one day make use of it myself. I probably should have found you a great big Carrington heirloom, or something, but—'

'No,' she interrupted, touching the cool stone. 'No...'

'"No" as in no good? Or "no" as in you like it?'

'No, as in I am about to cry again.'

He smiled and took the ring. 'And you said you weren't excitable, my love...'

'I was wrong.'

He paused with the ring halfway on her finger, his eyes rising to hers, the deep dark sapphire sparking with heat. Then he slipped it on the rest of the way, his thumb brushing over it like a seal.

'We were both wrong about quite a few things. But not about this.' He kissed her finger just above the ring and then, very gently, her mouth. 'Make a birthday wish, Genny mine.'

'You have just fulfilled it, Kit.'

'Make another, then.'

'I wish to go swimming with you every day.'

'In winter too?'

'Don't ruin my wish with practicalities!'

He laughed. 'Every day. You can warm me afterwards. What else do you want?'

'You.'

His chest rose and fell. 'You ask for so little, Genny.'

'You aren't little at all, Lord Peacock.'

'Ah. You remember…?'

'Of course I remember. You thoroughly disliked me that first week, didn't you?'

'*Dislike* isn't the right word. You…rubbed me the wrong way. It merely took me a while to find out why. And what to do about it.'

'Seduce me?'

'May I remind you that you seduced me? Several times. And, no, when a spitting kitten is rubbing you the wrong way, all you have to do is turn around and then you discover that the rubbing is just right…'

His hand brushed down the length of her spine and she couldn't stop the reflexive arching of her back into the caress.

'Yes, just like that,' he murmured, pressing the words against the sensitive skin below her ear as his hand curved round her waist, turning her over. 'Just. Like. That.'

Epilogue

'**W**ell, this is a sad disappointment,' Genny said.

Kit took off his other boot and watched as his wife stepped further into Julius Caesar's fabled Rubicon River. She stood, hands on hips, frowning at the grassy incline and the woods beyond.

'Not what you expected, love?'

'Not at all. I had this image of a great river, like the Thames or the Tiber, and Caesar glaring across it at the wealth and power of Rome that were denied him. I knew it could not be anywhere near Rome itself, yet somehow... Fantasy can be so much more satisfying than reality.'

Kit stepped into the stream, sighing with pleasure as the cool water engulfed his feet.

'I beg to differ. I far prefer reality to the fantasies I had to indulge in until I came to my senses and kidnapped you.'

'Is it kidnapping if I came willingly?'

'Kidnapping or not, I've not regretted a moment since,' he said, planting his feet and sweeping her into his arms. She gave a yelp of surprise. '*Alea jacta est,* Genevieve Maitland. The die is truly cast, and this is the fate you've drawn—two perfect children and one imperfect husband. Resign yourself to it.'

She laughed. 'Kit! We'll fall in.'

'If Caesar had had so little faith in the Thirteenth Legion as you have in me, my little field marshal, history would have played out quite differently.'

She wrapped her arms around his nape and settled more securely against him, her lips brushing against his neck, just where she knew how to do the most damage. 'That's not true, Kit. I trust you wholly, without boundaries, with my life and my heart *and* our two horrid children.'

'I happen to be quite fond of the little devils—especially when they are far away in Venice with their aunts. Your daughter, Genevieve Maitland, looks likely to rival you in tyranny.'

'Why is it that when she is being brilliantly managing she becomes *my* daughter, yet when everyone says how sweet and beautiful she is, she is your daughter?'

'It is one of life's mysteries. Stop that, or we shall both end up in the water.'

She gave his ear a playful nip and blew gently on it. He groaned and let her slip down his body, holding her tight against him before leading her to the other bank.

'I told you my skirts would get wet.'

He eased her back onto the grassy incline and stretched out beside her, running his hand down her thigh and then slowly gathering the damp fabric so that it slid up to reveal her legs.

'You should have tied them up as you did that day in the bay. Then I could have the same pleasure untying them… smoothing them down…or up…definitely up.'

She sighed and stretched happily as his hand followed word with deed.

'I'm so glad we decided it was better that I accompany you on your voyages again now that Tom is old enough.'

'It wasn't a decision; it was a necessity, Vivi. You have no idea how much I missed you on my last voyage.'

'I beg your pardon; I have a very good idea. You had

your voyage to distract you. I had to spend every night in our bed alone.'

'I should hope so. And I had to spend every night in our other bed, alone, freezing my backside off in the Baltic Sea, with a ship full of snoring and shivering men. After a week I was ready to turn back. After a month I promised myself that next time you were coming with me—even if we had to let the children fend for themselves. After two months I was convinced you were quite happy not to be constantly disturbed by my carnal lust. After four months I was crying into my wine…a pitiable sight.'

She smiled, her fingers trailing patterns on his back and sending shivers of anticipatory pleasure to all the right places.

'That is very poetic—though a trifle dramatic and not quite accurate. After three months you were safely back in your bed with me, being mightily disturbed by a three-month accumulation of *my* carnal lust. In fact, I am feeling mightily disturbed right now.'

'You don't mind the ghost of Caesar watching on, then?' he asked.

'Not in the least. He might learn something from the best lover on earth, ever…'

He laughed and slipped his hand higher up her thigh, curving it over her warmth. Somehow her skin felt different from anyone else's. It made no sense, but there it was.

'Perhaps this was why he crossed the Rubicon—the poor fellow was looking for this.'

'This?' she sighed, her eyes closing again as he trailed kisses down her throat.

'This…' He eased her bodice down, punctuating each word with a kiss as he revealed inch after inch of warm skin. 'Happiness. Contentment. Challenge. Joy. Pain. Pleasure…'

He slipped the last inch from her tightly beaded nipple and bent to lavish a slow kiss over the sensitive peak that made her twist towards him with a moan, her fingers threading through his hair. But then he drew back, blowing a gentle soothing breath against the damp skin and looking up at her, holding her gaze as he spoke.

'…and love.'

She rested her palms against his cheeks. Her grey eyes were magnified by the welling of tears and her voice was hoarse when she finally spoke.

'I would cross any Rubicon for this, Kit. Fight any battle for you. You know that, don't you?'

Kit waited out the tightening of his throat. He hadn't completely lied. Perhaps he hadn't quite cried into his wine, but the depth of pain and fear that had caught at him all those miles from her had been as much a shock as falling so desperately in love in the first place. He had *needed* to return.

'I know that, Vivi. That is why I need you with me. I need you to remind me that you care for me almost as much as I care for you.'

She smiled his favourite smile—full of joy and promise and trust. 'Dear me, Kit. Are we competing again? I'll win, you know.'

'I'm afraid I outshine you there, sweetheart.'

She nudged him onto his back, tucking her bare leg between his, slipping her hand over his abdomen and under his waistband.

'We shall see. I *do* so love a challenge… Especially a hard one.'

* * * * *

*If you enjoyed this book, why not check
out these other great reads by Lara Temple*

The Return of the Disappearing Duke

*And be sure to read her
The Sinful Sinclairs miniseries*

The Earl's Irresistible Challenge
The Rake's Enticing Proposal
The Lord's Inconvenient Vow